SECRETS

A TRILOGY

by

ROBERT NOONAN

WILDFLOWERS

While overworked child laborers of the nineteenth century might have created the grist for the Industrial Revolution, even darker abuses were committed against them.

BRIDIE'S DAUGHTER

The Orphan Trains carried homeless children westward, altering their lives and the lives of the people who took them in ... for better or worse.

SECRETS

The orphan children, as well as the adults who adopted them, have secrets from their past. Some secrets are revealed; others better left untold.

SECRETS

The Third Story in the Orphan Train Trilogy

Robert Noonan

Author of *Wildflowers* and *Bridie's Daughter*

iUniverse, Inc.

New York Lincoln Shanghai

Secrets
The Third Story in the Orphan Train Trilogy

iUniverse books may be ordered through booksellers or by contacting:

iUniverse
2021 Pine Lake Road, Suite 100
Lincoln, NE 68512
www.iuniverse.com
1-800-Authors (1-800-288-4677)

Because of the dynamic nature of the Internet, any Web addresses or links contained in this book may have changed since publication and may no longer be valid.

This is a work of fiction. All of the characters, names, incidents, organizations, and dialogue in this novel are either the products of the author's imagination or are used fictitiously.

ISBN: 978-0-595-43628-6 (pbk)
ISBN: 978-0-595-69292-7 (cloth)
ISBN: 978-0-595-87954-0 (ebk)

Printed in the United States of America

Robert Noonan has presented us with a gift … three extremely well written novels highlighting a desperate time for children of our past. We may not enjoy reading about some of the challenges they faced but it is important that we learn of them. These books will become memorable additions to your historical fiction bookshelf.

—IP Book Reviewers

I dedicate this novel to my daughters, Alissa and Meris Noonan, for being the wonderful young ladies they are and the thrills they have given me through the years.

REMEMBER THE
CHILDREN

The Children's Aid Society in New York City began helping children in 1853. Their good work continues today, aiding more than 150,000 children and their families each year. For further information or to make a donation, see the following.

The Children's Aid Society
105 East 22nd Street
New York, NY 10010
(212) 949-4800

CHAPTER ONE

It was a warm August morning, with billowy white clouds passing slowly under an endless blue sky. Kate stood at the kitchen window watching Hillary ride Knickers inside the corral. She circled in one direction and then another, turning him to form large figure eights.

Hillary noticed Kate watching her and waved.

Kate smiled and clapped her Hands close to the window, so Hillary would know she was pleased with the way she was controlling the horse.

Kate believed Hillary was happy on the farm, away from the textile mill, the filth of Alton, Delaware, and that pig, Frank Dragus. Even though she appeared content with her new life, there were nights Kate heard Hillary crying in her bedroom. Losing both parents by the age of twelve was difficult to accept, as was being raped by Mr. Dragus, under the guise of paying a doctor to save her dying mother. Kate didn't know how many times it had happened, but she would continue to pretend she didn't know about it. If Hillary wanted to keep it a secret, then so be it. In turn, Kate intended to keep her secret that she'd killed Frank Dragus.

Kate looked up at the blue sky. *Laura? Jeremiah? Can you see your lovely daughter with her wavy blond hair? She'll be 14 years old in just three months. It's the year 1900, the beginning of a new century and a new life for Hillary. See how well she has learned to ride her horse in such a short time.* Kate's pensive mood changed, realizing, that if they could see their daughter riding, then they could have witnessed her being raped by Frank. *Can they see only the good, and not the bad?* she wondered. The ugly thought of Hillary's abuse put a quick end to Kate's affectionate ponderings.

She opened the window to let fresh air into the kitchen. The sounds of Knickers snorting and his hoofs pounding the ground entered the room with the morning breeze. Kate continued to watch Hillary ride, wondering when she would ask to return to Alton, Delaware, to visit her parents' graves, and her friends, Iris and Vera. A smile crept across her face, remembering the girls calling themselves "Wildflowers." Their secret club of three, pledged to be friends for life. Now, those girls didn't know where Hillary was, separated by hundreds of miles. Having left Alton sixteen months ago, she expected Hillary to mention it soon.

Kate stepped out to the porch and yelled to Hillary, "We're going to the Lantinos to say, 'goodbye' in about two hours. John said he'd be back here by eleven o'clock. You'll have to wash up before we go, and you still haven't snatched the eggs from the chickens."

Hillary stopped the horse by the corral fence. "I'm taking Knickers in now. My butt is getting sore."

"Then you're doing something wrong."

"I know. For some crazy reason, my timing is off today and I'm banging my bottom on the saddle."

Kate watched Hillary ride into the stable, before returning to the kitchen and the apple cakes baking in the oven. Again, she began thinking about Hillary and her desire to return to Alton, Delaware—a dangerous undertaking. *Does Crossroads Shipping still have the Sheriff and Wade Widner looking for John? Wade doesn't believe my husband killed Jesse Sharpe, nor does anyone else—just Tyler Sharpe, who wants revenge for his brother's murder. Hillary knows John can't go back to Alton, but she doesn't know I can't go back. Being that Frank Dragus was killed the morning we disappeared from Alton, I'm sure to be a sus-*

pect and the authorities will want to question me. No, I can't risk every-thing we have by going back. No one in Alton must know where we are.

Twenty minutes later, Kate was removing apple cakes from the baking sheet when Hillary entered the kitchen carrying a basket of eggs.

Hillary raised the back of her hand to Kate. "Look at this. Zelda pecked my hand when I went for her egg."

Kate turned and grinned. "Get me a magnifying glass, so I can see it."

Hillary responded quickly to Kate's lack of sympathy. "No, it isn't a big cut, but it hurt when she did it. Zelda is the meanest chicken we have." She smiled and elbowed Kate. "When's our next chicken dinner?"

"Forget it, she's one of our best layers." Kate took off her apron and laid it across the back of a chair. "Hurry and take your bath. John will be home in a few minutes."

"Why are the Lantinos moving so soon? Their farm isn't sold yet, and they'll still be living in Illinois."

"They've signed all the papers, so their lawyer can close the sale without them being here. To get the job he wants in Abingdon, Mr. Lantino has to start work next Monday. Besides, Joan wants to get their new house in order before Larry starts school. By the way, John told Joe we'd keep an eye on their place until the new owners arrive next weekend."

Hillary sat on a chair and began taking off her riding boots. "Do the new people have children?"

"Three, according to what John was told."

"How old and what kind?"

Kate chuckled. "What kind? They're not livestock. They're human beings." She looked at Hillary, grinning at her joke. "Girls are nine and twelve, and a boy sixteen."

"I hope they're nice people, especially with them living so close. Then I'd have someone to play with." Hillary started unbuttoning her blouse, then paused to listen. "I think I hear John's wagon rattling this way." She grabbed an apple cake and ran to the bathroom.

"Don't dally. Bathe quickly," Kate yelled after her.

Kate looked out of the window and saw John riding toward the barn. The color of his copper-red hair was intensified in the sunlight, looking almost as though his head was on fire. She put the coffee pot on the stove and placed an apple cake on a small plate, covering the others with a cloth. She watched John tie Cokie to the corral fence and walk toward the house. She went out to the porch and waited for him, sliding her arms around his neck when he came up the two stairs. Her mind, her heart and her body belonged to him. She looked at his freckled face, "I need to tell you I love you."

He smiled slowly, putting his arms around her waist and looking into her rosy-cheeked Irish face and brown eyes. "What brought this on? I can't remember doing anything special."

"You, just you, and the nice new three-bedroom house, the nice farm, and the wonderful life you're giving me."

He smiled at her. "Aw shucks, 'tain't nuthin,' Ma'am."

"If the people in Alton learned where we are, I'd die. The thought of losing you and our home has me in a constant worry."

John kissed her forehead and stroked her light-brown hair. "They'll never find us. This is a big country."

Kate smiled and they kissed, again.

John looked into her eyes. "By the way you're acting, I would say, Hillary isn't here, but I know better."

"She's taking a bath. Come in, I've got coffee and an apple cake waiting for you. I prepared a basket of them for the Lantinos."

John poured himself a cup of coffee and sat at the table. "That Bridie woman and two orphan girls are coming next Friday, right?"

"Yes, one week from today, but they haven't called to tell us which train they're coming on." Kate turned from the stove and whacked John on the shoulder with the spatula. "Those girls are no longer orphans, so don't call them that. They came to Newberry, Illinois on an Orphan Train from New York City. Catherine was adopted by

Bridie, and Pina was adopted by Richard and Eileen Campbell. They are very nice people and I'm looking forward to their visit. I'm sure you'll like them, too."

"I think you're anxious to get Biff and Bridie together. You met her and Catherine once, two weeks ago at the Scottish Festival. You really don't know much about them."

Kate carried a cup of coffee to the table and sat across from John. "Actually, there are different reasons why I'm looking forward to their visit. And yes, I am curious to see if Biff and Bridie will like each other."

John looked at her with raised eyebrows. "I think Biff's heart still belongs to Hillary's mother. I don't think it'll be easy for him to forget Laura and care for someone else this quickly."

"You're right, he loved Hillary's mother very much, but she's gone to Jeremiah. Maybe Bridie's the person who can soften him. Living alone isn't natural."

"What?" John questioned, quickly. "Many people live alone. For five years, Laura and Hillary lived without Jeremiah, and they did fine—under their circumstances."

Kate pinched a piece of John's apple cake and tossed it into her open mouth. "Yes, 'under their circumstances.' But they could have had a better life with a man around, having more income, and a better social life. Your cousin Biff and Laura were perfect for each other. Being that Laura was my best friend, I hoped they'd marry and move here."

John leaned back in his chair. "One night, months ago, Biff told me he loved Laura and would do what it took to bring her and Hillary here. Then, when he went back to Alton and found Laura dying, it hit him hard. Biff said to me, 'God must have wanted Laura and Jeremiah to be together.' He hasn't mentioned her often since, but I know he still thinks about her."

"I guess there's no sense wondering what will happen when Bridie comes. We'll know in a week." Kate sipped her coffee and added,

"The people who bought the Lantino farm are moving in next week-end. I don't want to snub them, but we'll be busy with our guests."

Hillary came out of the bathroom wrapped in a large towel, scurrying toward her bedroom. "I'm as clean as a new born babe," she hollered.

Kate laughed. "If you think a new born babe is clean, you're grossly mistaken."

"You know what I mean. I'll be ready in ten minutes." Hillary pushed her bedroom door shut and yelled, "Now that we're talking about babies, when are we going to have some around here for me to take care of—like you promised?

Kate and John smiled at each other before Kate responded, "Don't give up. We've been talking about it."

Hillary opened her door to reply. "You've said that before."

"And we may say it again, but don't give up hope," John added.

"It's not the *if* I'm concerned about, but the *when*. I'm not getting any younger you know, and I won't be around here forever."

"She's right," Kate said, quietly. "She may not be here much longer."

John looked startled. "What the hell are you talking about? She's only thirteen."

"Almost fourteen, but that's not the issue. When Hillary returned from visiting her friends in Newberry, she told me Catherine gave them a tour through her school. It's a private school. I think the name is Bradbury. The girls receive advanced studies in the arts, social graces and a better education overall, than she would get in a public school."

"It'll teach her to be a snob. Is that what you're saying?"

Kate put her hand on John's wrist. "No! It'll teach her to fit in at all levels of society, so she would never feel out of place. Plus, she'll get a good education."

John reached under the cloth that covered the basket and took out an apple cake. "Has Hillary asked about going there?"

"No, not at all. She seemed interested, as she was telling me about it. For all I know, she may not want to go to Bradbury."

"And the cost, is?" John whispered.

"I'm sure we can handle it, but I believe her Uncle Biff would want to pay the tuition."

"You're probably right."

Hillary stuck her head out of her bedroom. "Is Uncle Biff coming this weekend?"

"I'm sure he will," John shouted back. "If you're here, he'll be here."

Kate smiled. "She loves calling him Uncle Biff, even though they aren't related."

The next morning, in Newberry, Illinois, Bridie knocked on Catherine's bedroom door passing her bedroom. "It's Saturday, 9:00 a.m., and we have shopping to do for our trip to Galena, remember?"

"Yes, I remember, and I'm sure Pina does, too. I'll be downstairs in twenty minutes."

Bridie paused at the top of the stairs. "She can make it faster than that," she mumbled. She turned and shouted down the hall, "I forgot to tell you about a letter you got from Brian yesterday. It's on the desk in the parlor." Bridie smiled and descended the stairs.

Seven minutes later, Catherine was in the kitchen holding Brian's letter. Bridie didn't comment about Catherine's earlier estimate of twenty minutes. "Do you want your eggs up, over, or scrambled?"

Catherine picked up a knife from the table to open the envelope. "Up, please." The rest of the world disappeared until she finished reading Brian's letter. "He says he loves his architectural drawing class, because he can put his ideas on paper." Her face was aglow, placing the letter back into the envelope. "In a year and nine months, he graduates."

Bridie looked over her shoulder, admiring Catherine's pretty face and strawberry-blond hair that matched her own. "How many minutes and seconds?" Bridie joked.

"If I knew, I'd tell you."

"You turned sixteen just a month ago. Enjoy your youth, because once you are married with children, your life is not your own."

Catherine went to the stove for the kettle of hot water. "I'll make the tea."

"Good! The fried potatoes are finished, just sitting on the stove keeping warm. And the eggs will be ready in a minute."

Catherine filled the teapot with hot water and hung a tea ball inside. "Pina is meeting us at Carrie's Dress Shop at eleven o'clock. She's quite anxious to see Hillary's farm and horse."

Bridie dropped eggshells into the garbage container under the sink. "So am I. Four days on a farm sounds delightful." She scraped the fried potatoes onto a platter and handed it to Catherine. "While we're at Carrie's, do you need to buy clothes for the coming school year?"

"I don't believe so. Then again, I may see something while we're there."

Both were quite hungry when they sat at the table. The only sound in the room was from the clock on the wall, ticking steadily. Occasionally, Catherine would glance at the clock's pendulum, swinging from side-to-side.

"I have a question," Bridie said, breaking the silence. "Has Pina ever mentioned being interested in attending your school?"

"No. I'm sure she would love to attend Bradbury, but I don't know whether her parents can afford it. Why do you ask?"

"It was just a thought. She's a nice girl and it would help her prospects for marriage in the future." Kate wiped her mouth with a napkin. "Pina is fourteen years old, isn't she?"

"Yes, about the same age as Hillary."

"She's a nice girl, too."

Catherine looked at Bridie who appeared to be deep in thought. "What are you thinking about?"

"To be honest, I was wondering if both girls would be interested in Bradbury. It would do more for them than the public schools they're attending now."

Catherine placed her knife and fork on her empty plate. "We don't know if either of them could afford it."

"True. But if they didn't have to pay room and board, maybe they could manage it?"

"Are you implying, what I think you're implying?"

Bridie straightened her back before continuing. "These are just thoughts, so don't get excited. Pina, like you, lives here in Newberry, so she wouldn't have to pay room and board. Hillary could avoid that expense, if she lived with the Campbells. If that were a problem for them, it is possible that she could live here with us."

Catherine laughed. "You've been thinking about this long before now," she insisted.

"I have, but it is just thinking, nothing more. We know Hillary fairly well and we'll know her and her parents better after we spend a few days with them."

"I certainly like the idea, but why are you interested in arranging this?

Bridie looked at her, thoughtfully. "The week Hillary was here, you girls had such a good time I hated to see it end." She nodded her head at Catherine and smiled. "I'm sure you did, too. I truly enjoyed watching you girls and that is how the idea came to me. I decided, what harm would it do to discuss Bradbury with the others?"

Catherine carried the dishes to the sink and began washing them. "There is one problem. Hillary won't be fourteen until November."

"No, that isn't a problem. A girl can attend the school, as long as she turns 14 the year she enters Bradbury." Bridie paused to sip her tea. "Another reason I'm interested in arranging this, is because, the three of you are intelligent girls and I believe you should be given a good education. All you girls, and your boyfriend, Brian, I might add, were orphans with an uncertain future. Now, if better schooling is possible, I would like to see you get a good start in life. Not that, *their* lives are any of my business."

Catherine laughed again. "No, they aren't your business, but I appreciate what you're thinking. School starts in twelve days. How could we manage it in such a short time?"

"It's possible, but more than likely we'd be talking about the following year. I can't imagine the Campbells and Hanleys deciding so quickly." Bridie got up from the table and put her teacup into the dishwater. "Whatever you do, don't mention this to anyone until we decide whether this is the right thing to do—not that I think Kate and John are people who have anything to hide."

CHAPTER TWO

Late Sunday morning, Hillary fed the chickens and horses, while Kate and John walked to the Lantino farm to see that their house wasn't disturbed. Soon after Hillary returned from the stable, the telephone rang.

"Hello. Were you out riding Knickers?" Pina asked.

"No. I just finished feeding the animals, but I plan to ride him this afternoon. Kate and John are looking in on our neighbor's vacant house. They moved to Abingdon, Illinois, and the new people don't move in until next weekend, while you're here. We promised to keep an eye on the house for them."

"My, what nice people you are," Pina joked. "Now, let's get on with why I really called. Our train will be arriving around 2:20 on Friday afternoon—if it's on time. Catherine and I are dying to see your farm and Knickers. As a matter-of-fact, Catherine told me that Bridie is as enthused about this trip as we are."

"Good!" Hillary shot back. "I hope she remains enthused when she meets Biff."

"Me, too. By the way, did you get my letter?"

"Yes, I did, and thank you for mailing my letters to Alton, Delaware."

"You're welcome," Pina replied. "The Thompsons should be getting them about now."

"Iris and Vera will be so surprised when the Thompsons give them my letters. I'd like to see their faces when he does. Remember, we must be careful not to mention these letters to anyone when we're together next weekend. Kate and John would be very upset if they knew I was writing to people in Alton."

The following evening, in Alton, Delaware, Wade Widner left his office at Crossroads Shipping and walked toward his apartment. Along the way, he stopped at Thompson's Grocery Store for a few cans of fruit, especially peaches. As he entered, a small bell above the door jingled. He exchanged greetings with Avery Thompson who was standing next to the cash register looking at his mail. Mr. Thompson's wife, Sari, was tending to the fresh vegetables along the back wall.

Wade's tall, muscular body caused the floorboards to creak as he walked to the canned goods section. He scanned the selection and cradled three cans of peaches in his arm. While deciding whether to buy a can of cherries or pears, he heard Avery yell, excitedly.

"Sari, a letter from Hillary Cook! My God, I don't believe it." He raced to Sari, waving the letter over his head.

Sari dropped the ears of corn she was holding and turned to Avery. "My prayers have been answered. Finally, a letter."

Wade was stunned by what he was hearing. Immediately, he wondered where the letter came from. He saw Avery with the letter, but not the envelope. He realized that the envelope with the return address must still be by the cash register. He walked casually to the front of the store and placed the cans of fruit on the counter. There, on top of the other mail, was a large opened envelope with more letters inside. He glanced at the Thompsons, who were unaware of everything, except Hillary's letter. He reached over the counter and turned the envelope, so he could read it. There it was, *H. Cook, 715 Oakley Avenue, Newberry, Illinois.* He removed a pencil from inside his jacket and began looking for something to write on. On the floor was a sales receipt. He picked it up, turned it over and began copying the address.

Later, at his apartment, Wade placed a can of peaches in the icebox to cool, then sat in a stuffed chair to ponder his discovery. It had been well over a year since Kate and Hillary disappeared and he hadn't put much effort into searching for John in recent months, but he had thought about Kate. He assumed they were married by now, but then there was a possibility that she may have changed her mind—especially since John ran from Alton without her. If so, and he could find Kate, he could try to win her hand.

Wade was about to get up from his stuffed chair, when he remembered something else. Frank Dragus was killed the day Kate and Hillary disappeared. He also recalled that Frank had a liking for young girls, and because of his wealth, had his way with many poor girls working at his mill. He began pondering possibilities for Frank's death. *Perhaps one of the girl's parents killed Frank for revenge? If not, and Kate, Frank's secretary, did kill him, as some people suspect, did she run away without ever having made contact with John? Maybe they don't know where each other are? If that's the case, then chances are Kate is raising Hillary by herself, which will make her more receptive to marrying me. After all, she had shown interest in me.*

Wade decided to go after Kate. He would explain what he had learned to his boss, Tyler Sharpe, at Crossroads Shipping. He'd let Tyler believe that he was going after John. Wade knew Tyler Sharpe couldn't leave the shipping company and would be more than willing to pay the expenses to find his brother's killer. The fact that he was really looking for Kate would be his secret.

At 9 a.m. the next morning, Wade went to Tyler Sharpe's office to explain what he had learned. As Tyler listened, fire returned to his eyes. "Go find him. Leave today. You've got two and a half hours to catch the train."

Wade boarded the train at 11:47 a.m. It would be a three-day ride and he was looking forward to it. He would sit back and relax, enjoying free meals and a ride through a part of the country he hadn't seen before—while getting paid for it. In addition, there was a good chance he would see Kate, again. The train was due to arrive at Newberry, Illinois, Friday morning.

While Wade boarded the train, Avery Thompson was sitting in the back room of his store, pondering how to approach Iris and Vera about their letters from Hillary. Her letter to him stressed the importance of keeping the Newberry address a secret.

Sari entered the back of the store and sat across from him. "I'm anxious for the girls to get their letters."

Avery held the two letters in his hand. "I think I'll invite the girls here Sunday, being they work until evening the other six days. They can read Hillary's letters and write to her in this room. I'll have pencils and paper for them. They won't need her address, because I'll mail the letters for them."

Sari rested her arms on the table. "Since Hillary moved from upstairs, the girls don't come to our store as often and we don't know where they live. How will you get them here, if they don't stop by on their own?"

"Today is Tuesday. We can wait until tomorrow night to see if they stop by. If not, our neighbor, Dick Zulkie, works at the mill and I'll have him tell Vera to bring Iris on Sunday, around noon."

Sari smiled. "Those girls will be so thrilled to get a letter from Hillary. They were devastated by her sudden disappearance. I'm sure they have millions of questions and tons of news to tell her."

Friday morning, Wade's train slowed, pulling into the Newberry station. He was somewhat disappointed, because he was enjoying his ride into new territory. He removed his suitcase from the overhead rack and walked to the back of the train. Through the window, he could see a woman and two girls waiting to board. As he descended the stairs, one of the girls he'd just seen through the window was about to climb up the stairs. He saw the woman take the girl by the arm, saying, "Wait, Pina, let the man off first." The girl stepped back and Wade disembarked, giving the three a friendly smile.

Wade went inside the train station to inquire about hotel accommodations. The man at the ticket window suggested he stay at Langrick House, across the square, opposite the train station. The man guaranteed it had "first-class accommodations and good food," then smiled with a wink, telling him that it was a "full-service" hotel. Wade thanked him and moved on.

Crossing the square, Wade looked at Lincoln's statue. It was made of bronze and he thought it a good likeness of the President. He waited for a furniture wagon to roll past, then walked quickly toward the hotel entrance.

A man, wearing a black vest over a white shirt and red tie, was standing behind the reception desk. "Good morning, Sir. May I help you?"

"Yes. I need a single room for three or four days, preferably one flight up."

"Very good, Sir. I have a nice room near the stairs, if that is what you prefer?"

"I do. By the way, is there a Telephone Exchange nearby?" Wade had been instructed to call Tyler Sharp, as soon as he found John Hanley.

The man handed Wade a pen and turned the registry book, so he could sign in. "Yes, there is, and it's open seven days a week. When you exit the hotel, turn right to the corner and turn right again. It's at the end of the block." The man tapped a bell twice for the bellboy.

Once in his room, he lay across the bed, thinking of how he would approach their apartment without being recognized by Kate. Hillary had never seen him, so she wouldn't be a concern. He decided it would be better to verify their address during the day, assuming Kate would be at work. Being it was Friday he would have to do it today, before four o'clock. He hoped their name would be on a mailbox, so he would know immediately if it was the correct address. If they lived in a house, which he doubted, it would only take a second to verify a name on a single mailbox.

After three days of riding a train, Wade was desperate for a bath. He soaked in the tub, thinking about his favorite meals. The dining room served lunch at eleven o'clock and he was there as it opened. He ordered a roast beef dinner and a glass of red wine. The fact that Tyler Sharp would be paying the bill, made his meal doubly delicious.

Before leaving the dining room, Wade asked for directions to Oakley Avenue. The waiter told him, "six streets north of the hotel."

He stepped outside into a sunny afternoon, ready for a leisurely stroll after eating a large meal. Within twenty minutes, he was at Oakley Avenue. He looked to his right and left, observing that it was a street of private homes. Wade was standing at the end of the 900s, block, so he turned left toward the lower numbers. He was curious about Kate's position, being she lived in a house and not an apartment. He was disappointed, assuming she must be married to John. Together, they could afford a house.

As Wade approached house number *715*, he put his handkerchief to his face and pretended to blow his nose. It was a modest, white frame house, with bedrooms upstairs. A gray mailbox was mounted on the wall next to the entrance door. He saw a small white tab and assumed it displayed the occupant's last name. As he got closer to the house, Wade tried looking through the windows, searching for movement inside. He couldn't see any activity at all, so he quickly turned up the walk to the house and read the name on the mailbox. Wade was surprised to see the name *Campbell* printed on the tab. Without, delay, he retraced his steps back to the sidewalk and continued down the street, wondering if he'd made an error copying the address from Hillary's envelope.

Wade decided to return to that house after dark. It would be easier to see people in lighted rooms. He started back to the hotel when he had another idea. He decided to go to the Telephone Exchange to inquire about subscribers named, Cook, Moran or Hanley. This way, he could avoid wasting the afternoon, waiting for it to get dark. He walked a little faster now, anxious to learn what he could.

He entered the Exchange and approached the young woman behind a highly polished wooden counter. "Excuse me, I just got into town and I'm trying to find relatives of mine. I'm not sure if they have a telephone and I don't know their exact address. I believe they live on Oakley Avenue."

With a smile, the woman was very willing to help. She placed a pencil and pad of paper in front of him. "Print their name here and I'll look for it on our subscriber sheets."

"I really appreciate this," Wade assured her. "I haven't seen them for over twelve years, and since I was passing Newberry, I thought it would be nice to visit them." Wade wrote, *Hillary Cook, Kate Moran* and *John Hanley* on the pad and pushed it toward her. "It's three branches of the family tree, so I'm giving you all the names."

The woman took the pad and started toward a desk and file cabinet. "I'll see what I can find for you. It won't take long."

Wade leaned against the counter waiting, wondering what went wrong when he copied the address. He watched the woman to see if she would write something, a sign she found one of the names. He was disappointed when she rose from the desk, returning to him without having written anything.

"Sorry, but none of these people are telephone subscribers. You could inquire at the Post Office, but I'm not sure they can help you. They just deliver mail to an address. I don't believe they have a list of everyone's name."

"You looked at all of your subscribers?" Wade questioned.

"Yes, Sir, all the last names that start with the appropriate letters."

Wade stepped back from the counter and hesitated. "Where are your public telephones?"

"Through that door, there," she said, pointing. "Pay here when you're finished. The operator will tell me the cost of the call."

"Thank you." Wade entered the room and saw twelve telephones widely spaced along one wall. Two telephones near the door were in use by what appeared to be businessmen wearing dark suits. In an attempt to have privacy, Wade walked to the far end of the room. He planned to quiz an operator, believing she would know almost everyone in town.

Wade picked up the receiver, surprised by the immediate response. "May I help you?"

"I hope so," Wade answered. "I just got in town and I'm trying to find relatives here in Newberry. I went to what I believe is their house, but there was a name I don't recognize on the mailbox. I may have a wrong address."

"Give me your relatives name and I'll see what I can do. I know almost everyone in town."

"Actually," Wade said, sheepishly, "It could be one of three family names."

"Give me one at a time and I'll see if I know them."

Wade believed a telephone would be listed under a man's name. "John Hanley."

There was silence for a moment. "That name is vaguely familiar," she said. "But I can't recall a Hanley living here. Give me another name."

"Kate Moran."

"No. Don't know that one at all. Next?"

"Hillary Cook is the other."

"That name seems familiar, too, but I don't believe that person lives in Newberry. I've been an operator here for a long time and I can't place that person in our town, either. Sorry."

Thinking aloud, Wade said, "I'll go back to the Campbell's house tonight and see what they know."

"Campbell?" she repeated quickly. "I know Richard and Eileen Campbell." There was a short pause. "How silly of me—of course, I know them. You saw their name on the mailbox because they live here." There was another short pause. "Wait a minute. Campbells ... Hanley? Let me think a moment."

Wade repeated the names, "Cook, Hanley and Moran."

"It's coming. Hold on," she mumbled. "Yes!" she said, smartly. "Now I remember. Hillary Cook is a friend of the Campbell girl. Hillary visited them for a few days this summer." She fell silent again. "Aha! I've got it. When the Campbells telephone Hillary, they ask for John Hanley's residence in Galena, Illinois. Yes, that's it. I remember it clearly, now. That's where they live."

"Galena, Illinois?" Wade questioned. "Are you sure the name is John Hanley?"

"Absolutely. I've connected them to that number a few times."

"You're a dear," Wade said. "Thanks for your help."

"If you do meet them, tell them their operator, Cora, saved the day."

CHAPTER THREE

That afternoon, Hillary and Kate were at the Galena, Illinois train station, waiting for their guests. Hillary watched with fervent anticipation, as the engine moved slowly toward them with its bell clanging a warning. Kate covered her face with a handkerchief to avoid inhaling the black smoke that was about to engulf them. They stepped away from the train and waited to see which passenger car their friends would come out of. Six people got off the train. Hillary's stomach seemed to sink, wondering if they weren't on the train. She looked at Kate to see if she was concerned.

"Look again," Kate said, smiling. "They're getting off now."

Hillary jerked her head back to where she had been looking and ran to them, shouting, "You're twenty minutes late. Get back on the train and try it again."

Pina spun around to face Hillary, causing her short black hair to flare like a spinning skirt. "Nuts to you," Pina responded. "We're here to stay."

Hillary hugged and kissed her friends, and greeted Bridie. She carried one of Bridie's two bags and led them to where Kate was waiting.

Kate smiled, being Bridie and Catherine weren't blood relatives, but had the same strawberry-blond hair. "Welcome to Galena," Kate said, enthusiastically. "Did you enjoy the ride?"

"Absolutely," Bridie answered. "I love riding trains."

"We saw five Indians a half hour from here," Catherine said. "Are there many around here?"

"We see them occasionally," Kate replied. "They come into town to trade or buy goods, mostly for hardware and groceries."

"Follow me," Hillary said, walking toward the end of the platform. "Biff's father is letting us use his coach this weekend. Five of us can fit in it easily." She leered at Pina. "Otherwise, you'd have to walk."

Pina stuck her tongue out at Hillary. "Do you want to sleep in my basement the next time you come to Newberry?"

Kate opened the large trunk on the back of the coach and filled it with luggage. She turned to Hillary. "Who's driving us home, me or you?"

"I interpret that as an invitation. Yes, I'll drive."

"You're going to drive this big coach?" Catherine questioned.

Kate looked into Catherine's green eyes, as she was about to climb aboard. "When you live on a farm, you learn to handle all kinds of wagons and buggies. Actually, this isn't really a coach. It's just a large buggy."

Hillary climbed up the other side and picked up the reins. "This coach doesn't bounce like smaller buggies and buckboards, but still, be prepared for bumps." Hillary flicked the reins and directed the horse through town.

Kate glanced back at Bridie and the girls. "If the road outside of town is too dusty, we can put the top up if you'd like?"

"I'll let you know," Bridie answered. "By the way, is anything playing at the theatre this weekend?"

Kate chuckled. "Yes. *Joan, the Beautiful Typewriter Girl.* It's a melodrama."

"How cute," Bridie responded. "Melodramas are quite charming. I like them."

"What's a melodrama?" Pina asked.

Hillary shook the reins and glanced quickly over her shoulder. "They're fun. We get to yell at the actors."

"I'll explain, so Hillary can concentrate on what she's doing," Kate insisted. She elevated her voice, so she could be heard over the noise of steel wheels rolling over the brick street. "It's a play of heroes, heroines and villains. Every time the hero or heroine enters the stage, the audience cheers. When the villain comes on stage, the audience yells, 'Boo,' or hisses at them. Sometimes, a person will throw a tomato or head of lettuce at the villain."

"You're kidding?" Catherine gasped.

"It's true," Hillary assured her from above. "People are allowed to yell at the actors, but you really shouldn't throw things at them."

"We must see this," Pina remarked, leering at Catherine.

"It sounds like a good idea to me," Bridie said. "I haven't yelled at anyone for a long time, and I'm overdue."

"Turn up Kouts Street," Kate said, suddenly. "We might as well buy the tickets now, being everyone is interested in the melodrama." Kate turned her head slightly, so she could be heard. "We have three choices, Saturday afternoon and evening, or Sunday afternoon."

"Not in the afternoon," Hillary insisted. "It would break up one of our days."

Kate nodded to Bridie. "That makes sense. Since your time here is limited, an evening performance would be better."

Bridie smiled at Catherine and Pina's pleading eyes. "Saturday night at the theatre sounds good to me." Bridie looked at the shops and people walking the avenue. She was pleased to be visiting Galena again.

"Biff and John will go with us, won't they?" Pina asked.

Hillary glanced at Catherine and Pina, understanding it was a way to guarantee that Bridie and Biff would meet. "I'm sure they'd like to go with us. Melodramas are fun for everybody."

Hillary stopped the coach in front of the theatre. Kate got out of the coach swiftly, so there wouldn't be any arguments as to who paid for the tickets.

On her way back to the coach, all three girls simultaneously asked, "Did you buy tickets for Biff and John?"

Bridie rolled her eyes, at their obvious plotting.

"I did," Kate said, waving the tickets. "I had mentioned the melodrama to John and Biff earlier this week and they agreed to come with us."

Soon, they were riding down the main street, parallel to the Galena River. Bridie sighed, riding past the De Soto Hotel, where she had stayed on previous visits. She felt as though John McTavish was nearby. They came to Galena, just four months before they were to be married. *Why was he taken from me,* she wondered.

The brick street ended and they entered a dirt road leading them from town. "How long will it take to get to your farm?" Pina asked.

"With me driving, a short half-hour, because I'm fast," Hillary joked. "But then, if we run into bandits or Indians looking for our money or scalps, it'll take a little longer."

Kate noticed Pina and Catherine cringe. "Stop teasing," she insisted. "Tell fibs like that and they'll never come here again."

"We'll get even with her," Pina assured Kate. "Catherine and I aren't helpless."

"I imagine you're not," Kate laughed.

Catherine leaned forward and tapped Kate's shoulder. "How far is the Mississippi River from here?"

"About three miles," Kate answered. "We can go there this weekend, or when you visit again, if you'd like. Have you ever seen it?"

"No. But I'd like to some day."

"Uncle Biff and I ride our horses there sometimes," Hillary said, boastfully. "I pack a picnic lunch and we eat along the river bank, watching the water roll by. The river is wide and powerful." Hillary began singing "Ole Man River." Catherine joined in and the others followed.

When they neared the farm, Kate pointed up the road. "Look! The new neighbors are moving in now." There were three large wagons of possessions being unloaded. Men, women and children were carrying things into the house, returning to the wagons for more. When they got closer, Kate waved.

A woman wearing a bonnet waved back, neither knowing for sure who the other person was.

They entered the path to their farmhouse as John was coming out, wearing his denim work clothes. He held the horse by the bridle, keeping the coach steady until everybody was on the ground. "Welcome to Hanley Farm," he greeted, looking at Bridie and the two girls. He noticed Bridie was the same size and height as Kate.

Kate stood next to John and made the introductions. "John will help carry your bags inside and then we'll have a cool drink."

Bridie put an arm around Catherine and Pina. "The girls and I would like to thank you for this weekend vacation. The scenic coach ride through the countryside has me relaxed already."

"Our pleasure," John said, removing the two largest pieces of luggage from the coach's trunk. He set them aside for himself.

"I thought you'd be helping our new neighbors move in?" Kate questioned.

John handed smaller bags to each of the girls before they went inside. "I went over there, but Tom said they had enough help. He thanked me for the offer and said we'd get together after the weekend."

Kate took one of the bags from John. "What's his wife's name?"

John removed the last piece of luggage from the trunk and handed it to Bridie. "Ruth. Tom and Ruth Roddy." John noticed Kate staring at him, waiting for more information. "They appear to be very nice people. The children, too."

Kate smiled and turned for the house. "Let's have that cold drink."

The three girls were putting ice in brown pottery mugs. Hillary asked, "When is Uncle Biff coming?"

"Tonight," John replied. "He'll be here to have supper with us."

"What time?" The girls stared at him, waiting for an answer, so they'd know when he would meet Bridie.

Kate stepped in front of John before he could answer, glaring at the girls, so they would stop being obvious about matching Biff and Bridie. "I imagine between five and six o'clock," she said, firmly. "I'm making one of his favorite summer meals." Kate turned to Bridie and pointed to a framed piece of paper on the wall. "That's a list of Biff's favorite meals. I try to have one of them when he comes, but he'll eat anything I prepare."

"What are we eating?" Hillary asked, licking her lips.

Kate looked at Bridie. "Being today's a hot day, I'm serving a cold meal. Do you mind?"

Bridie put her hand to her chest. "Not at all. In this heat, I'd do the same."

"What's the cold meal?" Hillary asked again, pouring iced tea into the mugs.

"Did you notice a ham shank in the icebox?"

"Yes, I did," she answered, sheepishly. "I guess we're having ham."

"Correct! With sliced tomatoes and corn-on-the-cob, which has been cooked and will be served cold."

Pina passed the mugs around after Hillary filled them. Bridie was served first, on Kate's guidance.

John took his first swig and deliberately groaned, "Aaahhhh! Now that I did that, all of us can do it—if you wish to."

All three girls followed his lead, while Bridie and Kate ignored them.

Bridie went to one of her two bags and removed a nicely wrapped package, then handed it to Kate. "This is a hospitality gift for you and John. When I saw it, I had to get it for you."

Kate unwrapped the package and showed the gift to John. It was a small porcelain, mantle clock with farm animals painted on it. "Isn't this perfect for us?" she asked, holding it up to him.

John chuckled. "I like it. It is perfect for here in the kitchen. We can put it on top of the spice rack near the stove. Thank you, Bridie."

"I think it should go there, too," Kate agreed. "I love it. Thanks for being so thoughtful."

Kate took Bridie by the arm. "I'll take you to your room. It's almost four o'clock, so by the time we freshen up it will almost be time for dinner." She pointed at Hillary. "You take the girls to your room, so they can freshen up, too."

Twenty minutes later, Biff rode onto the farm and went directly into the stable. He removed his saddle and blanket from Creo, before removing the bridle. He looked into her eyes and patted her neck. "You're a good girl." He was taking the bridle to the tack room when he heard voices coming from the house. He stepped to a window and looked across the yard. Hillary and three others were coming out of the house. He assumed the woman to be Bridie McDonald, and the girls, Pina and Catherine. He had memorized their names, so he wouldn't blunder when talking to them. All he needed to know was—which name went with which girl. He tried to get a good look at Bridie, but she was too far away.

Biff was about to hang the bridle on the wall, when he noticed the leather rein coming loose from the bridle ring. While repairing the bridle, he heard voices and footsteps approaching the stable. He looked out the window again. A rush of blood flew through his body. He was momentarily dazed and took a step back. He watched her closely, noticing the way she moved. Her figure and voice were very similar to Laura's, as was her skin and hair coloring. Staring at her, his breathing became difficult, feeling Laura's presence. He started taking rapid, deep breaths, trying to slow his heartbeat before they reached the stable. His legs weakened, so he began walking in a circle, con-tinuing to take deep breaths. It was working. Soon, his pulse slowed and his legs returned normal. Quickly, he prepared himself mentally for their meeting. As they got near, he walked out of the tack room and met them by the stable entrance.

Hillary ran to Biff and threw her arms around him. She looked back. "This is my Uncle Biff." Hillary looked up at Biff. "This is my friend, Catherine. The others will be along in a minute."

Chapter Four

Biff was sitting in the living room, thinking about Laura and how strongly Catherine reminded him of her. Their faces weren't the same, but similar and equally beautiful. Seeing her at a distance, or from the back, she *was* Laura.

Biff heard Bridie and Kate talking on the front porch and the girls in the kitchen washing dishes. He decided it was a good time to socialize with Bridie and learn more about her. He avoided the kitchen and went directly to the front porch where the ladies were enjoying the porch swing.

"Feel like little girls again?" he asked. "Or do you feel old enough for a hard drink?"

Bridie waved her hand and laughed. "I'm not sure how old I feel, but I feel wonderful. I think being in the country has caused it—so much so that I don't need a drink to feel good."

"I'll pass, too," Kate said. "Maybe later."

Biff sat on the porch railing, looking toward the barn. "Is John doing a chore, or is he inside the house?"

"Tossing hay," Kate replied. "He'll be back soon."

Bridie looked carefully at Biff, agreeing with Hillary that he was handsome, though she thought he looked more Scandinavian than Scottish. His hair was blonde and he had a nice wide smile. She grinned at him. "Kate tells me that besides your farms, you own a bank."

Biff smiled in return. "I'm in partnership with my father. The bank has been in the family for fifty years. It's an interesting business."

"She knows," Kate interrupted. "Bridie also has a partnership in a bank."

"You do? A bank in Newberry?"

"Yes. Like yours, it's been in the family for many years."

"I've got money *in* a bank," Kate quipped. "Does that qualify me for anything?"

Bridie laughed. "Why yes, you qualify for interest earnings, my dear."

Biff laughed with them. Pleased to find Bridie was not a reserved, rigid person, but friendly and easy to talk to. Observing her through dinner convinced him she was a pleasant person.

Giggling and laughing could be heard from inside the house. As the sound got closer, Kate remarked, "Here come the girls. They must have finished the dishes."

Hillary came out first. "It's eight o'clock already. We're going to the stable, so I can show them Knickers before it gets dark." She looked at the three adults. "Does anyone else want to come along?"

"I would love to see your horse," Bridie answered, eagerly. "I've heard so much about him, I feel he's a relative."

They walked toward the stable, with Biff lagging behind, watching Catherine. It was difficult for him to not watch her. Yet, he knew he had to hide his interest in a girl so young.

John surprised them by walking Knickers out of the stable. "I only put his bridal on, so you could see all of him."

Hillary watched the others respond to Knickers. They seemed genuinely impressed.

Bridie brandished a huge smile toward Hillary. "No wonder you love this animal. He's very handsome."

Pina pet his nose and kissed him, turning her soft, gray eyes to Hillary. "I'm jealous."

Catherine stroked his neck, slowly, studying all of him. "I'm jealous, too." She looked at Hillary. "Your name for him is perfect. He definitely appears to be wearing knickers."

Hillary felt immensely rich at that moment, not only because of her horse, but also because she had good friends and family. *Where would I be now, if Kate and John hadn't taken me into their lives?* she wondered.

"I wish Brian could see Knickers," Catherine remarked. "He'd probably want one just like him."

"Who's Brian?" John asked.

Catherine was running her hand across Knicker's back. "He's my friend. Brian's fond of horses, too."

Pina turned to John, "By friend, she means, sweetie."

Biff looked at Catherine, thinking, "*Of course, a girl like her would have a fella. Lucky guy.*"

Kate glanced at the others. "Now that you've been introduced to Knickers, is everyone ready for blueberry pie?"

Hillary and Pina looked at each other, licking their lips. They led the others back to the house, while John returned Knickers to the stable. Biff walked a few steps behind Catherine.

An hour later, after eating pie, the girls decided to go outside for girl talk. Hillary yelled to the adults in the parlor, "We're going outside to wail at the moon."

"Stay near the house," John replied. "Remember, there are wild animals around here."

"Wild animals by the house?" Pina questioned, stepping out to the porch.

"Deer mostly, but rarely a bear or wolf," Hillary assured them. "They're more afraid of us than we are of them. Besides, the full moon has the grounds lit up nicely."

Catherine searched the surrounding area. "Are you telling us animals will only eat us if we're in the dark? I don't think so."

Hillary took her friends by the arm and led them toward the corral fence. "We need to get away from the house, so they can't hear us."

"True," Pina agreed, searching the grounds for wild animals.

"What do you think?" Hillary asked. "Have either of you noticed any signs of interest between Biff and Bridie?"

"It's too early to tell," Pina answered. "They just met this evening. We'll have them sit together at the theatre tomorrow night. Maybe that will inspire something?"

Catherine leaned against the corral fence. "We can't make anything happen. We've got Bridie and Biff together. Now, it's up to them. All we can do is wait."

"They've certainly been getting along nicely," Hillary declared. "I think there's a good chance they'll like each other."

"I've noticed something," Pina said, mysteriously, "But I'm keeping it a secret until I know for sure."

The following morning, Kate and Bridie prepared ham, eggs and fried potatoes for breakfast. Biff and John had four eggs, a thick slice of ham and potatoes before going out to put up fences.

Bridie was standing at the stove with a spatula in her hand, looking at the men. "I don't think I'll eat breakfast this morning. I'm getting full just watching you men."

Kate laughed. "I've felt that way at times, but I still end up eating."

John winked at Kate. "We'll finish our work by noon, then spend the rest of the day with you ladies. Think about something you'd like to do this afternoon."

"Don't tire yourselves out," Kate suggested. "Remember, we're going to see a melodrama tonight and I don't want you falling asleep in the theatre."

Bridie placed more ham in a frying pan and leaned toward Kate. "I don't think they'll fall asleep at a melodrama, especially with the audience yelling at the actors."

"True," Biff agreed. "The audience can be as entertaining as the performance."

John drank the last of his coffee and looked at Biff. "Ready to go?"

Biff stood at the table. "Ready." He looked at Kate and Bridie. "Thanks for the great breakfast."

The women watched them cross the yard and climb onto the buckboard filled with fencing supplies.

"It's nice having a man around, for many reasons," Kate remarked. "Especially if you have a good one like I have." She looked at Bridie. "Sorry about you losing your man."

Bridie walked back to the stove. "Me, too." She didn't want to tell Kate the truth about John McTavish at this time, deciding to keep it a secret until later. "When I see how well you and John get along, it pains me that I never had that kind of relationship … but could have. John McTavish and I were a good match, like you and your John."

Kate wanted to say more, including something about Biff, but didn't want to appear a matchmaker. Fortunately, the three girls could be heard making their way to the kitchen, putting an end to their conversation.

Pina entered the kitchen first, her arms extended from her sides. "Watch out ladies, here we come."

Kate and Bridie laughed when they saw Catherine and Pina dressed in matching blue bib overalls over red shirts. Hillary was wearing denim pants and a cotton-sack shirt.

Bridie pointed at the girls. "Your farm hands look adorable."

Kate glanced at them, her hands clasped together with delight. "We should go to town and have pictures taken of the girls dressed like this."

Bridie nodded. "I agree. A souvenir of our visit to Hanley Farm."

Kate continued admiring the girls. "We'd have to do it this morning. The photographer is closed tomorrow and you leave for home Monday. If the pictures aren't ready before you leave, I'll mail them to you."

Hillary's eyes widened at the suggestion. "I think we should, too. We can have it framed and hang it in my bedroom."

Kate looked at Catherine and Pina. Their grinning faces revealed they liked the idea, too. "Let's do it." She faced, Bridie. "We can have a picture made for each of the girls. After all, they're making memories for the future."

Bridie started breaking eggs into the frying pan. "I think it's a great idea. It's only eight o'clock, so eat fast and we can be back by noon, when the men are through working. Besides, I'd like a picture of the girls for myself. Catherine won't be living with me forever and she'll take the picture with her."

"Hurry girls," Kate insisted. "Bridie and I have eaten. You have to gather the eggs and pump water for the animals before leaving. We should be able to go within the hour."

Hillary began placing ham on the three plates. "We can leave a note for John and Biff, so they know where we are."

Catherine grabbed the pan of fried potatoes from the stove and scraped the contents onto the plates. "We can have the dishes soaking while we're gone. We'll wash them when we return."

"Don't worry about the dishes," Bridie said. "Kate and I can wash them, while you girls are tending to the animals."

Pina went after a pencil and paper on a small desk next to the telephone and began writing. When finished, she turned and faced the others. "My note reads, *Gone Fishing. Back by noon.*"

Kate chuckled. "That's fine. They'll understand the meaning."

"Eggs are about ready," Bridie announced. "Bring your plates over."

Two hours later, Kate reined in the horse, stopping in front of John Harte Photographers. Before entering, they looked at photographs displayed in the window, trying to decide if Kate and Bridie should have their picture taken, too.

"You could dress as cowgirls," Catherine suggested.

"Or painted ladies," Hillary giggled.

"Let's go in," Bridie said. "I'm sure Mr. Harte will have plenty of ideas for two inane women."

A woman sitting at a desk stood and walked over to them. "Good Morning. How may I help you?"

We didn't come here for tomatoes, or saddles, Hillary thought to herself.

Kate stepped forward. "We'd like to have pictures of these girls … and a picture of us women … in costume. We're in a very silly mood, and if we don't do it now, it won't get done."

The lady smiled. "Silliness is part of our business." She glanced at the three girls in work clothes. "I understand why you'd want a picture of them. They're darling in those outfits." She backed away and sat at her desk. "My name is Helen Harte. My husband is in the back room, developing some plates. He'll be out shortly." She wrote their names and address on a card and pointed to a light-gray backdrop. "You girls stand over there, please."

The girls tittered and grinned, lining up where the woman pointed. Kate and Bridie were enjoying the girl's enthusiasm. "We want five of these pictures," Bridie instructed her.

Helen tapped a small, silver bell on her desk. In less then a minute, John Harte came from the back room. "From what I could hear, you ladies are out for a good time."

"You're right," Kate responded. "We didn't know we'd be like this when we got up this morning, but here we are."

Mr. Harte stepped into the studio part of the room and stood behind a large, black box camera on a tripod. He placed his head under a black cloth draping the back of the camera. "Take one step back, girls." His directions were muffled, but distinguishable. "Let's have the bib overalls on the ends and the cotton-sack shirt in the middle."

The girls stood as directed.

"Smile!" A bright flash of light blinded the girls.

"Where is everybody?" Pina asked.

"You'll get your vision back in a moment," Mrs. Harte said. "Don't move. Stand there until you can see properly."

Mr. Harte looked at Kate and Bridie. "You're next."

"We want to wear a costume," Kate said. "What do you have?"

Mrs. Harte led Bridie and Kate to anther room. Kate held up her hand to the girls. "Wait here. Bridie and I will do the choosing. We'll surprise you."

Fifteen minutes later, they returned wrapped in Indian blankets and a single feather standing in the back of their hair. Kate was carrying a peace pipe and Bridie a hatchet.

The girls began laughing, vigorously.

"We want five of their pictures, too," Catherine squealed.

Hillary pointed at them, tears of laughter rolling down her cheeks. "Do we have to admit we know them?"

Kate looked at Bridie. "Come, Chumsa, we go to magic box."

"Ugh!" Bridie responded.

After being blinded by the flash, they removed their Indian blankets. Bridie fanned her face. "It's warm under that blanket, especially on a hot day like today."

Still amused, Hillary pointed to their heads. "Don't forget to take out the feathers."

Bridie reached for her feather. "Thank you, Hillary. I would have forgotten. Wouldn't I look silly riding down the street with that in my hair?"

"No more than in here," Catherine chuckled.

"When will the pictures be ready?" Kate asked Mrs. Harte.

"Mr. Harte is leaving in minutes to take pictures at a private residence and he'll be working with them all afternoon. I don't believe they'll be ready until Monday afternoon."

A subtle groan emanated from the girls.

Kate noticed Bridie's disappointment. "I'll mail them Monday," she assured her. "They'll be wrapped, so they can't be damaged."

"Thanks. I guess we don't have a choice. It'll give me something to look forward to, once I'm home."

Mrs. Harte stepped up to them. "What time are you leaving town Monday?"

"About two o'clock," Kate answered for Bridie. "She's taking a train."

Helen patted Bridie's forearm. "Stop by for the pictures on your way to the train station. I'll see that John has them ready for you by noon Monday."

Bridie's face brightened. "Thank you. I really appreciate that."

"We appreciate it, too," Pina joined in.

"Let me ask *you* a favor," Mrs. Harte queried. "Would you mind if I display your two pictures in our window? We like to have a variety."

Kate glanced at the others. The girls were smiling and nodding their heads, anxious to have their picture displayed for the public to see. "I can see the girls would like that, but I'm not sure I want to be displayed like an idiot." She peered at the smiling girls again and replied, reluctantly, "We'd be delighted to have our pictures in the window."

CHAPTER FIVE

Returning home, they passed their new neighbors' house. Only one of the three wagons was still parked outside. A teenage boy was sitting at a picnic bench reading a book. Everyone in the coach waved to the boy. He looked up, raising his book slightly, as if undecided about responding.

"I guess that was some kind of a hello," Hillary muttered.

"It appears most of their helpers are gone," Kate remarked. "I wonder if the other wagon will be leaving today?"

"It could be their wagon." Hillary suggested.

Kate shook the reins to move the horse faster. "You're probably right. I'm anxious to meet them. John said they appear to be a nice family."

"Look!" Pina shouted, looking toward the house. "Two girls just came outside and they're waving to us."

"It appears the girls are friendlier than the boy," Hillary commented. She and Pina waved back. "How old did John say their children are?"

Kate smiled at Hillary's interest in her new neighbors. "The girls are nine and twelve, the boy is sixteen." She guided the horse to the front of her house, searching the grounds for the men. "Everybody out. It's time for a cold drink and a change of clothes."

Hillary looked over at the stable. "I don't think the men are back. I don't see John's wagon."

"I'm sure they'll be here shortly," Kate assured her. "It's almost twelve o'clock. Go inside and start pouring iced tea. I'll be there in a minute."

"Is there something I can do to help?" Bridie asked.

"No, Chumsa, just make self comfortable."

"You bet'chum, Chief."

"Listen to those two," Catherine teased. "They're pretending to be on an Indian Reservation. How cute."

"I think we should lock these crazy squaws out of our tee pee." Pina joked.

"That's it," Hillary shouted. "We'll call Kate, Crazy Squaw, and Bridie, Nutty Squaw."

"And I'll call you late for the melodrama tonight," Kate laughed, driving off to the stable.

The girls ran to the house, their feet pounding on the porch. Bridie sauntered in behind them and went directly to her room to wash and change her clothes. Minutes later, Kate brought her a mug of iced tea.

"Thank you, Kate. I need something cold to drink." She sat on the edge of the bed and sipped her tea, then took a deep breath. "I must tell you, I'm enjoying myself immensely, and looking forward to the melodrama tonight."

"Me, too. This morning was fun."

"It's strange how you can have so much pleasure doing something spontaneously, and when you plan an event, it's a disappointment. In Newberry, I would never have a chance to do what we did this morning. It was great getting silly with the girls." She sipped her tea again. "The difficult part is knowing the girls will leave us in a few years." Bridie hesitated, giving Kate an apologetic glance. "Sorry about that. It's my problem, not yours. You haven't started your family yet."

Kate sat next to her and asked, "Do you still think about getting married and having a family?"

Before Bridie could answer, Hillary came running down the hall to Kate. "The new girls are waving for us to go over there. Their mother and brother are sitting at the picnic table, too. What do you think? The men aren't back yet."

Kate glanced at Bridie. "Would you mind Catherine and Pina going over there?"

"Why not? It's Spontaneous Day."

Kate held Hillary's arm, so she couldn't run away. "You can go, but come home as soon as they go inside. If you're still there when John and Biff come back, we'll come over and introduce ourselves."

They could hear Hillary racing through the house until the screen door slammed shut.

"I'd better change my clothes now," Bridie said.

"Me, too. See you in a few minutes."

The girls walked through the field of golden hay, swaying in the summer breeze. They could see the girls standing near the wooden table, waving to them. Both wore flowered, cotton dresses and black shoes. Approaching the picnic table, the woman stood. The boy, however, remained seated, staring at them as if they were a curiosity. He had a comely face and blond hair draped his forehead.

"I'm Trish," the younger girl shouted.

The woman, tall and slender, stepped toward the girls. "Welcome, girls. I'm Mrs. Roddy. We were hoping you'd come and visit. Would you like something to drink?"

The three girls looked at each other and shook their heads. "I guess not," Hillary answered. "Thank you anyway." She smiled at the older girl and Trish. "I'm Hillary and these are my best friends, Pina and Catherine. They live in Newberry, Illinois."

The older girl gave a sincere welcoming smile. "My name is Marnie." She turned to the boy. "This is our brother, Adam."

"Hello!" he mumbled unenthusiastically, closing the book he was holding. His eyes danced back and forth between the three girls before settling upon Hillary. "Do you have a brother?"

Hillary thought it an odd first question, as though he preferred she be a boy. She looked at him suspiciously, "No," she responded, with a frown.

Mrs. Roddy recognized Hillary's irritation with Adam's inappropriate question and interceded. "Mr. Roddy should be home soon. We've been anxious to meet you and your parents." She faced Pina and Catherine. "How long will you girls be visiting?"

Pina took a step forward. "We're leaving Monday."

"This is our first time here," Catherine added, quickly. "We only arrived yesterday."

"Sit down, if you like," Marnie suggested, sitting next to Adam. "Were you coming from Galena when we saw you this morning?"

The three girls sat opposite Marnie and Adam. He opened his book and began reading again.

"Yes! We went to have our pictures taken," Pina said, giggling. "We were in a silly mood and we all had our pictures taken in costume. Their mothers dressed like Indian squaws."

"You're kidding?" Trish questioned. She turned, looking up at her mother. "We should do that."

Adam looked up from his book of short stories. "We haven't been to Galena, yet. Maybe this week." He began reading again.

"Adam!" Mrs. Roddy said, firmly. "Don't read now. We have guests."

He looked up at her, appearing startled and contrite. "I guess," he said, closing his book again. "Sorry."

Hillary wondered if Adam hated girls, or was it bad manners.

"Where did you people move from?" Catherine asked.

Marnie leaned forward, clasping her hands together on the table. "We moved from Rockford, Illinois. It ain't far from here."

"It *isn't* far from here," Mrs. Roddy corrected her. "Not, '*aint*.'"

Marnie looked over her shoulder at her mother. "Yes, Ma. I knew better. It just came out wrong." She faced her guests again. "Our father had a pharmacy there, but always had a 'Hankerin,' as he calls it, to own a farm. He lived on a farm when he was a boy. One day, he came home from the pharmacy and announced, "We have the money to buy a farm, so we're doing it."

"We all liked the idea, and now we're here, talking to our new neighbors."

"Hillary loves living on a farm," Pina remarked. "She even has a beautiful horse of her own."

A feeble smile appeared on Adam's face, looking at Hillary. "Do you really have your own horse?"

"Yes. My uncle bought him for me. He's brown and black. I named him Knickers." She stared directly into his eyes. "Girls, as well as boys, can ride horses."

Catherine chuckled. "When you see him, you'll understand why she named him that,"

Ruth Roddy stood above the children, her gray calico dress fluttering in the breeze. Her eyes quickly swept over the children, pleased that they were accepting each other so readily. She glanced at Adam and gave a shallow sigh, wondering when he would adjust.

"Hillary, what kind of animals do you have?" Marnie asked.

"Right now, we only have eighteen cattle and a couple dozen chickens. We expect to buy a few pigs next year. John is more interested in grain than animals."

Adam leered at Hillary, baffled as to why she called her father John, instead of Dad or father.

"Here comes Pa," Trish said, pointing to the field behind their house. They watched him rock in his saddle, riding toward them. Two men in a wagon came over the rise behind him.

"John and Biff are following him." Pina said.

They sat silent, watching the men ride to the side of the house. Ruth waved to Tom. "Are you finished for the day?"

Tom climbed down from the horse and gave her a quick glance. "Yep. Time to visit with the neighbors." He was a tall, barrel-chested man with a narrow waist. He waited until John and Biff climbed down from the wagon, then they walked with long easy strides over to the bench. "We were looking around to see what fencing work needed to be done. John and Biff volunteered to help us get started. Fortunately, most of the fencing is in good shape."

Ruth stepped up to the men. "Thank you for your help. It's surely appreciated." She extended her hand. "I'm Ruth. Would you care for something to drink? It won't be cold 'cause we don't have ice yet."

The men accepted Ruth's hand carefully and introduced themselves. "Water would do just fine," Biff replied.

Adam got up from the bench, brushing blond hair from his forehead, and started for the white frame house. "I'll get it." He looked over at the two men. "I'm Adam."

John and Biff gave him a nod and smile. Adam stopped suddenly, pointing toward the field of hay. "Looks like your women are coming."

All heads turned. "Yep! It's Kate and Bridie," John said. "In hay up to their waists."

Biff walked to the edge of the field to meet them, taking the baskets they were carrying.

Kate shouted ahead, "It looked like everybody was here but us, so here we come."

"Glad ya did," Tom Roddy shouted back.

Ruth turned to her daughters. "Trish! Marnie! Get twelve glasses and cups, and tell Adam, enough water for twelve people."

"Thanks," Tom said, to the passing girls.

Biff placed the two baskets on the table and stood next to John.

Kate stepped closer to Ruth and made the introductions.

Ruth smiled at the two women. "Nice to meet you, ladies. My name is Ruth." She looked toward the men. "My husband, Tom, seems to be well acquainted with your men already." Ruth looked at Bridie. "Which man is yours?" In an instant, she realized by the sudden silence and rigid faces, she asked a delicate question.

There was a faint glint of laughter in John's eyes. He cast a brief peek at Biff, who was trying to ignore the uncomfortable inference.

The three girls held their breath, waiting for a response from Bridie.

Bridie smiled at Ruth. "I'm visiting. I don't have a man here."

Ruth put her hand to her mouth, her eyes pleading for forgiveness. "I'm sorry. I just assumed …"

Bridie grinned at her. "It's okay. I would have assumed the same."

"What's in the baskets?" Hillary asked, intentionally ending the uneasiness.

"I brought sandwiches, apples, pickles and cookies." Kate gripped Ruth's wrist for a moment. "I know you're not fully settled into your house, so this will fill your family's stomachs for a while."

"Thanks. We appreciate it."

"Watch out, water coming," Marnie yelled, running up to the table carrying cups and glasses. Adam followed, staggering and leaning to one side, carrying a heavy bucket of water.

"Adam," Ruth shouted. "Take the water by the tree and pour there, so you don't spill on the table." She watched him pivot around the heavy bucket dangling from his arm and shuffle toward the tree. "You girls hold the cups for Adam."

Bridie removed the cloths covering the two baskets, inviting the men to come and eat. Catherine stood and backed away from the table. "You adults eat here. We can sit on the grass." The other children vacated the table, waiting for the adults to take their food.

Ruth nodded and smiled at Catherine. "That was considerate of you children. Thank you." She turned to the men taking food from the baskets. "Take a water and sit where you like."

John led Biff to the end of the table and sat across from Tom. The women selected what they wanted to eat before Kate passed the basket to the children. Ruth sat between Tom and Kate. The only seat unoccupied was next to Biff.

Bridie sat down, handing him a napkin. "Here, you didn't get one."

Biff smiled at her. "Thanks."

Pina was watching them from under the tree. "Biff and Bridie are sitting together," she whispered to her friends. The three girls took a quick peek and smiled at each other.

Kate turned toward the girls. "We only have another half-hour to be here. The play starts at six and we have to freshen up before five o'clock."

Adam took quick glances at Hillary, trying not to be caught admiring her pretty face. "What play?"

"We're going into Galena to see a melodrama tonight," Hillary answered, firmly. "It's something a girl would like more than a boy."

"What's the name of it?" he inquired, with a smirk.

"Joan, the Beautiful Typewriter Girl."

Adam rolled his eyes, taking a bite of his ham and tomato sandwich. Guilt settled within him for being unpleasant to Hillary. She appeared to be nice, so he decided to say something pleasant. "I hope you girls enjoy the play. I'm sure it will be fun."

Hillary took a long look at him, surprised by his kind statement. "Thank you, Adam."

"It will be exciting," Pina insisted. "We'll tell you about it tomorrow."

"Please, bring us the program?" Marnie asked. "They're brief, but it will be fun to read and see the drawings."

"Maybe *we'll* be lucky enough to see a melodrama someday," Trish said loudly, looking over at her mother.

"I heard you Trish," Ruth responded, without turning around. "We will eventually."

When they finished eating, the children gathered the garbage and put it into a wooden crate. "I'll burn it all tonight," Adam said.

"I want to do it with you," Trish said. "I like to throw things into the fire and watch it burn."

"I like to watch fires, too," Hillary agreed. "Watching the sparks drift skyward and float away ... similar to fireworks."

Adam called to his father, "Could we add wood to this and have a bonfire tomorrow night, then our neighbors could come."

"Don't see why not," Tom replied. "Contain the garbage, so it doesn't blow around before then."

"Alright, children, time to go home and clean up," Kate called, rising from the table. She faced Tom and Ruth. "It was nice meeting you. It appears we'll be seeing you again tomorrow for a bonfire."

John and Biff shook Tom's hand and nodded to Ruth. "See you tomorrow."

Marnie and Trish waved.

Adam stood silent, watching them walk through the field of hay.

Back in Newberry, Wade Widner was sitting on his bed at the hotel, examining his train ticket, reassuring himself the day and departure time were correct for Monday. He laid it on the nightstand next to the bed, leaning back against the headboard, thinking about Kate and how he would like to have her for his own. He figured if John was arrested and jailed for many years—or possibly be hung—then Kate and Hillary would be self-providing and possibly need help financially, giving him an opportunity with her.

Wade also realized Kate must never know he would be the one to reveal John's location to Tyler Sharpe. She would hate him for that and never allow him near her. He needed a promise from Tyler Sharpe he'd never tell who discovered John's whereabouts. He left his room and walked to the telegraph office to send a message to Tyler Sharpe, requesting an immediate response.

CHAPTER SIX

The girls stood on the porch wearing pretty dresses, anxious for their evening at the melodrama. They fussed with each other's clothes, so they would hang perfect. They waited for the adults to come out, while Biff drove his father's coach to the front of the house.

"Biff's here with the coach," Hillary shouted into the house. "It's time to get-a-goin'."

John stepped out onto the porch, wearing brown pants and a tan sport jacket. "They're on their way," he assured the girls. He watched Biff climb down from the coach. "Doesn't your Uncle Biff look dapper in those new gray slacks and blue jacket he just bought?" He grinned at the girls. "Think he's trying to impress someone?"

Biff jerked his head in John's direction, frowning. "Let's not make something out of nothing. I bought them because I needed them."

John walked to the edge of the porch. "You needed them for some time, but didn't buy them until now. Too coincidental for me, I'd say."

"Them's powerful words," Hillary said, smiling at John. "One would think you're implying something?"

"Seems purposeful to me, too," Pina laughed.

"Enough," Biff insisted. He looked at Catherine with her hands clasped together, grinning, but not saying a word. "Whatever you're cooking up to say, don't."

Kate walked out onto the porch wearing a brown skirt and white blouse. She held the door open for Bridie and stepped aside, so Biff could see Bridie in her green dress. "We're ready to go."

"You women look fantastic," John said. His eyes flashed at Biff, coaxing him to say something complimentary.

"I agree," Biff added. "Any man would be proud to be seen with you two ladies. Let's go, so we can show you off."

Hillary placed her hands on her hips. "Does anyone want to show us off?"

Biff held his hand out to her, helping her down the two stairs. "I'm always proud of you, you know that," he said, giving his hand to Pina and then Catherine, focusing on the touch of her soft, warm hand.

Walking to the coach, Kate took John's arm. Bridie took Biff's arm and followed. When the women and girls were inside the coach, John and Biff climbed up to the driver's bench. Biff cracked the whip and they rolled toward the road. When they passed the Roddy house, Marnie and Trish were sitting at the picnic bench waving to them.

At the theatre, the three girls entered their row of seats, Hillary deliberately stutter-stepped to make sure that the adults were aligned where Biff and Bridie would be sitting together.

While waiting for the play to begin, a man in a black suit entered from back stage and sat at a piano below the stage. He began playing, *My Old Kentucky Home* as the curtain opened.

Joan, the beautiful typewriter girl, was sitting at a desk, typing.

The audience cheered and applauded the heroine.

> *A bent woman with white hair opened the door and entered the office carrying a basket with Joan's lunch inside.*
> The pianist began playing a few notes from the song, **Clementine.**

The woman set her basket on the edge of the desk. "Here, my dear, I brought hardtack, two apples and dried beef. I'd like to give you something better, but we don't have enough money and the mortgage is due at the end of the month. Mr. Miserly said, 'If we don't make our payment on time, he'll throw us out of the house.'" The woman feigned crying.

Joan stood and placed a gentle arm around the woman. "Don't cry, Mother. I work eight hours every day at this office and Mr. Opportune gave me a job at his boarding house, cleaning and cooking. I'll be working another six hours every day. If we're lucky, we'll have enough to pay the mortgage this month."

Her mother pulled a white handkerchief from the sleeve of her tattered gray dress and began dabbing her eyes. "You're a good daughter. You do so much for your poor mother." With heavy heart and sad eyes, she looked up at Joan with hopeful yearning. "Do you think you and Randy will marry soon?"

Joan looked to the ceiling. "I don't know, Mother. I can only hope." She looked down at her mother again. "Randy came back from a month of fur trapping today and is at the Trading Post selling his pelts now."

"Let's hope he gets a good price," her mother said, woefully. "I'm going out on the street to see if I can sell some of my knitting." She kissed Joan on the cheek. "I'll be asleep when you get home from your second job. Get as much rest as you can, my dear. God loves you." She walked out of the office.

Joan began typing again. Moments later, a man flung the door open and entered the office with long strides, as though he owned the place. He was tall and slender, wearing a black suit and cape with a tall stovepipe hat. A long, black handlebar mustache hovered above his lips.

The piano player thundered out a portion of **Woodman, Spare That Tree.**

Immediately, the audience began yelling, "Boo! Hiss! Cad! Scoundrel!"

Joan turned to him, with the back of her hand in front of her mouth, obviously frightened by his presence. "Go away!" she screamed.

"Go away?" he scowled. "Why would I go away, when you know I want you for my bride?"

Joan raised a halting hand to him. "Never, never," she moaned, as he came closer.

"We'll see about that," he sneered. "If you don't marry me, I'll throw you and your mother off of my property."

Spectators began yelling, "Boooo! Hiss!" The jeers resounded throughout the theatre. One man stood and threw a turnip at the villain, landing on the stage floor near his foot.

"My God!" Hillary gasped to her friends. "Did you see that?"

Mr. Miserly looked out at the audience and shouted with anger, "Bah!"

A carrot appeared in flight, wide of its mark.

Joan laid her head on the desk and began crying.

"Tears won't do you any good," Mr. Miserly laughed. He pulled a paper from his pocket and slammed it on the desk. "Look at this," he demanded. "It's the mortgage on the house. It says you must pay me every month for another eleven years. If you don't pay, you must get out of the house and lose all you paid to date." He twisted the ends of his mustache. "Unless you agree to marry me."

"Get away from her," came a voice from the doorway. It was Randy, tall and handsome with broad shoulders. "She'd never marry a scoundrel like you."

*Strong notes from, **Hail Columbia**, raced out of the piano.*

The audience went wild, clapping and cheering. "Yeah! Our Hero! Bravo!"

Mr. Miserly spun around and stepped back. "Curses! When did you get back in town?"

"Today, and I sold my fur pelts for cash an hour ago. Tell me, what is owed on that mortgage?"

"How much is owed?" Mr. Miserly snickered. "More than you can pay, to be sure."

"Pay him," came a shout from the audience.

Randy pulled a wad of cash from his jacket pocket. "How much does Mrs. Sweet owe, damn you? I want you out of their lives forever."

Mr. Miserly rubbed his hands together and leered at Randy. "It's ninety-eight dollars," he replied. "Do you have that much?"

Randy glanced at Joan and his shoulders sagged. "I only have eighty-six dollars." He stood tall again, bellowing with confidence, "I can borrow the difference. I know I can. I'll be at your office tomorrow."

The pianist strummed out **The Battle Hymn Of The Republic.**

The audience cheered for Joan and Randy. "Yeah, Randy! Pay the cad."

"You can raise twelve dollars by tomorrow?" Mr. Miserly questioned. "That's nice, but there is a clause in the mortgage where they pay for all damage done to the property, and there appears to be a lot of damage—probably another twenty dollars worth. Can you get twenty dollars more, than the twelve?"

"Oh, my God," Joan moaned, falling back against the desk. "We could never get that amount of money."

An apple flew up onto the stage. "Kill the bastard," came an irate voice.

"You liar," Randy bellowed, shaking his fist at Mr. Miserly. "I did fixin' at that house and it is in better condition now than when they bought it."

"Heh! Heh!" Mr. Miserly goaded. "Can you prove it? If not, another twenty dollars, please." He turned to Joan again. "Marry me, rather than this poor joke of a boy, and you can have whatever you want."

Joan gasped, placing her arm against her forehead, "No! I'd die first."

"Then die you may," Miserly snickered.

"Boo! Cad! Scoundrel!" heaved through the theatre.

Hillary glanced at Catherine and they smiled, agreeing that the play was fun. She looked at Pina and saw a tear running down her cheek. Hillary elbowed Catherine and pointed to Pina. "We can tease her about this later."

Pina's head turned slowly to her friends. "What are you whispering about?"

"We can't believe you are crying over this play." Hillary responded.

"It's sad," Pina said, earnestly.

Kate leaned toward the girls. "Be quiet, you're disturbing the people around us."

Hillary smiled at Kate. "Can we leave and buy vegetables before the second act starts?" She and Catherine began laughing, covering their mouths to muffle the sound. She glanced at Kate again. "Sorry. We'll stop."

Randy took a step closer to Mr. Miserly. "I don't believe such a clause is in that mortgage contract. Let me read it."

Mr. Miserly unfolded the contract and held against his chest. "Come and look," he said, pointing to the bottom of the page.

Randy examined the names on the mortgage and read the brief contract. He faced Joan. "Where is your copy of the mortgage?"

Embarrassed for not having one, Joan looked toward the floor and answered meekly. "We've lost it. We don't know where it is."

Randy stepped back and squared his shoulders. "You'll get paid, one way or another, but you aren't throwing them out and you'll never marry Joan."

Mr. Miserly started for the door, looking back over his shoulder. "We'll see," he snarled. "We'll see."

The curtain lowered, ending the first act.

Hillary noticed Bridie and Biff talking and smiling. She leaned back against her seat, satisfied with their progress.

John looked over at the girls. "Are you enjoying the melodrama?"

"Absolutely," Catherine answered, with a smirk. "But I think Pina is enjoying it more."

Hillary giggled when she saw Pina sitting stubbornly, her arms folded tightly across her chest, seemingly irritated by the teasing. She patted Pina's leg. "I'm sorry. We were just having fun."

> Suddenly, **My Old Kentucky Home** loomed again and the curtains parted slowly.
>
> *Randy had his arms around Joan, trying to console her.* "What can I do?" *she pleaded, with her hands over her heart.* "If we don't pay, we'll be thrown out of our house."
>
> *Randy raised a fist, looking toward the door.* "I noticed something rotten about that contract and I'm going to get to the bottom of this. I'm going to the sheriff's office. I'll be back later."
>
> *Joan stared up at Randy, placing a hand on his chest.* "Please, my love, do whatever you can."
>
> *After Randy walked out of the office, Joan returned to her desk, buried her face in her hands and began sobbing.*
>
> The piano player strummed more of **Oh, My Darling Clementine.**

Sympathetic moans spread through the theatre and the stage went black for a few seconds. When the lights came on again, a man's arm shot out from behind the curtain, holding a sign reading, *TWO HOURS LATER.*

> *Joan's mother entered the office again, slowly shuffling toward her daughter.* "I sold three doilies for forty-five cents, my dear. That will help toward paying the mortgage."
>
> *Joan gave her mother a pitiful look and smiled.* "Yes, Mother, that will help." *Suddenly, they heard loud voices coming their way.*
>
> *Randy and Sheriff Good entered the office, deep in conversation. The sheriff tapped his index finger on Randy's chest.* "If what you say

is true, he'll have to accept your money to pay off the mortgage. But you'll have to prove your accusation."

"I can," Randy insisted. He stood by Joan and her mother. "Mrs. Sweet, soon you'll have Mr. Miserly out of your life. I believe he has forgery in that mortgage and I intend to prove it. The judge and Mr. Miserly should be here any minute."

Clapping and shouts of "Yeah! Good boy, Randy," resonated.

Joan looked at her mother. "Did you hear him? We may be free from Mr. Miserly forever." Joan laid her head against Randy's chest. "You are wonderful."

"I see them crossing the street now," Sheriff Good announced. "I sure hope you are right, Randy. That evil man needs a good comeuppance."

Judge True entered the office with Mr. Miserly flailing his cape covered arms, trying to convince the judge his contract was binding and the meeting was a waste of time.

"Hiss! Boo! "Hang him, Judge," spectators called out. Nothing was thrown onto the stage for fear of hitting someone other than Mr. Miserly.

"Good afternoon, ladies and gentlemen."

"Same to you, Judge True," Joan replied, meekly.

The judge faced Randy. "You say the mortgage contract between Mrs. Sweet and Mr. Miserly contains forgery. Can you prove it?"

Randy held his hand out to Mr. Miserly. "Show us the contract, so the judge can read it."

Mr. Miserly stepped back. "It's legal. Everything needed, is printed there."

"If you have nothing to hide, show it to us," Judge True demanded.

Mr. Miserly reached inside his coat and unfolded the contract. "Here, look for yourself. Everything is there, legal-like."

The judge read the contract, rubbing his chin. "I don't see anything wrong with this agreement. Everything Mr. Miserly claims is here."

Randy took the contract from the judge and laid it on the desk. "Look here," Randy said, pointing to various words on the paper. "Notice the difference in the printed paragraphs above the signatures, with the paragraph below the signatures. All the letters are not of like kind, meaning they were printed on different machines. The part about paying for damage to the house was added below all the signatures—not above in the body of the contract, as it should be. Obviously, it was added later and is not part of the original mortgage agreement."

Judge True looked at Mr. Miserly. "Some of the letters are different. How do you explain that?"

"I don't know," he replied, slyly. "That's how it was printed originally. I'm not a printer."

"I'd have to be an idiot to believe that," Judge True responded. "This contract has definitely been tampered with. Mrs. Sweet may have lost her contract and does not understand what you did, but I do. I suggest you take full payment from Randy, or go to trial and possibly jail for fraud. You and Randy meet me at the courthouse within two days to finalize this."

Mr. Miserly twisted the ends of his mustache and glared at Randy. "Curse you!" he snarled. "I'll get you for this." He slithered out of the room, with another turnip flying after him.

"Hooray! Yeah Randy!"

The curtain closed, while the audience applauded wildly.

Kate stood to face the girls. "That was fun. It's time to eat. And don't forget to save a program for Marnie and Trish."

CHAPTER SEVEN

The next morning, Hillary showed Pina and Catherine how she fed the horses and collected eggs from the chickens. Hillary broke bales of hay into small portions, so each of them could carry hay to the five horses. "Let the horses see the hay before you walk in the stall, then they'll be glad to see you," Hillary assured them. She fed four horses, because Pina and Catherine were busy talking and petting the first horse they fed. When they finished, they brushed straw dust from themselves and walked to the chicken coop. "I have to be careful of Zelda because she's mean and might peck me."

"Which one is Zelda?" Pina asked.

"I'll show you in a minute." Hillary picked up a wicker basket lying next to the coop entrance and handed it to Catherine. "You hold this, I'll put the eggs in." Hillary stopped at the first hen, pushing it aside with the back of her hand before taking the egg. She looked to her friends, smiling. "See, it's that easy ... except for Zelda." She pointed to a hen in the row of nests across from them. "That's Zelda, the reddish-yellow one. I'll take her egg."

"Good," Catherine sighed. "But, I'd like to collect an egg."

"You both will," Hillary assured her, taking the basket from Catherine. "You saw how I did it, so get the next one, then Pina can take the one after that. As a matter of fact, you two can collect all the eggs, except for Zelda."

Catherine pressed her lips together, then gently pushed the hen aside, grabbing the egg. "That was easy." Very carefully, she laid the egg in the basket Hillary was holding.

Hillary looked at Pina. "You're next, old friend."

With squinting eyes, Pina leaned toward Hillary and glared at her. "I want Zelda's egg. And I want it now."

Hillary laughed. "Are you serious?"

Pina continued leering at Hillary. "Yesssss! I'm not afraid."

"She might peck you," Catherine moaned.

With shoulders back and chin raised, Pina insisted, "I'll take that risk to protect my friends from her."

"I get it," Hillary shouted. "Hooray! Our Heroine! Just like in the melodrama."

Catherine laughed. "Is that what you were doing? Convincing performance." She and Hillary began clapping.

Pina bowed. "Thank you. Thank you." She leered at Hillary again. "I really want to take Zelda's egg."

Hillary agreed, and led them to Zelda. She leaned close to the hen. "My friend Pina desperately wants *your* egg. Do you understand, you nasty hen?"

Pina walked to Zelda. "Thank you for the introduction, Hillary." She bent forward and stared at Zelda. Suddenly, with the back of her hand, she whacked Zelda's side, tumbling her out of the nest. Pina smiled at the startled hen and removed the egg. "Thank you."

"Bravo! Very brave," Catherine shouted.

"Good girl," Hillary howled. "I guess I shouldn't be gentle with Zelda. Look at her. She's still not sure what happened."

The girls collected the remainder of the eggs and brought them to the house. Bridie and Biff were sitting on the porch talking about banking. The girls frowned at each other, wondering why they were talking about business instead of something more romantic.

Hillary held the basket of eggs toward Kate. "Here, and the horses are fed."

"Put the eggs in a bowl, then into the ice box," Kate responded.

"I enjoyed doing that," Catherine said. "What else can we do?"

Kate removed her apron and laid it on the table. "Nothing at the moment. It's almost noon and Biff is taking Bridie for a buggy ride to show her his farms. This was her idea, not his, so she really seems to enjoy the country."

The girls looked at each other. "Good!"

"They seem to be getting along nicely," Pina remarked.

Kate smiled at the little matchmakers. "It seems that way, but appearances can be misleading. Give them time."

"Time?" Hillary whispered. "They live many miles apart." She gave Kate a sly look. "That means Bridie will have to come here often, with my friends."

Kate tapped Hillary on the nose with her finger. "You seem to have forgotten about school, my dear. And then there is winter, which isn't loads of fun around here."

"It's always something," Hillary pouted, leading her friends outside toward the stable. Hillary stopped, looking back at Biff. "Want us to hitch up the buggy for you?"

Biff winked at Bridie. "Excuse me, I should do that." He stepped from the porch and waved them off. "I'll do it." He followed the girls, his eyes devoted to Catherine. For a moment, he let himself go, imagining she was Laura.

In Alton, Delaware, Avery Thompson stood at the door of his corner grocery store, waiting for Iris and Vera. He looked up and down Union Avenue, hoping to see them coming.

"Relax," Sari said. "Mr. Zulkie said the girls will be here at noon and they've got five minutes yet."

"I know. I know. It's just that I'm excited for them. I want to see their faces when we give them Hillary's letters. God, they'll be happy."

"Take the empty boxes to the back of the store. That will occupy your mind."

"Later," Avery snapped.

Sari shook her head, joining him at the door. "Standing here isn't going to bring them sooner."

Avery stepped outside, to see further down the street. He dashed back into the store. "They're coming! Are the letters in the back room?"

"Of course," Sari assured him. "Calm down."

"Look busy," Avery said.

Sari put her hands on her hips. "Why should I look busy?"

Avery glanced at Sari, but couldn't answer her question. He went to the counter for two licorice sticks from a jar.

"They're crossing the street," Sari announced, concentrating on Iris's short, black hair and beautiful light-gray eyes. The girls were the same age, but Vera was big-boned and a head taller.

Avery held the licorice behind his back, waiting for the girls to enter. His eyes were fixed on their faces. "Good afternoon!" he said, nervously. "I forgot you were coming."

Sari rolled her eyes.

He smiled. "We haven't seen you girls for a while."

The girls noticed his hands behind his back, which meant he had a treat for them. "Good afternoon," they echoed, with a smile.

Avery presented the licorice sticks to the girls. "Here's a little something for you."

They thanked him and looked at him with suspicion, noticing he was nervous. Both girls glanced at Sari for a clue as to why he was acting strangely.

"Is this why you wanted us to stop by today?" Iris asked.

"We certainly appreciate it," Vera added, quickly. "You've always been kind to us."

"No!" Sari responded. "We have something very special for you. The surprise is in the back room. Follow me."

Vera and Iris glanced at each other, wondering what was going on.

Avery followed on the heels of the girls. In the back room, he pulled two chairs from the table. "Sit," he suggested, watching Sari remove two envelopes from a shelf. "This is a very special surprise." He stepped back to watch the girls. "You give it to them, Sari."

Sari laid an envelope in front of each girl. "They're letters from Hillary Cook."

There was a moment of disbelief, then both girls screamed, "Hillary? They're letters from Hillary?"

"Where does she live?" Vera shouted.

The girls stared at Mr. Thompson, waiting for an answer.

Avery moved closer to them. "When you finish reading the letter, I'll explain about Hillary and why you can't know where she lives. Right now, enjoy Hillary reaching out to you."

The girls laid their letters on the table, staring at the pages. Their grinning faces revealed excitement, as they read. When Iris finished reading, she stared at the paper a moment, then lifted it against her face and began crying.

Sari and Avery glanced at each other, understanding her emotion.

Sari rubbed her hand across Iris's back. "Happy tears, I assume?"

With her face still buried in the letter, Iris nodded.

Vera didn't cry, but the expression on her face revealed she was pleased. She looked to Sari. "Hillary said, we'll always be 'Wildflowers,' no matter what."

Iris wiped her eyes with the back of her hands. "She believes she'll visit us, but doesn't know when. Until then, we can write." She looked at the letter again, fighting back another rush of tears.

Sari removed two pencils and paper from a desk drawer. "Here, girls, write Hillary now, and Mr. Thompson will mail them. Where she lives, must remain a secret."

Hillary sat on a porch step, watching Bridie board the buggy, wearing a gray shirtwaist and a black, full-length skirt and boots. She was impressed with Bridie's fine taste in clothing. Next to her, Pina and Catherine were leaning against the porch railing.

Biff took Bridie's hand, helping her into the buggy. He turned to the others. "We'll be back in about two hours."

Bridie waved, as they rode away.

"There's no rush to get back," Kate yelled after them. She walked over to the girls and removed a handkerchief from her dress pocket, wiping road dust from her face. "John has Cokie hitched to the buckboard, so you girls can go for your ride whenever you want."

Hillary stepped to the ground and faced her friends. "First, we'll stop to see if the Roddy kids can come with us."

The girls ran to the stable where Cokie and the buckboard were standing. Hillary untied the reins from the corral fence and joined her friends up on the seat. She shook the reins and Cokie pulled them away.

Kate watched them enter the road and go in the same direction Biff had. "I hope they aren't following Biff," she mumbled. She watched them turn toward the Roddy house, breathing a sigh of relief.

Marnie heard a wagon approach their house and looked out the window. She smiled, seeing three girls on the buckboard. "Trish!" she yelled, "Hillary and her friends are here."

With a book in hand, Adam left his bedroom and sauntered down the stairs, as if uninterested in the arriving trio. "It seems your friends are coming and I planned to read outside."

"You still can," Marnie responded. "No one will bother you."

Adam looked down at her. "Trish was in the backyard. Now, she's out front. I guess she saw them coming before you did."

Marnie opened the front door and ran to her new friends, shouting, "Where are you headed?"

Hillary pulled on the reins, stopping Cokie. "Nowhere special. We thought we'd come by and see if you wanted to ride with us."

Marnie stepped up to the wagon. "Sure, but I'll check with Ma." She glanced at Trish. "Go ask Ma, and hurry."

As Trish turned to run to the house, Ruth came through the doorway. "You can go, but don't be gone more than an hour."

Marnie looked at Hillary, to see if that was agreeable with her.

Cokie took a step forward and Hillary pulled back on the reins. "That's about how long we planned to be gone."

Pina looked at Adam, sitting at the table reading. "How about you, Adam?" Do you want to go with us?"

He leaned over the book and smiled up at her. He was interested, but wasn't sure he wanted to be with five girls. He began turning pages, randomly. "Thanks, but I'll stay here and read. Maybe another time."

Well, at least it was a polite rejection, Hillary thought.

Ruth watched Adam, wishing he would go with the girls, thinking it may help break him from his solitude. She believed he really wanted to go with them.

Marnie and Trish climbed into the buckboard and sat on a bench seat at the side of the wagon. "Back in an hour," Marnie shouted to her mother.

Hillary glanced over her shoulder. "I'll drive slow, so you don't get bumped too badly,"

"Thanks," Marnie replied. "Where are we going?"

Hillary guided Cokie into the field behind the Roddy house. "Let's go to the creek and see what animals we can find. Besides that, we can pick wildflowers and give them to our mothers. They'll like that." The word "Wildflowers" turned Hillary's thoughts to Iris and Vera. *I wonder if they received my letters?*

"What kind of animals could we see?" Catherine asked.

Pina looked at Hillary. "Not bears, I hope?"

"I can't say we won't *see* a bear," Hillary answered. "Bears run away from people, because they are more afraid of us, than we are of them."

Pina gritted her teeth. "Not in my case, I'll tell you."

Catherine nudged Pina with her elbow. "Where is your melodrama spirit?"

Pina squinted at Catherine. "I only have bravery for chickens."

Trish shouted to Hillary, "Did you bring a program from the melodrama?"

"I have an extra one you can keep. I'll bring it tonight at the bonfire. Hold on," Hillary shouted. "There's a deep rut here."

"There's an animal over there," Catherine shouted, pointing to some brush. "What is it, a wild dog?"

"It's a racoon," Hillary answered. "Like I said, it's running away from us like all animals do." She pointed to a ridge ahead of them. "The creek is just beyond that little hill in front of us."

"How are we going to know when an hour is up?" Trish asked.

Hillary turned her head slightly. "Don't worry, I can pretty well tell time by how far the sun moves to the west."

"You're a true pioneer, aren't you?" Pina joked.

Hillary smiled. "You learn to use nature when in the country."

The wagon rolled over the hill and down to the creek, to an array of wildflowers. Hillary stopped Cokie, "See that big log sticking out of the water? There's a turtle on top of it, sunning itself."

"Where?" Pina asked.

"I see it," Trish shouted. "The log by the Lilly pads."

Catherine climbed down from the wagon and walked along side, as Hillary moved it close to a tree. She stood in tall grass waiting for the others to climb down. "Too bad your brother didn't come with us. He'd be some protection, if animals came at us."

Marnie and Trish glanced at each other, remaining silent.

Hillary noticed, but didn't question their actions, being they did it on the sly. She reached for the reins and tied Cokie to the tree.

"Let's start picking flowers," Marnie suggested, attempting to change the subject. She and Trish led the others to the flowers, picking their favorites.

"I'll pick some for Bridie," Pina yelled to Catherine.

The girls wandered through the flowers selecting the prettiest, cradling them in their arms. "Don't take too many," Hillary suggested, "Just take what we need."

When they gathered enough flowers, the girls walked to the edge of the creek and peered into the water. "Look at all these tiny fish," Trish said, pointing into the water. "There must be a hundred of them."

"Minnows," Hillary explained. "They're good bait for catching bigger fish."

"Quiet," Pina whispered. "I hear something walking in the brush on the other side of the creek. It sounds big."

Catherine started walking back to the wagon. "I'm leaving and I suggest you all come with me. If it's big, I don't want to become a meal."

Hillary looked up at the sun. "It's time to start for home, anyway."

As they rode away, the girls kept looking back, hoping the animal would show itself.

Hillary recalled Trish and Marnie acting oddly, when Adam's name was mentioned earlier. She wondered what it was about. She cleared that question from her mind and began singing her favorite song, *Buffalo Gal*. The others joined in, singing all the way home.

CHAPTER EIGHT

That evening, Kate saw Biff on the porch, waiting to have an after-dinner drink. Kate went out and stood next to him. "Bridie will be coming soon." She paused, before continuing. "She seems to be a very nice person."

Biff agreed. "Yes. Yes, she does."

Hillary and her two friends came out of the house, announcing they were going to the stable to see Knickers before walking to the Roddy house. Kate watched the girls stroll toward the stable, when suddenly Catherine's likeness to Laura became apparent. *My God! Why hadn't I noticed before?* She looked at Biff, his eyes fixed in the direction of the girls. Kate took measure of Catherine again and glanced at Biff. He was still looking toward the girls. She believed that Biff, too, had recognized Catherine's likeness to Laura, and was experiencing her presence. Kate looked straight ahead and cautiously asked, "There's a strong resemblance, isn't there?"

Biff didn't respond. His thoughts were far away.

Kate stared at him and repeated her question.

Biff jerked his head toward her. "I'm sorry, what did you say?"

She paused, gazing into Biff's eyes, repeating her question. "I said, there's a strong resemblance, isn't there?"

He immediately understood Kate's meaning. His shoulders dropped slowly, as he looked away. "Yes."

"I didn't notice until just now. When did you become aware of it?"

Biff looked down at the ground. "The day she arrived."

Kate knew by the tone of his voice that he was hurting. She wanted to console him in some way, but didn't know how. "Is it a problem for you?"

"Yes, and I have to do something about it." He moved closer to Kate, put an arm around her and took a deep breath. "Face on, I know who she is, but from a distance, or from the back of her, I see Laura. The way she moves, her voice, her hair is so much like Laura." He looked down at Kate and smiled. "It's a good thing Catherine lives in Newberry and isn't here all the time."

It was almost eight o'clock when Trish looked out of her bedroom window. She saw her three new friends walking through the field of hay toward her house. She stepped out of her bedroom, noticing Adam in front of the bathroom mirror putting pomade on his hair. Trish was surprised. She'd had never seen him use pomade before. She hurried downstairs and ran to her mother in the kitchen. "Maaa! Adam is combing his hair and he used pomade."

Ruth looked down at Trish and smiled, serenely. "He did, did he? Well, my guess is, one of the young ladies coming here tonight has plucked Adam's heart strings."

"Which one, I wonder?" Trish questioned, with a big fat smile.

Ruth wiped her hands on a dishtowel. "I believe he will let us know by his actions. Adam will probably give extra attention to the girl he likes, so all we have to do is watch him." Trish was about to run away when Ruth grabbed her by the arm. "Don't mention this to your sister, or anyone else. The last thing Adam needs is teasing. We'll watch him and it will be our secret, until it becomes apparent to the others. Promise?"

Trish skipped away. "I promise."

The sun was like a huge yellow ball, getting ready to settle behind the distant hills. Marnie was standing on the edge of the grassy slope when Trish joined her. They could see the melodrama program in Hillary's hand, as she ran toward them.

Marnie held out her hand. "Thanks for remembering the program."

Hillary handed it to her. "You didn't have to worry about that. Kate made sure I didn't forget."

Pina heaved a great sigh of relief, reaching the top of the slope. "When are we going to have the bonfire?"

Catherine laughed. "When it gets dark, of course."

Pina crossed her eyes, "I asked a dumb question."

"Let's sit," Trish suggested, leading the others to the picnic table.

When seated, Adam came from the house, walking slowly toward the girls. His carefully combed hair was noticed by all of the girls.

Trish smiled to herself. *Show me which one she is.*

Marnie began reading the Theatre Program, while Trish watched Adam. She intended to observe him constantly. "Where do you want to sit?" Trish asked Adam, believing he would sit near the girl he liked.

To Trish's disappointment, Marnie invited him to sit next to her, by shifting sideways and patting the seat. Trish glared at Marnie. *That was no help to me.*

Adam dropped onto the bench, folding his arms. "I collected enough wood and trash for a big bonfire tonight."

"Where will it be?" Pina asked. "We can't have it by the house, or hay field, right?"

"We'll have it in the dirt field behind the house. It's the safest place."

Ruth and Tom came from the house carrying two jugs, one of cider and the other iced tea. They placed them on a level patch of ground near the oak tree. Tom nodded toward the hay field. "Here come the rest of your people."

Catherine giggled. "I get giddy when I see Bridie walking through that field of hay. I never dreamed she'd be at home in the country."

"Give them the table," Trish said, quickly, "Us kids can sit in the grass like we did yesterday." She wanted to see which girl Adam sat next to.

The children were gathering by the tree, when Tom called, "Adam, go into the house and get twelve mugs and glasses, please."

Trish watched Adam turn from the group and run toward the house. *"Darn!"*

John and Biff were the first ones up the slope, greeting the neighbors. "Here," John said, handing Tom a jug. "I brought some hard cider for the adults."

Tom took the jug and shook hands with the men. "Thanks. I'm sure we'll put this to good use." He gestured for the ladies to sit.

It wasn't long before daylight faded and the temperature began dropping. Ruth noticed Kate and Bridie wearing shawls across their shoulders. "Wearing a shawl is a good idea. I'll have to get mine soon."

Adam ran to the adults, with mugs and glasses cradled in his arms. He placed them on the table and raced for the tree.

Ruth turned and called for Adam to get the shawl from her bed.

Trish looked down her nose, falling back against the grass. *What ... again?*

After giving Ruth her shawl, Adam went directly to the girls. Trish sat up and watched him sit between Pina and Hillary. *Who will get the most attention?* She wondered.

"I'm thirsty," Marnie said, looking at the others.

Hillary and Pina agreed.

Adam jumped up. "Wait here, girls. I'll get six glasses."

Trish pondered his action. *Adam went for the glasses because Pina and Hillary said they were thirsty. That doesn't tell me which one he favors."*

Adam gathered the six glasses from the table when Hillary called, "Kate, can we have some of what you're drinking?"

Kate frowned at her. "What do you think, young lady?"

Adam looked at Hillary. "Why do you call your parents, John and Kate, instead of mother and father?"

Hillary smiled. "Because they aren't my parents. They adopted me."

Adam stopped abruptly and slowly lowered the glasses back to the table. "You're adopted?" he repeated, in disbelief. He looked to Kate and John, searching for affirmation.

"That's right," Kate assured him. "Her parents were our best friends, so when her parents died, we adopted her."

"Me, too," Pina added. "I was adopted."

"Bridie adopted me," Catherine added.

Adam leaned against the table, as if his legs were too weak to hold him. He spoke as though the words came hard. "You three, beautiful girls … were orphans?"

With raised eyebrows, Ruth glanced at Tom, surprised by such a bold statement from Adam.

Pina raised a hand to fluff her hair. "He called us beautiful."

He thinks all three of them are beautiful, Trish pondered. *This is getting complicated.*

Shocked by this sudden revelation, Adam looked at Ruth and Tom.

Ruth placed her hand on top of Adam's hand resting on the table. "Like I told you, there are millions of orphans, and they are loved, as we love you."

Adam looked at the girls again and methodically announced, "I'm adopted. Ruth and Tom are my aunt and uncle. Trish and Marnie are my cousins." Adam's feeling of being an outsider to his adoptive family began to evaporate.

"Then you're a grape like us, so join the bunch," Hillary jested.

Ruth's affectionate touching of his hand and Hillary's levity about, "joining the bunch," lessened his notion of being tolerated. Adam collected himself and looked to the five girls under the tree. "Let's start piling the wood and trash for the bonfire. It'll be dark soon."

"Good idea," Hillary and Marnie cheered together.

Trish stood. "We can take a glass of cider with us."

Bridie stood and poured cider into six glasses. "I'll play mother this time. I've never done that before."

John and Kate glanced at each other and smiled, wondering if the feeling of *"family"* was filtering through Bridie.

The children thanked Bridie for the cider and raced past the white, two story house. At the back, there was a porch its entire width.

When they were well beyond the back of the house, Trish sipped her cider and carefully placed the glass on a flat rock. She joined the others, unloading a wagon of wood and trash, throwing it into a heap. By now, the sun was settling behind the distant horizon.

"Another half-hour and we can torch it," Adam shouted.

"Let me torch it," Marnie yelled back to him.

"Fine, but I'll stand next to you in case something goes wrong." Adam noticed Catherine carrying a log toward them. It wasn't big, but it appeared heavy for her. He ran to Catherine and took it from her arms.

Catherine smiled. "Thanks. I was about to drop it."

Trish watched Adam take the log from Catherine. "Hmmm? Could it be her?" she mumbled.

Pina collected a small pile of weathered wood and dried grass she found scattered around the field. She walked up to Adam and laid the scraps near the pile of debris. "This will help start the fire."

"Good idea!" Adam said. "That's exactly what we need." He began stuffing the bits of wood and grass under the pile of debris.

The sun was gone and the moon hovered in the distance. Catherine looked up, thinking of Brian, wishing he were there. It had been a couple of wonderful days she would like to have shared with him. Voices coming from the back of the house broke her concentration. She looked through the darkness and saw the adults carrying chairs from the lantern–lit kitchen to the rear porch.

Marnie ran to get stick matches from her father. On her return she was shouting, "Dad said, we can start the fire whenever we want."

"We want," Pina hollered.

Adam moved next to Hillary and nodded toward the wagon. "There are small pieces of wood in the back of the wagon. You can throw them in after the fire has started."

Hillary looked fixedly at him and smiled. "Thank you. You remembered I like doing that." She had sensed warmth in his voice that was more than casual. *He is certainly nicer today than he was yesterday,* she thought.

Trish lifted her glass of cider from the flat rock and watched Adam and Hillary.

Marnie lit a match and circled the pile, lighting it at different places, while Adam walked with her. Soon, the fire was reaching skyward. The children retrieved their glasses of cider and stood around the fire, their faces and bodies aglow from the flames.

Tom circled the porch, offering hard cider to his guests holding partially filled glasses. "The fire may not be the only thing glowing, if we keep drinking." He smiled at Bridie. "But what the heck, we don't get to do this often."

Bridie smiled back at him. "Hardly ever in my case, and I am enjoying myself." She held her glass up to Tom. "As you said, 'What the heck.'"

Kate offered her glass to Tom. "Top it off, neighbor."

Ruth watched the children standing around the fire, talking and laughing. "Kids sure begin friendships fast. It's a shame adults aren't as good at it."

Tom looked down at her. "It's seems we adults are doing fine." He raised the jug of hard cider. "More friendship, anyone?"

Ruth glared at him. "You know what I mean." She grinned and raised her glass. "Yes, more friendship, please."

Tom filled her glass and set the jug on the deck, next to the porch railing. "I'd like to say, Ruth and I are very happy with our new home and neighbors. We've only known you a couple of days, but we believe you are fine people. Moving to a new area is always a gamble and we were lucky to have located near you. And, it's not the cider talking."

"We feel fortunate, also," John smiled. "If we work together, we'll turn both our farms into good, productive investments. Welcome!"

"Yes, it's been a fruitful weekend and the children appear to be happy here," Ruth added.

Kate looked at Ruth, casually suggesting, "Why don't you send the children, or one of them, to our house in the morning for eggs? We always have more than we need."

Ruth raised her glass to Kate. "I'll do that, thank you. We can always use eggs."

Bridie looked at Kate and John, thinking about her visit the past two days. She was convinced the Hanleys were good people, as she had thought. She decided to ask them about Hillary attending Bradbury School when they returned home.

Later, when the fire faded, Adam returned to the house and pumped water into a bucket to pour on the embers. He looked up at the adults sitting on the porch. "The end of a good evening," he said, with a big smile.

Ruth observed him walk back to his friends and began to speculate. *I haven't seen him this happy and outgoing since he's been with us these eight months. I wonder which girl it is?*

At ten o'clock, the girls were in Hillary's bedroom talking about the past three days. The men were in the stable bedding down the horses, while Kate and Bridie sat at the kitchen table drinking tea. Bridie was expressing the fun she was having and decided it was a good time to mention the Bradbury School.

"The children start school soon, and I wanted to discuss something with you. I guess it's none of my business, but I'd like to present an idea I have for Hillary's schooling."

Kate grinned at her. "Two years at the Bradbury School?"

Bridie was surprised by Kate's immediate mention of the school. "You know of it?"

"Only what Hillary told me. When she returned from her trip to Newberry, she mentioned Catherine showed her the school. She didn't ask to attend, but during the discussion I detected desire in her voice." Kate looked down into her cup. "I've mentioned it to John and we both like the idea, but we need more information from you. I was planning on asking you about it before you left, so now we are."

Bridie leaned back, pushing her cup and saucer aside, then explained the advantages in attending the Bradbury Finishing School. "Hillary could live with me and Catherine, if the Campbells feel their accommodations are insufficient. But then, I still haven't presented the idea to the Campbells. If Hillary decides to attend, I'll talk to the Campbells immediately. I think they'll like the idea of the three girls schooling together."

"You've made a generous offer," Kate said. "I guess the next step is to talk to Hillary. It will have to be her decision."

"Of course, but if she decides to attend this year, we must move fast to get her registered. I'll take from you, what information is needed for the application, and then it can be mailed to you and John for your signatures. I have a close relationship with the faculty, so I can sign a document for your character references."

Kate stood, looking down at Bridie. "You leave tomorrow, so I'd better talk to Hillary tonight. Something could happen tomorrow morning and I'd never get a chance to discuss it before you leave." She looked above the spice rack at the porcelain clock Bridie gave her two days before. "It's getting late, so I'll talk to her now, before they go to bed. You keep the other girls occupied, while I take Hillary outside."

Bridie agreed and waited until Kate and Hillary were gone. She went into the girl's bedroom and began talking about the wonderful time they were having.

Kate and Hillary passed John and Biff coming from the stable. "Where are you two going?" John asked.

Kate waved them by with her hand. "We need privacy to talk about school."

John gave her a knowing nod and continued on.

Hillary gave Kate an inquisitive look. "What do you mean—talk about school?"

Kate stopped at the corral fence, smiling at Hillary. "I'm talking about a special school. How would you like to attend the Bradbury Finishing School with Catherine, and possibly Pina?"

Hillary was completely surprised by the offer. "Are you serious?"

"Yes, John and I are serious. We've talked about it and decided it would be your decision. As you know, it's only a five-hour train ride away and you could come home when you wanted to … and bring friends, if you like."

Hillary found it difficult to answer. "It appears to be a very good school … but leave you, John and Biff … and Knickers?"

"Remember, you can come home some weekends."

Hillary bit her lip. "Yeah! That makes it easier." She continued to look uncertain. "Wait a minute. You're not going to have a baby soon, are you?"

Kate laughed. "No! I'm not pregnant. Besides, you could tend to the baby on weekends and through the summer."

Hillary threw her arms around Kate and smiled. "Yes, I'd like to go to Bradbury."

Adam stood at the window of his dark bedroom, looking across the field of hay. He watched Kate and Hillary walk from the corral toward their house. "I'm glad she lives next to us," he mumbled. "I'll be able to see her almost every day."

CHAPTER NINE

The next morning, the girls were up early collecting fresh eggs for the Roddy family. John and Biff were out feeding the cattle, wanting to have some chores completed before ten o'clock, when they would take their guests to Galena.

After washing the breakfast dishes, Kate and Bridie sat on the porch talking about Bridie's home in Newberry. Being that it was a large home, Kate asked how she maintained her property.

Bridie paused, deciding whether to tell Kate the whole story about Jack.

Kate noticed Bridie's hesitation. She looked at her with a friendly smile in her eyes, realizing she raised a sensitive subject.

Bridie looked into the distance toward the hay field. "I'll tell you a concise story about myself and the man I was to marry, but it doesn't have a happy ending." She turned to Kate, again. "His name was, John McTavish, handsome and strong, but gentle in spirit. In an attempt to save two little boys from drowning, John jumped into a river and saved one boy. When he went after the second boy, a raft of debris swept over them, holding them under the water. The boy drowned, but John survived ... in a sense. By that, I mean, he was under the water long enough to cause him brain damage due to lack of oxygen. Marrying him and having children was out of the question. He was a powerful man reduced to a somewhat feeble condition. His mother, Doreen wanted to keep the memory of her son, John. So, after the accident, she began calling him Jack, the informal name for John—as though he was a different son. I didn't mind going along with her fantasy, so now we call him Jack."

"Is he living in an institution?"

Bridie leaned back in her chair and forced a smile. "He's the man that does the heavy work around my house."

Kate was puzzled. "He's able to work?"

Bridie nodded. "As I said, he is somewhat feeble, but Jack is quite strong and capable of doing un-complex labor—the kind I need to have done at the house."

Kate shifted in her chair to look more directly at Bridie. "Does he live nearby?"

Bridie sighed. "Yes, he lives with his mother, just a few streets from me. I have a bed for him in the basement in case he needs a nap, or if the weather is too bad for him to walk home." She glanced into Kate's eyes, then to the field again. "End of a condensed story, and in good time, because Ruth and the kids are heading this way."

The children ran toward them, with Ruth trailing behind carrying a basket cradled in an arm. Kate stood and yelled, "The girls are in the hen house." The children immediately changed direction and ran to where Kate pointed. She remained standing until Ruth approached them. "Good morning, Ruth. I see you've recovered from last night's hard cider."

Ruth laughed. "I had enough, but not too much, so I'm feeling fine." She laid the basket on the ground and climbed the two stairs. "How are you ladies doing?"

"I'm just dandy," Bridie answered, cheerfully.

Kate started for the kitchen. "Sit in that chair. I'll get another one."

Bridie watched Ruth turn the chair to face her. "I thoroughly enjoyed meeting you and your family. It appears you and the Hanleys will have a good relationship."

"We feel very fortunate to have them as neighbors." She began to smile, as she went on, "My children love Hillary and her two friends. Adam seems to have ..."

Kate stepped out of the kitchen and set a chair between her guests. "Iced tea, anyone?"

With a raised hand, Bridie declined.

"No, thank you," Ruth answered. "I was just telling Bridie about how my children love Hillary and her friends. It's a shame they don't live around here. They get along so well."

A roar of laughter shot from the hen house.

Bridie grinned at Ruth. "It appears you're right."

Kate looked at Ruth, thoughtfully. "I agree, but all three girls will be gone soon. Catherine and Pina leave today, then next week Hillary will join them for school in Newberry."

Ruth stared at Kate and moaned, "Hillary is going away to school?"

"Yes. We just decided last night."

Ruth put a hand to her mouth. "This will be a big disappointment for my children."

Bridie brushed back a wisp of hair. "Maybe they already discussed it in the hen house?"

Ruth glanced in the children's direction. "That could be, but if they had, one of my girls would have pouted her way over here and told me."

Suddenly, another scream could be heard from the hen house. "Damn you, Zelda!"

Kate laughed. She recognized Hillary's voice and could picture what had just happened.

Ruth was confused by the name. "Who's Zelda?"

Still grinning, Kate answered, "She's a mean hen that occasionally pecks Hillary's hand when gathering her eggs." She nodded in the direction of the hen house. "I guess they've had enough of the hens for a while. They're coming out now."

Catherine came toward them carrying a basket of eggs, while the others went to the stable. She handed the basket of eggs to Kate. "Zelda got Hillary again."

"I heard," Kate laughed. "What are they doing now?"

Catherine backed away to join the others. "Hillary is showing them Knickers."

The women sat silent for a moment, watching Catherine run to the stable.

Ruth sighed. "They are three beautiful and well-adjusted girls."

Bridie laughed. "Adam seems to think they're beautiful. He said so."

Ruth smiled back. "Not only that, yesterday, Adam combed his hair and used pomade, something he's never done before. I think one of the girls has caught his eye."

Kate chuckled. "Poor boy. Whoever she is, she won't be here much longer. He'll have to pine away by himself."

Ruth took a deep breath. "Though they don't know it, those three girls have been a big help to Adam. He had been a problem since he came to live with us, believing he was a burden and not really wanted. He had been distant with us, until last night, when he learned these three delightful girls had been orphans. Now, he seems to have a different outlook. Last night, before he went to bed, he gave me a hug and a *Goodnight* kiss on the cheek. It was the first time." Ruth folded her hands on her lap and looked at the children by the stable. "I believe he is home now, because of your girls."

Kate reached over and touched her arm. "I hope that's true. He appears to be a nice boy. This weekend he compared himself with others who were orphans. Maybe he's discovered having been an orphan isn't something to be ashamed of."

Ruth smiled, serenely. "I'd like to believe that, but will he revert back to who he was, when the girls are gone?"

Bridie tried to console her. "Hillary and her friends will come here some weekends, so it's not as though they'll be gone for months at a time. As long as Adam knows that, I believe he'll stay the course."

Ruth leaned forward in her chair, ready to stand. "That makes sense. You two have given me a better outlook on the situation." She gave Kate a grateful smile. "And you've given me eggs, too." She stood. "Thanks. Now, I'll make breakfast for my family."

Kate waved her hand at the basket of eggs. "Take them all as they are. We can exchange baskets another time."

Ruth gave Bridie a friendly smile. "Have a safe trip home, and I look forward to seeing you again."

As Ruth walked away, Bridie rose from her chair. "When you learn which girl Adam is interested in, let me and Kate know."

Ruth grinned and waved. "I'll do that."

John and Biff rode up to the house a few minutes before ten o'clock. Luggage was standing on the porch, waiting to be loaded onto the coach. John jumped from the wagon and went into the house, while Biff drove to the stable where he hitched Cokie to his father's coach.

John entered his bedroom, as Kate was putting on her dress. He closed the door, gave her a kiss on the neck and a pat on her butt. "Biff is getting the coach ready."

"Is he as dirty as you?"

"Probably. We did the same work."

Kate shook her head. "Then he'll be dirty when he says "goodbye" to Bridie."

John grinned. "Such is farm life. I'm sure she understands that."

Hillary and her friends ran from their bedroom, racing down the hall shouting, "We're ready! We'll meet you outside."

Kate turned her back to John. "Button me, please."

He did as she asked, then kissed the back of her neck, again.

"You seem to be in a kissy mood today."

"Our guests are leaving." Suddenly, a thought occurred to him. "Wait a minute, if Hillary goes away to school, we'll be alone most of the time."

Kate looked at him askew. "You just thought of that now?"

John heard the coach pull up to the house. "Bye, lover, time to load the luggage."

When he got outside, Biff was standing at the back of the coach. John heaved the luggage, a piece at a time to Biff, and he placed them in the back compartment of the coach. John faced the girls with his hands on his hips. "Why so glum? You'll all be together in a week or so."

Hillary's eyes shifted to John. "We know. It's just that "goodbyes" are always sad." She turned to her friends. "Smile, see you in a few days."

Pina and Catherine forced a smile, but remained silent.

Bridie stepped out onto the porch. "I've had a wonderful time and I hate to leave."

Biff walked over to her. "Then come again. We enjoyed having you."

Kate came out of the house and pulled the door closed. "I guess it's time to go? It's ten minutes after ten."

Biff opened the coach door and helped Bridie inside.

Once she was in the coach, John pushed Biff aside and took Kate's hand, helping her inside.

John leered at Biff. "See, I too, can be a gentleman."

"Not too often," Biff scoffed.

The girls entered the coach and the men climbed up to the driver's seat. Biff shook the reins and yelled, "Giddap!"

The moment Biff stopped the coach in front of Harte Photographers, the coach door flew open and the three girls dashed out to the studio window, looking for their pictures.

"There they are," Pina squealed, pointing.

"They're right in the middle," Catherine muttered, in a pleased voice. She turned to Kate and Bridie, exiting the coach. "You two will be the topic of conversation in Galena. Your picture is …" Catherine hesitated. She couldn't select the proper word.

Bridie held up her hand to stop Catherine from explaining. "Let me and Kate decide how we look. I'm sure it isn't flattering." She and Kate stepped up to the window and gasped.

Bridie placed her hand against her chest. "What on earth possessed us to do this?"

Kate leaned close to Bridie. "We can deny that it's us. But then, you don't have to worry. No one in town knows who you are."

The girls hurried to the door, with the women following. Kate looked at John and Biff, "Are you coming in?"

John shook his head. "No, my squaw. We'll look at the pictures in the window."

When they got inside, Kate and Bridie saw Biff and John laughing hysterically.

Kate glanced at Bridie. "It's a good thing *we* have a sense of humor."

Helen Harte came from the back of the shop carrying their photographs. "I saw you outside, so I immediately went for your pictures. I know you have a train to catch."

Hillary's excitement showed in her eyes. "We love them, and thank you for putting them in the window."

Bridie and Kate gave each other an empty stare, revealing that they weren't as enthused.

Bridie blocked Kate's hand, so she couldn't pay for the pictures. "This is my treat. You've given me a wonderful weekend and I insist on buying the pictures as a remembrance."

Kate smiled. "If you insist. Thank you."

They all examined the pictures before Helen put them into large envelopes. She looked at Bridie. "Have a nice trip home and come back soon."

Kate opened the door and looked back at Helen. "I'll make sure they return."

John and Biff were still grinning, as they assisted the ladies into the coach, refraining from making humorous remarks.

At the train station, the ladies and girls hugged and kissed, while exchanging pleasantries. Kate and Biff walked Bridie to her coach for a final farewell. Kate said a few friendly words then walked away, so Biff and Bridie could have time alone.

Bridie extended her hand to Biff, and smiled. "It was a pleasure meeting you, and I had a wonderful time, including the tour of your farms."

Biff took Bridie's hand and bowed slightly. "It was my pleasure. If agreeable with you, I could go to Newberry to see you again, and you could show me your bank and newspaper?"

Bridie nodded. "I would like that." The train whistle blew. Bridie turned and entered the coach.

That evening, Kate and John were standing on the porch steps, while Hillary visited with her friends at the Roddy house. Kate reached for John's hand. "Has Biff made any comments about Bridie, you know, like what he thinks of her?"

"Nothing meaningful. But they seemed to enjoy each other's company."

Kate squeezed John's hand. "Biff should think about getting married soon, if he'd like to have a family—which I know he does." They sat passive for a while, pondering the last three days and relishing the evening breeze. Kate was bothered by two problems Biff and Bridie would have in a relationship. *Bridie still has John McTavish in her life, and Biff sees Catherine as Laura.* She wondered if they could overcome those obstacles.

Kate looked at the setting sun, contemplating the end of another day, another month and another year. She nudged John and looked into his eyes. "It's probably a good time for *us* to start a family, don't you agree? The farm is well established and we're earning a good income."

John put an arm around her. "Yes, I agree, but *when* is up to you."

She laid her head against his shoulder. "I can't think of any reason why we should wait any longer. Time is marching on."

John chuckled. "Hillary would be angry if you had a baby, while she was away at school."

Kate gave John a fleeting glance and a faint smile. "Count the months, John. If I got pregnant now, the baby would arrive when school ends and Hillary would be home for the summer."

John kissed her forehead. "Our guests are gone and I'm sure Hillary won't be back for an hour or more."

Earlier that afternoon, Wade Widner rocked to the motion of the train, looking up at the cloudy sky. He wondered if it would be raining when he arrived at Galena. He looked at his pocket watch, surprised he'd be there in less than an hour. He decided to stay at the De Soto Hotel, which was highly recommended by another passenger. He planned to relax at the hotel for a while then walk Galena's streets, deciding how to go about finding the Hanley residence the next day. He was convinced it would be easy to do.

He lay back in his seat and began pondering what might be. *Are John and Kate living together, but not married?* He wondered. *Do they have a child of their own, besides Hillary?* He closed his eyes. *I'll decide what to do when I learn their circumstances.*

CHAPTER TEN

The next morning, Hillary woke to the sound of a talkative robin, sitting in a tree outside her bedroom window. She rolled out of bed and crossed the room to look out the window. The Robin, startled by her sudden appearance, flew across the yard and landed on the stable roof to begin chirping again. Hillary surveyed the farm she'd be leaving soon to attend school in Newberry. She liked the idea of being away with her friends, while still having the farm to come home to.

Hillary dressed to do morning chores and ride Knickers before bathing. When she entered the kitchen, Kate was making buckwheat cakes and maple syrup. Hillary put an arm around Kate. "It sure smells good in here. I'll do the dishes after my chores."

Kate flipped two buckwheat cakes into the air, catching them on a platter. They both laughed. She handed the platter to Hillary. "I wasn't sure I could do that."

Hillary was still laughing when she sat at the table. "You could get a job in a circus."

Kate put two cakes on another platter and sat across from Hillary. "Bridie is calling Pina's mother today to ask her about the Bradbury School. She'll let us know what they plan to do. Either way, I believe you'll be leaving next weekend."

Hillary sat pensive, looking down at her food. "I wonder who I will be living with, Pina or Catherine?"

"Like I said, we'll know when Bridie calls. I'm not sure the Campbells have enough room for a permanent guest." Kate noticed Hillary grinning to herself. "Are you excited about schooling there?"

Hillary nodded and swallowed a bite of food. "Minutes ago, I was thinking about how lucky I am to be schooling in Newberry, yet have a farm home with you and John." She smiled at Kate. "Thank you."

"Thank your Uncle Biff. Once he learned about you going off to school, he insisted on paying for it."

Hillary stuck her fork into another piece of buckwheat cake. "That isn't a surprise. He's always been good to me. I will definitely thank him."

Kate straightened her back and wiped her mouth with a napkin. "We may have a surprise for you next spring."

Hillary looked at her askew, swinging her fork back-and-forth like a pendulum. "The way you said that can mean only one thing, and you better not have a baby while I'm gone."

"We're timing it for June, when you *are* home."

"That's perfect. Try hard."

In Galena, Wade Widner stepped out of the De Soto Hotel, into a sunny Tuesday morning. The street was busy with people, wagons and horses moving in both directions. He decided to go to the Postal Station first to learn what he could about the Hanleys. He walked to the corner and turned right, as the desk clerk directed, leisurely strolling past numerous shops displaying their wares in the window.

When he arrived at Harte Photographers, he scanned the variety of photos displayed in the window. He always found photographs amusing. He laughed, when he saw two white women dressed as squaws. He wondered what would possess two white women to dress like that. He looked at other pictures, before returning to the squaws for another laugh. This time, the smile of one of the women caught his eye. He examined the photo closely and mumbled, "My God! That's

Kate." He scrutinized the other pictures, hoping to see one of John. Eventually he spotted Hillary and two other girls in a picture near Kate. He smiled. "They definitely live in Galena." He looked at Kate's picture again, muttering softly, "Except for that feather growing out of her head, she looks the same."

Wade dashed across the street, avoiding a horse drawn wagon bearing down on him, then entered the Postal Station. He paused by the entrance, wondering if it would be wiser to get directions to their house from here, or the photography shop. Surely, Kate and John went to the postal station more often than to the photographer, where they could hear about a stranger inquiring about them. He stepped outside and ran across the street.

Wade entered the photography shop, greeted by a lady, rising from her desk.

"May I help you, Sir?"

"I hope so. There's a picture in your window that caught my eye."

Helen smiled. "I know. I saw you grinning."

Wade chuckled, somewhat embarrassed. "Yes. Yes you did. I was looking at the picture of the two white squaws at the center of your window."

"I just put it in the window yesterday. Do you know them?"

He nodded. "Just Kate. I don't know the other woman. I'm an old friend of Kate's and John Hanley. I'm here for only two days, so when I saw Kate's picture, I had to inquire as to where they live so I could visit them." He looked into her eyes and smiled, trying to appear friendly. "Would you give me that information? I would love to surprise them and share a couple of hours."

Helen scrutinized him quickly, deciding he was a gentleman. She stepped to the window and pointed down the street. "Take this straight out of town for a bit more than a mile. On your right is a farm with a new house and barn. You can't miss it, because it's the only new farm out that way."

Wade started for the door. "I appreciate your help. Boy, will they be surprised!" He paused at the door. "Is there a stable nearby, where I could rent a horse?"

Helen looked into his face, pointing in the other direction. "To the corner, then go right two blocks. Across from the town's meeting hall, you'll see Monogan Stables."

He thanked her again and started for the stables, mulling in his mind what he would do. *I'll ride out there to learn what I can, then make a decision.* He entered the stable office. No one was at the battered wooden desk. The walls were of rough wood with pictures of horses scattered about. He called out, "Hello?"

He heard a muffled voice call back, "I'm out here."

Wade walked behind the office, toward the direction of the voice. He passed through an open doorway with a horseshoe nailed above it. Beyond, was the stable where a man was bent over, brushing the flanks of a horse. "Good morning. I'm interested in hiring a horse for a couple of hours, or possibly half a day," Wade said.

The man straightened up and took a long look at Wade. "I assume you're an experienced rider?"

Wade nodded. "I was an artillery officer for a few years. I could even ride 'em bareback, but not today."

The man chuckled. "No, you won't ride these bareback." He extended his hand to Wade. "I'm Bill Monagan, owner of this beautiful place." He dropped his brush onto the straw covered floor. "I don't rent for less than a half day."

Wade carefully shook Bill's small hand. "That's fine with me. I'm here for two days and decided I'd like to see your countryside. What better way, than by horseback?"

Bill Monagan turned away and walked deeper into the stable. "Follow me, I'll show you a nice mare that's fast and easy to control." He stopped at a caramel colored horse, with a white patch on her forehead. He backed her out of the stall. "Now this one is ..."

Wade held up his hand. "You don't need to sell me on her. I know horses, and she looks fine. I definitely would like to ride this pretty girl."

Bill nodded, then turned his head and yelled, "Jake! Get Kimby ready."

A husky black man, with curly gray hair, came from around the corner. "Kimby, it is, boss." His white teeth showed through his wide smile. "She's my favorite. Be ready in a few minutes."

They walked toward the office to make the final arrangements. Wade gave Bill the money and signed a receipt for the horse, declaring he'd be gone for three to four hours. When they stepped outside, Jake was already leading Kimby toward them. Wade tilted his head to the side and examined the horse. "Yes. She sure is a beauty." He climbed into the saddle and waved, as he rode off.

At the edge of town, he galloped for about a quarter mile then held Kimby to a walk. A quarter mile later, he galloped the horse again, enjoying every minute of being on a horse once more. As he neared, what he guessed to be a mile, he walked the horse, searching ahead for a new farm on his right. If Kate or John were to come his way, he planned to ride away from the road, so he wouldn't be recognized.

A short distance ahead, he could see a new farmhouse and barn. Passing high ground of the neighbor's property, Wade saw a blond girl riding in a corral next to a stable. A man and woman were standing at the corral fence watching her. The sunlight illuminated John's red hair. He galloped past the farm, so he wouldn't be exposed to the Hanleys for too long a time. Wade smiled, watching Hillary put her horse through a drill. "That's Kate, the squaw," he muttered.

John turned and waved to the passing stranger. Wade waved politely and continued on. *They look content*, he thought. *I'm sure they would be troubled if they knew they'd been discovered.*

Wade rode on, enjoying his ride with Kimby, pondering what he would do when he got back to Alton. He leaned forward and patted the horse's neck. *I think I'll stay another day and ride this beauty. If I take a train Thursday, I can report to Tyler on Monday. I have no schedule for when to be back in Alton. I can tell Tyler whatever I want. As long as he learns where John Hanley is, he'll be satisfied.*

It was dusk and Hillary had been playing with her friends at the Roddy house. When she returned home, Kate was sitting on the porch in one of two kitchen chairs. She patted the empty chair next to her. "John is bathing. Sit with me."

Hillary spun around and dropped onto the chair. "I'll sleep good tonight."

"I'm sure you will. I could see you running around with your friends all evening." Her voice softened, as she continued. "It looked like Adam was with you most of the time."

"Yeah. He seems to like me."

Kate grinned. "What do you think of *him*?"

"He's just another boy." Hillary looked at Kate from the corner of her eye. "But a nice boy ... with a nice smile."

Kate decided to change the subject and delay *that* conversation for another day. "Bridie called tonight, right after talking to Eileen Campbell. Which reminds me; I must call Eileen tomorrow and thank her and Richard. It appears all three of you girls will be attending Bradbury."

Hillary's face brightened. "A week ago this wasn't even a dream, now it's happening!" She shook her head back and forth. "I believe Bridie wanted it to happen, so she made it happen." Hillary searched Kate's face. "Do you want me to go away to school?"

Kate tilted her head. "I really don't want you to leave us, but I do want you to have good schooling. Obviously, I can't have both. Besides, you'll be coming home some weekends and it is only for two years."

Hillary sat grasping the arms of her chair. "Catherine has only one year of school left, so me and Pina will have classes different from hers. Of course, we'll still have plenty of time together." Fond recollections of her week in Newberry flashed through her mind. "I hope the Campbells aren't just being polite having me live there? It's not a big house like Bridie's."

Kate leaned forward in her chair, looking into Hillary's eyes. "Don't think that for a moment. Bridie told me the Campbells were delighted with the idea." She sat back in her chair again. "So much so, that Pina's father is building a wardrobe for you this week. He plans to stand it in the corner of Pina's bedroom."

Hillary grinned. "You mean I'm in demand?"

Kate placed her hand on Hillary's arm. "Tomorrow is Wednesday. I think we should go to town and buy your school clothes. You'll be leaving Saturday."

Hillary lifted her legs to leave and dropped them. "Am I traveling alone?"

"I think I'll go with you, and possibly, Biff. I'll ask him."

Hillary stared at Kate. "If Biff came with us, he could see Bridie again."

Kate smiled. "I've already thought of that, young lady."

"If he comes with us, I'd say he's interested in Bridie."

"I've already thought of that, too, young lady."

Hillary heard John's footsteps in the house. "John is washed. I'll go do the same."

Wade Widner rode Kimby another half day. On Thursday morning, he boarded a train that would take him back to Alton, Delaware. He planned to go to Tyler Sharpe on Monday, telling him about John Hanley. He didn't feel comfortable revealing where John and Kate were, but that was what he was paid to do. He wondered how fast Tyler would react to the news and how he would go about it?

It rained heavily Thursday evening. Hillary was in her room reading *Black Beauty* for the third time since Vera gave it to her on her twelfth birthday. She heard the telephone ring and Kate answer. Moments later, Kate called, "Hillary, a young lady would like to talk to you."

She knew it had to be Pina and rushed to the kitchen. Kate was sitting at the table drinking a glass of milk, the telephone receiver dangling against the wall. "Hello? Pina?"

"Yes, my dear, it's Pina. What time are you arriving Saturday?"

"According to the train schedule, we'll arrive at 2:27 pm." She listened for Pina's response, then replied, "Kate ... and Biff." She glanced at Kate who was pretending not to listen. "Yes, it is interesting, isn't it?"

Kate chuckled before taking another drink of milk.

Pina whispered, "I have another surprise for you."

Hillary waited a minute for Pina to continue. "Well, what is it?"

"Oh! Did you want me to tell you now?"

"Very funny. Of course I do."

"I wanted to be sure that's what you desired. Are you sitting down?"

"What difference does that make?"

"None! I'm just teasing you as long as I can."

"Get on with it, please."

"If you insist. Now, brace yourself." Pina cleared her throat. "I have mail for you from Alton, Delaware. If you don't know who it's from, I'll just throw it away."

"You know I do!" Hillary shrieked. She looked at Kate, frowning at her because of the loud outburst. Hillary had to keep Kate from knowing about her letters to Alton. She would have to lie, if Kate questioned her about her outburst. Hillary calmed her voice. "That's nice. You can show it to me when we're together."

Chapter Eleven

On Saturday, a hired coach waited at Newberry train station for Bridie's guests. Biff helped the driver load the luggage into the carrier. He looked at the man, "322 Root Street, please."

The driver smiled. "I know. Miss McDonald hired me."

Biff chuckled at his error. "Of course, you would know." He inspected the town closely, riding through the business district and into the residential area. Biff was impressed with its cleanliness and tranquil atmosphere.

When they approached Bridie's house, Pina's parents were inside with Bridie, while Catherine and Pina waited on the front porch. Biff's eyes scanned all of Catherine. When the coach stopped, he looked closely at the house, examining its grandeur. Bridie came outside, directing the driver to load Biff and Hillary's luggage into her buggy in the coach house. The plan was for Catherine to drive Biff to the Milton House Hotel later that evening.

Bridie hugged Kate, then kissed Hillary's cheek. She and Biff shared a pleasant greeting that appeared guarded, yet more than casual. Those that noticed kept it to themselves.

Bridie took Eileen's arm and brought her to the forefront, introducing her to her friends.

Eileen raised her brows and smiled. "Finally, we meet. I've been looking forward to this moment. Pina has nothing but praise for you." She turned to Pina. "You are right. He is handsome."

Biff smiled politely at Eileen and shook Richard's hand.

Hillary hugged Pina and whispered, "You didn't bring my Alton letters here, did you?"

Pina made sure no one could hear her reply. "No. I wouldn't take that chance. They're hidden in my bedroom."

Bridie raised her hands to her guests. "Dinner is ready, so let's go in and eat." She stepped forward, leading her guests into the house. "After riding the train for five hours, you must be hungry."

They walked through the foyer and into the dining room where open windows allowed a gentle breeze to pass through, giving a fine view of the flowerbeds.

Bridie and Catherine prepared roast duck, boiled potatoes and vegetables for dinner. Wine was served to the adults. Four times through the meal, Biff expressed how he was enjoying the dinner, generating quick glances around the table.

When they finished eating, Bridie addressed the adults. "I have arranged for you to visit the school tomorrow at noon. Mary Gutberlet, the school's Assistant-Principal, also a friend of mine, will give us a personal tour through Bradbury School. That way, you'll know exactly what the girl's curriculum will be and see the classrooms and laboratories for yourselves."

Kate folded her hands on the table and smiled at Bridie. "Thank you. I'm sure all of us are as anxious to see the facilities. That way, we can better understand what the girls are talking about in the future."

There was a satisfied expression on Richard's face. "Eileen and I are certainly delighted with that courtesy. We know the school has an excellent reputation, but to be given a private tour after our late enrollment ... is a pleasant surprise."

"Good! I was sure you'd want to see the interior of the school." Bridie glanced at her guests. "Do we want to stay seated at the table, or go out to the porch and garden?"

"Outside," Catherine answered, eagerly. Pina and Hillary nodded in agreement.

Realizing they were going outside; Kate rose from the table. "I would love to see your garden." She looked down at Hillary. "I think it would be a nice gesture if you and your classmates cleaned off the table before going outside."

At first, Hillary looked disappointed. She glanced at her two friends. "I guess we could do that."

Biff stood and laid his napkin on the table. "Outside sounds good to me."

Bridie led her guests to the rear porch, then onto the lawn and beds of mixed flowers. Eileen and Kate were admiring the beautiful variety of colors, while Bridie identified the flowers they were not familiar with. She took Biff by the arm and strolled to the next flowerbed, unaware that no one was following them. Kate and the Campbells were still engrossed in the first flowerbed. They noticed Bridie walking with Biff to beds of roses and dahlias. They hurried to catch up, so Bridie wouldn't be embarrassed upon discovering she was explaining flowers to only, Biff.

At eight o'clock, a man came and harnessed Bridie's horse, Bree, to her burgundy and black buggy standing in front of the coach house. Bree was Dapple-Gray, with a black mane and tail, ideal colors to compliment the handsome buggy. The man was muscular, with a damaged back, causing him to lean to one side. Catherine went to him, while Pina and Hillary, somewhat frightened by him, remained a short distance away.

When Kate saw the man working with the horse and buggy, she was sure it was Bridie's handyman, Jack, the man she was to marry before his accident. She looked up at Bridie, standing on the porch next to the Campbells. Their eyes met and Bridie gave her a confirming nod.

Later that evening, when Hillary and Pina arrived at the Campbell home for the night, they went directly to Pina's bedroom so Hillary could read the letters from her friends in Alton. Pina removed them from under a pile of sweaters in a dresser drawer and handed them to Hillary. "I'll leave you alone, while you read these." She smiled at Hillary and stepped out of her bedroom.

Hillary sat on the edge of the bed, staring at the three letters. She decided to read the Thompson's letter last. Iris's letter was on top, so she opened it, grinning as her eyes moved back and forth across the words. When she finished Iris's letter, she fell back against the bed, recalling her days with Iris and Vera, sitting among the patch of wildflowers along the Clarion River. Hillary sat up, wiped away a tear from her cheek, and began reading Vera's letter. Her words brought Hillary closer to the days that once were theirs, days she believed they would never repeat.

When Hillary finished reading the Thompson's letter, she laid back against the bed, again. An uneasy silence filled the bedroom, a heavy, somber silence. Guilt shrouded Hillary for having abandoned her dear friends without saying "goodbye." She folded the letter and slid it back into the envelope, deciding she had to go back to Alton and see her friends, no matter what.

After Sunday's tour of the Bradbury School, Richard and Eileen Campbell returned to their home, while Catherine took her two friends for a buggy ride into the nearby countryside, as they'd done weeks before. Bridie's best friends, Margaret and Tom Holmgren, were to be at her house at 3:00 p.m. to meet her guests.

They weren't home thirty minutes when Catherine and the girls rode up to the coach house. Bridie went to the front door to inquire why they were home so soon.

The girls ran toward the house, glancing down the street, as if looking for someone. "We were a short distance from town, when a scary looking man began following us on horseback. We looped around on Wrenn Road and headed back." Catherine turned and looked up and down the street, again.

Bridie held the door open for the girls. "You don't have to worry, now that you're home."

Pina searched both directions of the street, before entering the house. "I hope he didn't follow us here."

Biff got up from his chair in the parlor and went to the front door. "Do you see him?"

Hillary chuckled. "Maybe it was just a young man interested in meeting three beautiful young ladies?"

Again, Pina fluffed her hair with her hand. "That's right, we're beautiful. Adam said so."

Biff went outside and stood on the porch, looking for the rider. Soon, a man and woman rode toward him in a black buggy, pulled by a light gray horse. The black canvas hood was positioned above them, sheltering them from the sun. The man pulled on the reins and stopped in front of Bridie's house. Biff assumed it must be Bridie's friends, Tom and Margaret Holmgren. He watched the man assist the woman out of the buggy, then walked down the porch steps to greet them. "You must be Tom and Margaret?"

Tom tied the reins to a horse-head hitching post by the street. "That's right. And my guess is you're Biff?"

Margaret walked quickly toward him, brandishing a glowing smile. "Yes, Mr. Biff, we are the Holmgrens. Bridie told us what a wonderful time she had at the farm. So, of course, we were dying to meet you people."

Tom walked up behind Margaret, with his hand extended to Biff. "Delighted to meet you, Biff. We have an engagement in an hour, but we had to stop by and introduce ourselves."

Biff shook his hand. "I'm glad you did. I understand you are Brian's parents. Bridie boasts that he's smart and quite handsome, a perfect match for Catherine."

Margaret nodded. "A match made in heaven, as they say. He's six feet tall, with curly black hair and light-blue eyes. An Adonis."

Biff glanced at Tom. "I hope to meet your young man, someday. Catherine is quite enamored with him."

Tom couldn't contain a smile expressing his pride in Brian. "We were quite fortunate to find a boy like him. He's everything we wanted in a son."

Bridie greeted the Holmgrens at the door, introduced them to Kate and put her arm around Hillary. "I'm sure you remember Hillary from her visit here?"

Margaret grinned at Hillary. "Of course! You girls had a wonderful time together. You were so, so … girls."

Tom chuckled at Margaret's confusing remark about the girls. "Good to see you again, Hillary. It appears we'll be seeing a lot of you, now that you're a student of Bradbury. Welcome to the neighborhood."

Hillary's eager eyes looked up at Tom. "Thank you! I'm looking forward to the schooling and being with my friends."

Pina noticed Biff, standing behind the others with his eyes glued on Catherine … It made her feel uneasy. *Was he just interested in looking at her pretty face, or was there more to it than that?* She intended to keep it her secret, hoping it was just an innocent infatuation with a young girl.

Bridie closed the door and led her guests into the parlor. "Who would like something to drink? I have iced tea and water."

Margaret sat in the chair by the front window. "Before you do anything, I want to see that picture of Squaw Bridie and Squaw Kate. Where is it?"

The three girls laughed. "Yeah, show it, Bridie."

Catherine ran from the parlor and started up the stairs to the bedrooms. "I'll get it, and the picture of us girls."

Biff was leaning against the wall, laughing quietly. He knew Bridie wasn't pleased with her picture and was sorry she had it taken.

Bridie shrugged. "You might as well, you'll see it sooner or later." She started for the kitchen. "I'll have drinks set up on the kitchen table. When you're finished laughing, come and get a glass."

Pina went with Bridie to help her pour the beverages. "There's nothing wrong with your picture. It's funny, like it was intended to be. Remember how silly we were feeling? We knew the pictures would be ... different."

Bridie removed a pitcher of iced tea from the icebox. "You're right. It was intended to be humorous." She set the pitcher on the kitchen table. "It's just that it doesn't seem as funny now." Bridie cringed when she heard laughter in the parlor.

Pina glanced at Bridie and smiled. "Kate doesn't seem upset about the picture. Go out there and look at it with them. They know you were being humorous when you had it taken."

Bridie squinted at Pina. "You're right." She started for the parlor. "I'll go in there and laugh with them."

"Here comes the other squaw," Tom Holmgren snickered.

Biff walked up to Kate and put his arm around her. "Don't laugh, folks. The photographer was so proud of this picture he placed it in the center of his store window."

Standing amid the others, Margaret held the picture at different angles. "Actually, it is clever—different, but clever." She handed the picture to Bridie, and smiled. "Why don't you put it in the Newberry Times and share it with the community? You can claim her as an ancestor."

"Yeah!" Pina agreed. "You can do it, you own part of the newspaper."

Bridie held the picture to her chest. "My family history is already questionable. I certainly don't need to add to it." She walked to the fireplace and stood the picture on the mantle. "Now, everybody can look at it together and have a good laugh." Bridie stepped back and looked at it again. "It is clever, isn't it? How many people do you know who have a clever picture of themselves? I think I'm getting used to it. No—I like it."

"I love it," Catherine shouted. "We should keep it on the mantle."

Bridie patted Catherine on the back and laughed. "I can't say I like it that much."

Kate removed the picture of the three girls from a large envelope. "Now, this picture is adorable." She held it high, so all could see it. "Three precious farm girls."

Margaret fell in love with it immediately and cried out, "I want one!" She reached for the picture. "Is it possible to get another?"

Tom smiled, looking pleased. "Yes, could we? It would be a nice surprise for Brian when he comes home for Thanksgiving."

Kate was delighted with their response. She loved the picture, too. "I would think they kept the plates, especially since it's displayed in their window. When we get home tomorrow, I'll stop by their shop and ask."

Hillary forced a smile. "I already have it framed and hanging in my bedroom."

Pina looked at her. "What kind of frame do you have? I'm not sure what I want."

Hillary pointed to Biff. "My uncle made one for me. He made it from old weathered wood to keep a country theme. It's a perfect combination."

Catherine responded, crisply. "That sounds perfect." She glanced at Pina. "Let's all do it the same, so they match."

Pina agreed. "I'll have my dad make one for you and me."

"Do you have that kind of wood?" Tom Holmgren asked. "If he doesn't, I can get it from old sheds around the quarry."

Pina looked across the room at Tom. "I don't know, but I'll ask. Thank you."

Bridie addressed her guests. "Is anyone thirsty, I have drinks in the kitchen."

Biff walked with Tom, entering the kitchen. "Some day when I'm here, I'd like to see your quarry. I've never seen one in operation."

Tom picked up a glass of iced tea from the table. "I'd be happy to show you. We can arrange it for a day we're blasting a wall. *That* is interesting."

"I would imagine," Biff chuckled. "Let's go out on the porch. I'd like to hear more about your business."

Margaret noticed the men walking toward the kitchen door. "Tom! We have to leave in a few minutes. Don't get too involved."

When they stepped out onto the porch, Biff noticed Jack going into the coach house. He looked at Tom and nodded in Jack's direction. "He appears to be very strong. Do you think Bridie is safe with him, you know, being that he's mentally unstable?"

"Absolutely. He and his mother have been friends of Bridie's for twenty years." Tom wasn't about to tell Biff the full story about Jack. He knew Bridie was keeping it a secret from Biff, for now.

Biff leaned against the porch railing, facing Tom. "Hillary will probably be coming home every third or fourth weekend ... with girlfriends, of course."

Tom laughed. "Of course."

"There will be times when Kate or I will come back with her. When I plan to come, I'll call you in advance to arrange a visit to the quarry."

Tom smiled. "It's a deal. Maybe we could arrange it when Brian is home?"

Biff raised his glass to Tom. "That would be better, yet. And if you and Margaret are interested in coming our way for a farm stay, you're more than welcome."

Margaret opened the kitchen door and stared at Tom. "I think we should leave."

Tom gave Biff a friendly tap on the arm. "I enjoyed meeting you and hope to see you again, soon."

Biff remained on the porch, as the Holmgrens departed. He glanced over at the coach house, still concerned as to whether Jack could become violent.

Moments later, Bridie stuck her head out of the kitchen door. "Would you like a cold glass of iced tea or water?"

"No thanks." He turned to face the pond. "I've been watching that Labrador over there. He's quite interested in two ducks on the other side of the pond."

Bridie laughed. "That's an ongoing event. Actually, the dog, Roper, just wants to play with them. Only, the ducks don't know that."

"I guess you're right. He's not in a hunting stance—just wagging his tail and panting."

"He's not looking for a meal." Bridie moved next to Biff at the porch railing. "Now that I've mentioned the word, *meal*, are you hungry?"

Biff smiled, pleasantly. "Maybe in an hour, but I'd like to take you to the Highlander Restaurant for dinner. Tom Holmgren recommended it highly, and being that we are of Scottish ancestry, it sounded appropriate. Kate and I will be leaving tomorrow morning, so I thought it would be nice if the two of us dined together tonight." He paused a moment before continuing. "I've already discussed it with Kate."

Bridie returned his smile. "Well, if all the negotiating has been completed, I'd better agree. Besides, it sounds like a nice idea to me, too."

CHAPTER TWELVE

Monday morning, Wade Widner entered Tyler Sharpe's office.

Tyler looked up at him, with raised eyebrows. "You're back, so I assume you found John Hanley?" He sat back in his chair waiting for a reply.

"I did. I saw John, Kate and the girl from a distance, so they couldn't recognize me. John even gave me a friendly wave as I rode by, not knowing who I was."

Tyler stood behind his desk. "Exactly where is he?"

"A mile outside of Galena, Illinois. It's a three-day train ride through very nice country."

Tyler grinned. "Then it's nice country to be buried in."

Wade gave Tyler an uneasy stare. "Are you one hundred percent sure, John Hanley is the man you want?"

Tyler seemed irritated by Wade's challenging question, and answered firmly, "The murderer dropped his hat where my brother died, and the name inside of it read, *John Hanley*, who had been at the Delta Saloon that evening. That's all the proof I need. How else would John's hat have gotten there?"

Wade didn't have an answer, but still wasn't convinced John had done it. "When do you plan to go after him?"

Tyler sat down again. "Now that I know where he is, I can take care of him at my leisure. Since he owns a new farm, he isn't going anywhere. I'll make my move when I can break away from this business, probably this winter." Tyler leaned forward and folded his hands on the desk. "Go to your office, write his exact location, and bring it to me."

Wade nodded leaving the office, feeling uneasy about giving Tyler that information. He had no choice.

In Newberry, Bridie hired the same coach and driver to take Kate and Biff to the train station. She and the three girls said "goodbye" on the front porch, waving to them, as they rode away. Hillary stood a few feet away from Bridie, watching her closely for any signs of yearning because of Biff's departure. It didn't take long before Hillary was convinced she was correct in her assumption. *That face reveals disappointment, or she has gas. I believe Bridie has just revealed her true feelings for Biff.*

Bridie relaxed and turned to the girls. "Well, they left with a hardy breakfast to last them until they get home. What do you girls have planned for today and tomorrow? You start school Wednesday, then it's down to work until May."

Catherine leaned against the porch pillar and corrected Bridie's statement. "Wednesday we get our books and have Orientation. Classes don't begin until next Monday."

"You're right," Bridie admitted. "My mistake."

Pina peered over the railing, looking down at the row of dahlias in front of the porch. "If anyone needs school clothes, we could go shopping."

Bridie laughed, walking into the house. "Already, you girls are lost for something to do. It's a good thing you start school to keep you occupied."

Hillary waited until Bridie got further into the house, then whispered, "I watched Bridie as Biff was leaving. I really think she likes him."

Catherine moved closer to Hillary. "I think Biff likes Bridie, too. They appear to be quite cozy together."

Pina remained at the porch railing, thinking about what appeared to be Biff's interest in Catherine. "I think there's more to watch than Biff and Bridie, but I ain't saying what … a-i-n-t."

Catherine looked over at Pina. "What do you mean?"

Pina's eyebrows rose and dropped again. "I a-i-n-t saying until I'm sure, but keep your eyes and ears open when we're all together."

Catherine gave Pina a confused looked. "Why did you mention it, if you aren't going to tell us?"

Pina became flustered. "I really don't know. I'm sorry. I shouldn't have. Maybe so you'd know I knew before anyone else … if I'm right."

Hillary hopped down the porch stairs and stood in the lawn. "Since you're just guessing, you might as well keep it to yourself." She looked up at her friends. "Being that we don't have anything to do, why don't we write letters today? When school starts, we'll be busy with homework. I'd like to write my Uncle Biff and thank him for sending me to Bradbury School. I've already thanked him, but not as sincerely as I should."

Catherine sat on the porch steps, her elbows resting on her knees. "I like that idea, too. Thursday, I received a letter from Brian and I haven't written him, yet. Usually, I write Brian the day I get his letter."

Pina leaned over the porch railing again. "I don't have anyone to write to. I wish I knew where my brother is living. I'd write him a dozen letters." Despair showed in her face, as she went on. "I still remember his sad eyes, looking at me when I was adopted and he had to return to the Orphan Train." She looked up at the blue sky and white clouds. "God, please give Marcello a good life!"

Catherine leaned her shoulder against the stair railing and looked up at Pina. "You could write your parents and thank them for being who they are, and how much you appreciate what they are doing for you. An unexpected letter like that can be very powerful."

Pina thought about that for a moment, then nodded, smiling at Catherine. "You're right. No special occasion, just a letter of love. Yeah! They'd like that."

Catherine jumped to her feet and started for the door. "Let's do it. I've got plenty of paper and pencils. We can write them on the back porch and enjoy the flowers, while we're writing."

When Kate and Biff arrived at Galena, John was sitting on their buckboard near the end of the station platform. Biff carried their luggage from the train, as Kate hurried to John burying herself in his arms, kissing him.

John brushed her hair back from her brown eyes, and smiled. "Welcome home!"

Kate looked into his eyes. "Even though we had a wonderful time, I'm glad to be home."

"I assumed you'd have a good time. Is Hillary excited about starting school?"

"Very much so. I could see the excitement in Hillary's face, while given a private tour through the building and school grounds." Kate glanced at Biff, walking past them carrying the luggage. "You did a wonderful thing for Hillary and we want to thank you."

Biff nodded. "I loved doing it for her. She's a good girl."

John squinted at Kate and quietly asked, "How did he and Bridie get along?"

Kate glanced over at Biff to be sure he couldn't hear her whisper. "Extremely well. I'll tell you more about that when we're alone." She took John's hand, walking to the buckboard. "We need to stop at Harte's Photograpy Shop, so I can order more pictures of us squaws and the girls. Bridie's dearest friends, the Holmgrens, want a copy of both pictures. They are the people who adopted Brian, Catherine's sweetheart."

Biff looked at Kate. "You ride up there with John. I'll ride on the bench seat in the back."

"Thank you, dear Biff. I appreciate that." Kate took Biff's hand, to help her up to the seat. She smiled down at him. "You've become such a charming gentleman lately. Could it be Bridie's influence?"

Biff climbed into the back of the wagon. "Think what you like."

Kate glanced over her shoulder at Biff. "I was just teasing."

John shook the reins and Cokie pulled them away from the station. John tilted his head back and shouted, "Harte Photographers, next stop."

Riding along the avenue, Kate looked at the shops and the Galena River. She liked Galena and was elated to be living there. The thought of living in Alton, Delaware, again, appalled her.

At the photographers, Kate and John went inside to order the pictures.

Helen Harte came from the back room to greet them. "Good afternoon! Are you in a silly mood again?"

Kate laughed. "No. It seems the pictures of the girls and us squaws are very popular with our friends. I'd like to order one more of each. Do you still have the plates?"

Helen went to her desk to check the numbers of the two plates. "We certainly do." She sat down and took paper and pencil from the drawer to write the order. "This is Monday, so they should be ready Thursday."

Kate smiled at Helen. "We just got off the train from Newberry, where we visited friends. Our daughter, Hillary, will be attending Bradbury Finishing School for Girls."

Helen leaned back in her chair and looked directly into Kate's eyes. "When did you leave Galena?"

Kate was surprised at Helen's unsettled expression. "We left Saturday, two days ago. Why do you ask?"

Helen let out a sigh of relief. "Good! Then I assume you visited with your surprise guest early last week?"

"Guest?" John repeated, looking at Helen. "We didn't have a guest last week." He stared at Kate. "Did someone stop by the house, while I was away?"

Kate, too, was surprised at Helen's remark. "What do you mean—our surprise guest? No one came to our house."

Helen rose behind her desk and clasped her hands together. "Last week, Tuesday or Wednesday, a man saw your squaw picture in the window and said he was a friend of yours. He was nicely dressed and asked for directions to your house."

Kate glanced at John, then at Helen again. "What did he look like?"

Helen shrugged. "I'd say he was about six foot three inches tall. He was a big man, with broad shoulders. Rather good looking."

Kate and John looked at each other, again. Had they been discovered? Kate leaned closer to Helen. "Did he give you his name?"

Helen detected concern in Kate's voice. "No, he didn't. The man said he was here for only two days and stumbled across your picture in my window. He asked whether there was a stable nearby, so he could rent a horse and ride out to your place for a surprise visit."

John took Kate's arm and thanked Helen for the information. "I'll be back Thursday for the pictures." He led Kate out of the store.

Biff could tell that they were disturbed about something. "Is there a problem?"

John glanced up at him. "We don't know, for sure."

Biff was dumbfounded by their nervousness. "Well, something is bothering you."

Kate was shaking her head, looking at Biff. "Mrs. Harte said, a man was in their shop last week asking questions about us. He told her he was an old friend and planned to give us a surprise visit. Well, he never came to us."

Biff assisted Kate up to the buckboard seat. "Do you think it's someone from Alton?"

John was biting his lip, as he climbed aboard the wagon. "Who knows? But I'll be taking my rifle with me when I'm working in the field." John was about to shake the reins, then hesitated. "Last week," he mumbled aloud. He looked at Kate through puzzled eyes. "Early last week, we were watching Hillary ride Knickers in the corral when a stranger rode past. I waved and he waved back. Remember?"

Kate thought for a moment. "Yes! Yes, I do, and he *was* a big man, riding tall in the saddle. If he's the man, and he didn't stop by to see us, then his only purpose was to locate us."

John rested his forearms on his thighs. "Any ideas as to who, he could be?"

Kate looked skyward through narrowed eyes. "I sure do. Does the name, Wade Widner sound familiar? He fits the man's description. And after you fled Alton, his job was to learn where you went. I know, because he told me that."

John looked askew at Kate. "Wade and I were on friendly terms."

Kate avoided telling John about Wade's interest in courting her after John left Alton. "If that's what he's getting paid to do, then he's got to do it."

John stared straight ahead. "This is a big country. How could anyone have found us, without guidance?"

Biff leaned toward John. "When you bought your land and equipment, were you in contact with any business associated with the Alton area?"

John ran his hand through his hair. "I doubt it, but how would I know that?"

Kate placed her hand on John's forearm, reassuring him he wasn't at fault. "I'm sure a salesman working around here won't be doing business in Alton, Delaware."

Biff chuckled, cautiously. "True. But if a man works this area and his company transfers him to another area the following year, he could carry tales with him. With today's trains, a person can cross this country in just a few days."

Kate sighed, loudly. "Maybe someone just happened to see my picture in the window—nothing more?"

John shook the reins briskly and glanced back at Biff. "We need to keep alert for strangers from now on."

Kate had deep furrows in her brow. "We'd better keep our doors locked, too."

CHAPTER THIRTEEN

By mid-September, the girls completed two weeks of school. Hillary and Pina had adjusted to the school's routine, location of classrooms and varied personalities of their teachers. Every day, classes were dismissed at three o'clock and they met Catherine under a Weeping Willow tree on the school's lawn.

Surrounded by other students, Pina and Hillary walked out of the school, with books cradled in their arms. Catherine was under the tree, waiting for them. They ran down the stone steps, and raced across the lawn.

Hillary waved a piece of paper over her head, shouting, "We had a test in Etiquette today, and I learned I'm a pig."

"*We* are pigs," Pina added. "We need to change ourselves completely."

Catherine laughed. "I know exactly what you mean. Mrs. Davidson said most of my class, were pigs. Don't worry. She only wants you to be concerned about yourself, so you'll learn the proper ways of being a lady."

Pina sat in the grass, looking up at Catherine. "She's so skinny, she reminds me of a stick bug."

Hillary waved a finger at Pina. "Now, now, talking like that isn't proper etiquette. It appears you haven't learned anything these past two weeks."

Catherine opened a book and began turning pages. "This book is about flower arrangements. I want to show you one that is, absolutely beautiful."

Hillary laughed. "Oh, yeah! Flower arrangements—just what I need on the farm."

Catherine smiled at her. "Someday, your Prince will come and give you a beautiful home, so you need to be prepared."

Hillary laughed again. "My Prince will probably wear bib overalls and smoke a corn cob pipe."

"Here," Catherine said, opening the book. "Look at these beautiful flowers. It even tells you how long each flower stem should be at various locations in the arrangement."

Pina stood to study the picture. "Goodness! That is beautiful. It sure helps to know what you're doing."

Hillary fluttered her eyelashes. "That's why we attend Bradbury School. We must prepare ourselves for the good life."

Catherine closed the book and started walking home. "Right now, the good life for me is here in Newberry, living with Bridie." She glanced at the other two. "And then with Brian."

Pina looked up into Catherine's eyes. "You have your man already, but Hillary and I don't have anyone—not even a prospect."

Catherine smiled. "You will. Be patient, you're only fourteen."

Pina shifted her books from one arm to the other. "This isn't a big town, and I haven't seen anyone of interest, so far."

Hillary laid a hand on Pina's shoulder, slowing her walk. "Have you met all of Brian's boyfriends? I'm sure there must be one that is … interesting." She glanced at Catherine. "He does have nice friends, doesn't he?"

"Of course! I would say, Todd Hogan is … interesting, as you put it."

Pina laughed. "One! Is that the total number of worthwhile boys you can name? I don't even know him. Does he have two heads?"

Catherine looked at Pina, with expressionless eyes. "Your Prince can step out of the dark at any time, especially when you don't expect it. Who would have thought I'd meet my man in an orphanage."

"Enough of this Prince business," Hillary insisted, walking on. 'When he comes, he comes. Like Catherine said, we're only fourteen and there's no need to worry about marriage prospects now."

Pina turned away smiling. "We should marry well. Monica found Charles Belcher."

Catherine couldn't contain her laughter. "She's happy with him, and that's all that matters. Besides, she's elated about becoming a mother in a couple months."

Hillary tilted her head and looked at her friends. "Who's Monica?"

With pursed lips, Catherine and Pina cast a cryptic glance at each other.

"What? A secret?" Hillary asked.

Catherine stopped walking and faced Hillary, deciding to tell her about Monica's current situation, without including Monica's attack by Mr. Peters. "Monica came to Newberry on the same Orphan Train as me and Brian. She met a young man named Charles Belcher, who was born here, but is now a teacher at Knox College. Pina and I don't think much of Charles, that's why we're laughing. I guess we threw proper etiquette away for the moment."

Hillary's questioning eyes shifted back and forth between her friends. "What don't you like about him?"

Catherine started walking and the others followed. "He's a ... sissy type. You know, not manly."

Pina chuckled again. "He's not a young man you'd be proud to show off to your friends and relatives."

Hillary nodded at them. "I see, he's not exactly a Prince, right?"

"More like a Princess," Pina snickered.

The girls stopped at the street, waiting for a horse and buggy to pass and ran across the street. Hillary held up one of the books she was carrying. "I'm to write a two-page description of this short story for Monday. With this assignment and my other homework, I'll be very busy this weekend."

Catherine looked at the book's title. "I read *Juanita* last year, and enjoyed it. It's about a young Indian girl who lives in California."

Pina gave Catherine, a questioning glance. "Does she meet her Prince?"

Hillary slid the book between other books she was carrying. "Indians don't have Princes. Their men are called Braves, or Warriors."

"Unlike Charles," Pina snickered, producing one of her books. "I have to read and write a report on this story, *Tom Renn—Lumberjack.*

Catherine looked at Pina's book and laughed. "The girls who read that one hated it. None of us could figure out why a book like that would be assigned to girls."

Pina gave Catherine a glowering look, showing her disappointment. "Thanks! Now it will be more difficult for me to read, let alone write about it."

"You'll manage," Hillary assured her. "There'll be other assignments we won't like the next two years."

Catherine waved to a girl entering a house across the street. "She's in my Art and History classes. Her name is Grace and always gets top grades. She's a nice girl, too."

Hillary watched Grace until she closed her door. "There aren't many students who live in Newberry."

Catherine shifted the books cradled in her arms. "Only twelve, according to Mrs. Gutberlet, the Assistant Principal." She glanced at her friends. "Mrs. Gutberlet and Bridie went to grade school together. That's how long they've been friends."

"I imagine we'll be life-long friends," Pina surmised. "Even if one of us moves far away, we can still write or telephone each other—even visit."

The girls stopped at the corner where they parted to go home. Catherine looked at her friends and sighed. "Remember, as soon as we get home try and get as much homework done as possible, so we can have time together Sunday."

"And tonight," Hillary added, quickly. "After dinner, seven o'clock at Kitty's for ice cream—or whatever." The girls said goodbye and went their own way.

When they entered Pina's house, Mrs. Campbell came to the door with a letter in her hand. "This is for you, Hillary. I assumed you'd want to read it right away."

Hillary read the return address. "It's from A. Roddy." She gave Pina a perplexed stare and looked at the envelope, again.

Pina decided to tease Hillary about getting a letter from Adam. When her mother was back in the kitchen, Pina looked towards the ceiling and began mumbling names. "Let's see ... A. Roddy. Now who could that be? There's Ruth ... Tom ... Trish and Marnie. Oh, yes! There is also a young man named Adam Roddy. I guess it must be from him, since his first name starts with the letter 'A'." She looked at Hillary. "Wouldn't you agree?"

Hillary leered at Pina. "Very funny! Yes, I would agree, but I don't know why he'd write me. Kate must have given him my address."

"There's only one way to find out." Pina pushed on Hillary's back. "Go up to our bedroom for privacy and read it. When you're finished, tell me everything that's in that letter."

At seven o'clock, Pina and Hillary were in Kitty's Confectionary waiting for Catherine. Kitty set napkins and three glasses of water on their table. "You won't have long to wait. Catherine is crossing the street now."

Pina was about to burst, wanting to tell Catherine about Adam's letter to Hillary. She tried to hide her anxiety by pretending to read the menu. When Catherine entered Kitty's and walked to their table, Pina squealed, "Hillary's got a surprise to tell you."

There was disappointment in Hillary's voice, as she glared at Pina. "Why did you say that? I intended to mention it."

Pina blushed from embarrassment. "I'm sorry. I couldn't wait for her to hear."

Catherine sat down and faced Hillary. "Hear what?"

Hillary stared at Pina to keep her from answering. "I received a letter from Adam Roddy today."

Catherine sat back in her chair and smiled at Hillary. "Adam Roddy? Is there anything interesting in that letter, something you'd like to share with us? Or is the subject too personal to tell?"

Hillary looked to see whether customers nearby could hear what she was about to say. She spoke softly. "It was just a friendly letter, inquiring as to how I was doing with my school work and if I liked it here. Nothing more."

Pina leaned closer to Hillary. "In that friendly letter, did he ask when you would be returning home?"

"Yes, but he didn't dwell on my going home. It was just one question among others."

Catherine grinned. "Pina does make a good point. You're going home has nothing to do with school. It sounds more like he has a yearning for your return."

Hillary shrugged. "I don't see it that way."

Pina giggled. "I suggest you start seeing it that way, so you're prepared to deal with him when he gets, shall we say ... bolder."

Hillary spoke in a tone that was hard and even. "Up to now, he hasn't shown any sign of liking me. Remember how rude he was to us at first?" Suddenly, Hillary recalled the night of the bonfire. Adam had set aside scraps of wood, just for her, to throw into the fire. And how his voice seemed affectionate when he'd talked to her. She smiled and glanced at her friends. "On second thought, you may be right. He has been attentive in subtle ways."

Kitty came to their table for their food order. "I assume you've already had your dinner and are here for a treat. What will it be—besides girl talk?"

Pina raised an index finger. "Chocolate ice cream."

Hillary nodded, "Same for me."

Catherine looked over at the pastry counter. "I'd like to have a lemon tart, with milk, please."

Kitty returned the order pad to her apron pocket. "That's easy enough. No need to write that order down." She looked at the girls. "Anything special to talk about tonight?"

Pina leaned toward Kitty. "To be sure," she answered with a grin.

Kitty laughed and walked away. "Good. I'll leave, so you can continue."

Hillary tapped Pina's arm. "We just failed etiquette, again. When Catherine ordered her tart, she said, *please*. You and I didn't."

Pina rolled her eyes. "We're pigs, remember?"

Catherine smiled. "You usually say please. You just forgot this time."

Hillary unfolded her blue napkin and laid it carefully across her lap. "That's how a true lady employs a napkin. She doesn't shake it, then plop it on her lap. Did you observe that, Pina?"

"Employ a napkin?" Pina questioned. "I'm not sure I want to be a lady, if I must *employ* a napkin. Do you employ a washboard when you wash clothes?"

Catherine grinned at their antics. "I can't wait to employ my fork into my lemon tart. It's a much cleaner way of eating, than with my fingers."

Intentionally, Pina shook her napkin and plopped it on her lap. "Tell me, Lady Catherine, have you heard any murmurs from Bridie, regarding Mr. Biff Arley?"

Catherine thought for a moment. "Yes, but only a couple of times. Once, she mentioned something about him being Scottish, but I don't recall the other time."

Pina leaned forward, looking into Catherine's eyes. "The point is, if Bridie mentioned Biff a couple of times, she's thinking about him much more than she discusses him."

"Let's change the subject," Hillary muttered. "Kitty's coming with our food." She sipped her water and folded her hands on her lap. "I'm going home in two weeks. Can either of you come with me? Kate suggested I ask you."

Catherine and Pina looked at each other, waiting for the other's response. Kitty was amused by their silence, assuming they had stopped talking so she shouldn't hear. The girls thanked Kitty, placing their dessert in front of them. Kitty smiled and walked away, listening for their conversation to begin now that she'd left.

Pina's dark eyes smiled at her friends. "Did you notice, we all said, 'Thank you' this time. How's that for proper ladies?"

"Let's get back to our Galena discussion," Hillary insisted.

"I'll ask Bridie," Catherine promised. "I'd certainly like to go, and I hope we don't have tons of homework that weekend."

Pina fluttered her eyelashes at Hillary. "Then we'll be able to see A. Roddy again. He'll wish we weren't with you."

Hillary fluttered her eyelashes at Pina. "That is true. I'll get all of his attention, while he patiently tolerates your presence."

Catherine laughed. "You two are my entertainment. Only good friends could tolerate your shenanigans."

"Yes, we are good friends," Hillary assured her. "I'm still amazed that we found each other after being separated for what we thought would be forever." She sipped her water and addressed Catherine. "I consider you a good friend, too. I haven't known you as long as Pina, but I think you and Brian are great people."

Catherine lifted her fork and cut away a piece of her lemon tart. "Thank you. I feel the same about you."

Pina rolled her dark eyes and fell back into her chair. "I'm going to throw-up, if you two don't stop the lovey-dovey talk."

"We're finished," Hillary responded, with a silly smile. "Now, let's return to our discussion. Tonight, you two ask your parents about going to Galena two weeks from now. We need to plan ahead."

Suddenly, Catherine straightened up and smiled. "That would be the beginning of October, in time for the autumn colors."

"True," Pina agreed, enthusiastically. "Beautiful autumn colors for Hillary and a certain neighbor, A. Roddy. It may inspire romance."

Hillary pondered another idea. "It would be nice if Bridie and Biff were together during the autumn colors. Don't you agree? Ask Bridie to come with us. Say we're afraid to ride the train alone."

Catherine nodded and smiled. "That's a good idea. Saying we are afraid may convince her to go with us."

"Or give Bridie an *excuse* to go with us," Pina added.

When Catherine returned home, Bridie was sitting on the back porch reading a book about the Civil War. "Sorry to interrupt you, but we girls were wondering if you would go to Galena with us in two weeks?"

Bridie closed her book and laid it on her lap. "Actually, you aren't interrupting. It's getting dark and I should have quit reading minutes ago. I've been straining my eyes to see the words." There was a pleased expression in Bridie's face, as she repeated the question. "You want me to go to Galena in two weeks? Why don't you girls go by yourselves?"

Catherine sat in a chair next to Bridie, believing it wouldn't take much to convince her to go. "We're still nervous about traveling that far on our own. All kinds of people are on those trains."

There was a hint of eagerness in Bridie's response. "I certainly understand that. You girls are young and inexperienced travelers." She pretended to decide whether that date would be agreeable to her schedule. For a few moments, she sat silent; then drew herself up with a satisfied expression on her face. "Yes, I'll go. There doesn't seem to be anything I need to do that weekend."

"Good! I'll tell Hillary tomorrow."

Bridie held up her hand. "Wait a minute! Has Kate invited me and the girls, or is this something Hillary thought up on her own?"

Catherine shook her head. "No! Hillary received the invitation from Kate in her last letter. And it did include you."

Bridie smiled, pleased by the invitation. "Alright, we'll go."

Catherine started for the kitchen. "It should be a special trip. We'll be there for the autumn colors."

Bridie rose from her chair and straightened her skirt. "You're right, and I do enjoy that time of year. We can take the afternoon train on Friday and return Sunday evening."

Chapter Fourteen

Two weeks later, Bridie and the three girls arrived at the Galena station. Kate and Biff were there to meet them. The girls ran ahead to the coach and laid their luggage on the ground. Biff walked up to Bridie and took her luggage. "Being that it's 8:30, and it's getting dark, we're going straight home to eat there."

Kate came up to her other side and took Bridie's arm. "Supper will be simple, but it's better than riding these roads in the dark."

Bridie carried two shallow boxes. "I'm glad. These boxes contain chocolate cake and apple pie. The sooner we eat them, the better." She smiled at Kate. "With iced tea, of course."

Biff licked his lips. "Did you say apple pie?"

Kate gave Bridie's arm a gentle tug. "That's his favorite pie. So, you made a good choice."

He was pleased Bridie came with the girls. She was fun to be with and they had many interests in common. He also, found her attractive.

Riding out of town, Bridie breathed deeply and smiled at Kate. "I'm happy to be back. I thoroughly enjoyed my last visit."

Kate answered, evenly. "It shows, and we're glad you did, because we enjoyed having you."

"Thank you." Bridie pointed at the three girls sitting across from them. "They have fun no matter where they are, town or country."

"Of course," Hillary interrupted. "We're good friends, everywhere."

Bridie reveled in the passing scenery, though it was fading into dusk. Suddenly, it occurred to her, that as they rode through Galena, and past the De Soto Hotel, it didn't remind her of John McTavish, as it had before. She pondered the situation. *Am I distancing myself from John with the passage of time, or because of Biff?*

Approaching the farm, they could see Adam and his sisters entering the front of their lantern-lit house. When they heard Biff's coach, they turned and waved from the doorway.

Pina decided to give Hillary a little ribbing. "Oh, look! There's A. Roddy and his sisters."

Kate laughed. "Why do you call him A. Roddy, instead of Adam?"

"It's a private joke," Hillary answered, quickly. "I assume you're the one who gave him my Newberry address?"

Kate tried seeing Hillary in the dark. "Yes, I did. He came to me and asked if I thought you'd mind if he and his sisters wrote to you. I thought it was a nice gesture and assumed you'd enjoy getting mail from them."

Pina snickered, as the coach stopped in front of the house. "Hillary got a letter from A. Roddy, but not the girls." She jumped from the coach and faced the others. "Do you think he may have forgotten to give the address to his sisters?"

Kate gave Hillary a long look. "Is that true? He's the only one who wrote you?"

Catherine stepped out of the coach smiling. "I'm sure you will get a letter from his sisters … eventually."

Bridie looked at Hillary. "It appears Mr. Roddy's letter is causing you some embarrassment."

Rather than get upset, Hillary collected herself and started for the house. "I am not embarrassed by their teasing. They're jealous that he prefers me. Besides, they know I'll get even someday."

Biff assisted Bridie and Kate from the coach, then called to Hillary, "There's no reason to be embarrassed. You'll have lots of boys knocking on your door."

Hillary stopped at the door and looked back, grinning. "A. Roddy is just the beginning."

"Atta girl," Kate shouted. "We'll need a shotgun to keep them away."

"She'd rather you didn't," Pina quipped.

Hillary reached for the doorknob as the door opened. John bent down and gave her a hug. "Welcome home, Sweetheart."

Hillary closed her eyes and hugged him back. "It's good to be back."

Kate and Bridie went directly to the kitchen. Kate opened the icebox for the iced tea and Bridie opened the boxes of cake and pie.

The others entered the kitchen and praised the desserts. Hillary went to the cabinet for dishes and placed them on the table. "Thank you, Bridie. There's enough dessert for tomorrow night's supper, too."

Kate turned and faced the girls. "Sorry, but tomorrow night we adults are going to Galena for an early dinner. I'll have food prepared for you to eat here." She smiled at the girls. "It's not that we don't love you darlings, but I thought it would be nice if we adults had an evening alone."

Hillary looked at her two friends, giving them a devilish grin. "We'll have the whole house to ourselves. What a pity."

Catherine pulled a chair from the table and sat down. "Don't get too excited girls, we have homework to do, and tomorrow evening would be a good time to do it."

"True," Pina added. "That way, we'll have the daylight hours to be outside and visit with your neighbors, Trish, Marnie and A. Roddy."

The following morning, the girls dressed in denim pants and cotton shirts to collect eggs and fill the horse troughs with hay. On their way back to the house, John rode by in the wagon. He had a rifle next to him. When they entered the kitchen, Hillary placed the basket of eggs on the kitchen table.

Hillary stood next to Kate, drying the breakfast dishes. "Why is John taking his rifle with him today? I've never seen him take it into the field before."

Kate didn't want to tell Hillary about the stranger inquiring about them in Galena. She turned to Hillary, with a forced smile. "John has seen foxes around here lately and he wants to protect the hen house."

"He'd shoot a pretty fox?" Pina interrupted.

Kate feigned a laugh and wiped her hands on her apron. "He would shoot over their heads or at the ground to scare them. He'd only kill one if it was at, or in, the hen house."

Hillary looked puzzled. "We've never seen a fox around here before."

Kate started down the hall toward her bedroom, not wanting to continue the conversation. "Well, they're here now—unless they've moved on, to annoy another farmer."

She entered her bedroom and sat on the bed, thinking about the stranger, fearful that John could be taken from her ... one way or another. Kate wondered if the man was looking for John *and* her, being that she killed Frank Dragus, and was probably a suspect in his murder. She went to the window and looked at their new stable and barn and corral, then examined her bedroom. *I love this place and don't ever want to lose it.* Her thoughts turned to Hillary. *What would happen to her, if John and I were taken away? Could she cope with losing a second set of parents?*

That afternoon, Catherine and Pina helped Hillary saddle Knickers, intending to ride him in the corral. Hillary looked into Knicker's eyes and petted his soft nose. "These are my friends, so I want you to be gentle with them ... as you usually are." Hillary asked Catherine and Pina to come to the front of the horse. "Pet him and talk softly to him, so he gets to know you. I'll step back and hold the reins."

The girls stood at both sides of him, stroking his nose and neck, telling him what a beautiful horse he was and that they'd never been on a horse before, so he should be nice to them. Hillary could see that her friends were nervous about riding him, but still wanting to. To ease their anxiety, she made a suggestion. "To start with, I'll hold the halter and walk Knickers around the corral a couple of times. That way, you and the horse can get acquainted. Then I'll let go of the halter and you can guide him with the reins."

Catherine and Pina looked at each other and smiled, believing it was a safe way to begin. They followed Hillary out of the stable and into the corral, scaring off a pair of doves sitting on the fence. Hillary looked at Pina, pointing to a wooden box next to the fence. "Grab that box. We need it to step up to the stirrup and onto Knickers."

Pina chuckled. "Yes, Boss."

"Who wants to ride him first?"

Pina looked at Catherine. "You can go first."

Catherine bowed her head to Pina, "Thank you, I will."

Hillary held Knickers in place, while Catherine stepped onto the box and slid her foot into the stirrup. "Pina, push on Catherine's butt, so she can get up into the saddle."

Pina snickered, again. "Yes, Boss."

Hillary adjusted the stirrups for Catherine's legs, while Pina held the horse in place. Hillary looked up at Catherine and smiled. "Are you ready for your first ride?"

Catherine straightened her back and sat tall in the saddle. "I'm more than ready. I've waited years to do this."

Hillary held the bridle and walked Knickers around the corral twice. "You're on your own, Catherine. Remember, pull back on the reins, if you want him to stop."

Though somewhat nervous for being on her own, Catherine forced a smile. "Someday, I'd like to be good enough to ride fast."

"Kick your heels into him, if you want him to go faster," Hillary shouted.

Catherine looked over her shoulder at Hillary. "I don't want to kick him. He may not like it."

Hillary laughed. "Kick him to make him go faster; pull on the reins to slow him down. That's what they know."

After circling three-quarters of the corral, Catherine gritted her teeth, riding toward Hillary. When she was next to Hillary, she shouted, "What the heck!" and kicked her heels into Knickers. He responded immediately and began to trot. Unsure of the situation, Catherine frowned, but continued on. After circling the corral once, she felt more relaxed and sure of herself. On her next pass, she called to Pina, "Open the gate, I'm going to California."

Pina stepped up to Hillary, "Let her ride for a while. I can wait."

Hillary hooked her arm with Pina's, as they watched Catherine ride. "She's doing very well for a first time."

Pina agreed. "I hope I do as well."

In all, Catherine circled the corral ten times. She pulled back on the reins as she approached her friends. "That was fun. Your turn, Pina."

Pina walked over and helped her down from the horse. "You did good. I could see your confidence grow, as you rode."

"Thank you! I'm sure you will do as well." Catherine jumped from the box, looking toward the house. "Here comes Bridie and Kate."

"You were great," Kate shouted, crossing the yard. At the corral fence, Kate nodded toward Bridie. "We should give Bridie a chance to ride."

Bridie waved her hand at Kate. "No, thanks! It's been years since I rode a horse and I'd probably fall off. Besides, I'm wearing a skirt."

Hillary laughed. "That would be a sight, you straddling a horse wearing a skirt."

Pina stepped up on the box. "Well, I'm riding. Catherine, help me up into the saddle."

Catherine laughed and mimicked Pina. "Yes, Boss."

Pina held up a hand to stop Hillary. "Don't assist, I'll do this on my own." She took hold of the reins and Knickers started walking around the corral. From the other side of the corral, Pina yelled, "Calamity Jane has nothing on me." After making on full circle, Pina kicked Knickers into a trot. She began to giggle, while one hand held the reins and the other gripped the saddle horn.

"You're cheating," Catherine called to her. "I didn't hold onto the horn."

Pina bounced and came down hard on the saddle. "Because you didn't think of it," she wailed, painfully. Her face showed she wasn't pleased with her ride, as she continued to bounce on the saddle. After two trips around the corral, she pulled on the reins, stopping Knickers in front of her friends. "I'm doing something wrong."

Shaking her head, Hillary stepped up to her. "That's because you rode away before I adjusted the stirrups for you. Catherine's legs are longer than yours, so the stirrups are too low to support your legs."

Kate elevated herself by stepping onto the bottom rail of the fence. "Hillary will adjust the stirrups for you, then go around a few more times."

Pina slid off the saddle and dropped onto the box. "No, thanks. I'll ride another time." She stepped to the ground, rubbing the back of her pants. "My butt is hurting."

Catherine stepped forward. "I'll ride again, if you don't mind."

"Good!" Bridie cried out. "I want to watch you."

Before mounting the horse, Catherine looked into Knicker's eyes. "It's me again. Be a good boy." She stepped into the stirrup and flung the other leg over the horse. Feeling confident, Catherine kicked her heels into Knickers and rode off. She was smiling, because she felt good in the saddle.

Bridie applauded, as Catherine rode past the third time. "You're doing beautifully."

Catherine was excited, knowing she had performed well, especially for a first time. She rocked comfortably in the saddle, feeling as though she belonged there. Catherine looked beyond the farm, to the hills and fields in the distance, pretending she was riding free, over open land. The enthusiastic smile on her face showed she didn't want the ride to end.

Bridie was elated, watching Catherine ride with self-assurance and obviously loving it. She decided Catherine should have the opportunity to take riding lessons and see how well she could do. Eventually, if good enough, she could enter equestrian competitions. How perfect that would be, Catherine, a beautiful girl and graduate of Bradbury Finishing School, and an equestrian. She immediately began to ponder the idea of buying a horse and boarding it at a stable in Newberry. Another thought occurred to her. What if she and Biff were to fall in love and marry? Biff would have the means to keep a horse for her, too.

Bridie backed away from the fence, a breeze stirring a cloud of top dirt into the air. She was brushing dust from her blouse when a significant problem became evident. *What will happen to Jack when his mother dies? There are no relatives to take care of him and that could interfere with my relationship with Biff.* It was then, that she truly realized how she felt about Biff Arley.

At 3:30, John watched Biff drive up to the house in the coach, leaving a trail of dust behind him. He was dressed in a tan sport jacket and brown pants.

John came from the house wearing gray pants and a blue jacket. He stopped on the porch stairs and put his hands on his hips. "The ladies will be out in a minute." He looked up at the sky and nodded. "Looks like it'll be a nice evening."

When Biff climbed down from the coach, he could hear a breeze rustling the leaves of the oak tree next to the house. "Yeah, it's nice now, but if the wind picks up, we may be in for a storm before we get home."

John looked down from the porch, laughing. "Did you bring a raincoat ... Mr. Driver?"

"It's in the box under the seat ... Mr. Smarty."

The girls rushed out of the house, praising how beautiful Kate and Bridie looked. Hillary ran to Biff and gave him a hug, as she usually did when he arrived. She looked up at him, then at John. "You'd better compliment them on how they look, or you may be in trouble."

"Shhh!" Catherine said, quickly. "They're coming now."

As if on parade, Kate and Bridie, stepped carefully from the house, with the grace and dignity of royalty. Kate turned to Bridie, waving her hand through the air. "Come, Lady McDonald, our escorts are awaiting."

"Good, better them, than us, I hate waiting for people."

John was amused by their pretension. He stepped up to the ladies. "You're both so lovely, I'm not sure which of you I want to take my arm."

Kate pinched his arm. "Thee had better want me, or pay the consequences."

Biff walked up the two porch stairs and let Bridie take his arm. "May I have the pleasure of assisting you to the coach, my lady?"

Bridie fanned her face with her hand. "Why thank you, Sir Lancelot. I would appreciate that kindness."

Hillary wedged herself between her friends and whispered, "Biff and Bridie seem like a committed couple already."

Catherine nodded in agreement. "I've noticed it, too. And they've been together a few times already. They definitely appear to like each other."

Pina glanced at the other two. "I'll just say, Hmmm!"

As the coach pulled away, Kate looked out of the window and yelled, "Don't forget to do your homework."

"True," Catherine mumbled, apathetically. "Let's do it now, so we are free to play tomorrow morning."

Hillary walked slowly toward the kitchen door. "Remember, we have cake and apple pie we can eat, while studying."

Pina grinned. "Good idea. We can do our homework at the kitchen table." The girls went to Hillary's bedroom for their books and brought them into the kitchen.

"Look," Catherine said, passing the window. "Here comes the Roddy trio." She sat at the table, spreading her books and papers before her. "I'd like to spend time with them, but we need to do our homework."

Hillary went to the window, watching them run across the field. "You're right, they can't stay long. I'll have to tell them in a nice way."

Pina looked across the table at Hillary. "Tell them to come back in the morning, when we collect eggs." She grinned at Hillary. "We certainly wouldn't want to miss time with A. Roddy."

Hillary leered at Pina. "I don't even know the boy."

Catherine looked up from the table. "Like it or not, I have a feeling you're going to know him very well."

When the Roddy children were close to the house, the girls went out to the porch to meet them. Adam arrived first, with his two cousins close behind. Hillary greeted them with a hardy, "Howdy neighbors!"

Adam looked fixedly at her and smiled. "Howdy!" He stood silent for a moment, before asking what he really wanted to know. "When do you have to go back to school?"

Hillary leaned against a post supporting the porch roof. "Tomorrow afternoon, and we have homework to do tonight."

Marnie and Trish groaned with disappointment.

Pina jumped over the two porch stairs to the ground, raising a small nebula of dust. "Come in the morning and collect eggs with us, then we can play."

Adam looked back at his cousins, nodding in agreement. He look at Hillary again. "How long will it take to do your school work?"

"Until dark," Catherine interrupted.

Hillary watched them, turn and walk away. "Plan on 7:30. We'll meet you here in the yard."

Catherine turned and started back into the house. "I guarantee you, A. Roddy is interested in H. Cook."

Pina stepped up to the porch, following Catherine. "The question I have is—is H. Cook interested in A. Roddy?"

CHAPTER FIFTEEN

At seven o'clock the next morning, Kate and Bridie were in the kitchen making flapjacks and sausage. John spent the night at Biff's house because they were getting up early to remove a tree stump next to Biff's barn. The girls were in Hillary's bedroom, dressing to meet the Roddy kids at 7:30.

Bridie was turning flapjacks in the frying pan. "I truly enjoyed our dinner last night. The dining room was lovely and the food was excellent."

Kate rolled her eyes and smiled. "The drinks were good, too." She gave Bridie a side-glance. "I'd say you also enjoyed the man you were with. Am I correct?"

Bridie couldn't hold back her smile. "Yes, I enjoy him. The truth is, I haven't found anything I don't like about him."

Kate laughed. "It shows … to me, anyway. I don't know if Biff realizes it, though. Men aren't as attune to sensitive issues as women are." She looked down the hall to see whether the girls were coming, then whispered, "Women have subtle ways of letting a man know, right?"

"True, but a woman must be sure the man is interested in her before she does."

Kate thought of Biff, wondering how well he was dealing with Catherine's likeness to Laura. *Could he overcome that problem, or would it cause him to turn away from Bridie?* Kate removed the sausages from the frying pan and placed them on a plate. She paused next to Bridie. "You have Catherine, but are you interested in having a child of your own?"

Bridie didn't hesitate to answer. "Definitely. But I'm concerned about the difficulty of childbirth at my age. I'm thirty-eight, not the best age to start having babies."

Kate placed the plate of sausage on the table and walked back to Bridie. "I know Biff would love to have children. He pretends Hillary is his daughter. It gives him some semblance of being a parent."

The girls came from the bedroom and sat at the table. Bridie set a plate of flapjacks before them. "The Roddy kids will be here in twenty-five minutes, so you'll have to hurry."

Hillary looked through the kitchen window. "I'll know when they're coming. I can see their house from where I'm sitting."

"I'm sure A. Roddy will be here at exactly 7:30," Pina chucked.

"True," Catherine agreed. "He's more than anxious to see H. Cook."

Kate laughed, looking at Hillary. "So, now it's A. Roddy and H. Cook. Is there an implication there?"

"They're just being silly," Hillary insisted. "I don't even know the boy and these two are matching us up."

Pina looked at Kate and grinned. "Catherine and I believe there's more to their story than Hillary wants to let on."

Bridie gave Catherine a long foreboding stare. "It's nice to have fun, but don't let it get out of hand."

Hillary poured maple syrup over her flapjacks. She wanted to change the subject, so she asked, "When will the men be here? We must leave by one o'clock to meet the train."

Kate removed her apron and draped it through the oven door handle. "John said they'd be back by noon, all washed and ready to go."

Bridie waved a hand to Kate. "Let's go outside and revel in the cool morning air. I'm hot from cooking breakfast."

Kate nodded. "Good idea. Let's stroll to the south creek."

Within fifteen minutes, the girls finished their breakfast. Hillary looked across the field for the Roddys. "They're not coming yet, so let's wash the dishes before they get here."

Catherine removed Kate's apron from the oven door handle and tied it around her waist. "I'll wash and you two dry. We've got ten minutes."

Hillary jumped up from the table and got two dishtowels from a drawer. "The frying pans are greasy, so save them for later. We'll wash everything else."

Pina removed the teakettle from the stove to pour hot water into the sink, warning Catherine. "Don't put your hands in there until you add cold water."

Catherine began cranking the water pump next to the sink. "I know. I've been burnt before and I'm not about to do it again."

Hillary looked through the window, again. "They're not coming, yet."

Catherine looked over her shoulder, handing a dripping plate to Hillary. "Do we call them the Roddy kids, or A. Roddy and the other two?"

Pina laughed so hard she nearly dropped the cup she was drying. "That was a good one."

Hillary walked up to Catherine for another plate and asked, "When you get home, do you expect to find a letter from B. Hampton?"

"I hope so. I love my B. Hampton."

"Here come the Roddys," Pina yelled. "They're entering the field now. It'll be a couple minutes before they get here."

Catherine drained the water from the sink, while Hillary and Pina hurried to dry the remaining dishes.

Hillary opened the closet door and picked up the egg basket from the floor. "Let's go. It's time for Zelda and the gang."

The girls went outside and waited in the yard for their friends. Once again, Adam was the first to arrive. They started walking to the hen house where Trish and Marnie caught up with them. "Who takes Zelda's egg today?" Marnie asked.

Hillary held the basket for her to take. "You, if you want to."

She took the basket from Hillary, leading the others into the hen house. After collecting a few eggs, the children arrived at the matron of all egg layers. They gathered around Zelda, as if about to watch a hanging.

"Be careful," Trish warned, Marnie. "You know she'll peck you, if she gets a chance."

Pina walked up behind Marnie, holding her back. "Whack her off the nest with the back of your hand, sudden like. She won't know what happened. Then, grab the egg from the nest."

Marnie leaned over the nest, staring into Zelda's eyes. Zelda glared back at Marnie, as if daring her to steal the egg. Marnie intended to do what Pina suggested. She brought her hand back slowly, deciding when to strike. Just as she was ready to knock the bird off the nest, Zelda squawked and flew up into Marnie's face, causing her to fall backwards and drop the basket of eggs.

The other children laughed heartily. Zelda continued to squawk and run erratically around her nest.

Pina grabbed the egg from the nest and Catherine helped Marnie from the ground.

Trish retrieved the basket and gathered the unbroken eggs.

Adam grabbed a dirty rag hanging on the wall and scooped up the broken eggs. He held the mixture towards Hillary, "Where do you want me to put this mess?"

She pointed to a corner of the coop. "Thanks, Adam. There's a bucket over there by the door."

Adam waited until the others went outside, before asking, "Will your friends always be coming home with you?"

Hillary knew immediately why he asked. "Not always, I don't think. They like coming here, and we like having them."

Hillary followed him to the door, where he dropped the messy rag into the bucket, then joined the others outside.

Pina was staring at her in a suggestive way.

Hillary stuck her tongue out at her.

They ran and skipped toward the stable. Hillary noticed Kate and Bridie returning from their walk to the creek. They appeared to be deep in conversation.

It was almost noon when the girls packed their luggage and carried them out to the porch, waiting for the men. Kate was in Bridie's bedroom, helping her pack so she didn't leave anything behind. Kate looked at the small silver clock sitting on the dresser. "I hope the men are on time."

Bridie locked her luggage and took a last look at herself in the dresser mirror. "I'm as ready as I'm going to be. Shall we join the girls on the porch?" When they stepped outside, John and Biff were riding toward the house.

Bridie humorously announced, "Here come J. Hanley and B. Arley."

The girls laughed at her use of the men's initials. "That's our joke," Pina chuckled.

Kate looked at Bridie. "You certainly tickled their funny-bone."

Bridie beamed with pride. "I guess I did, but then, I enjoyed doing it."

After the men climbed down from the coach, John walked up to Kate and quietly asked, "Did you lock the door?"

"My God, I didn't," Kate answered. She removed a key from her purse and returned to the house.

At the train station, Kate and John watched the girls board the train. Bridie stayed back, with Biff at her side. They looked at each other, both wanting to embrace. Biff wasn't to be denied, so he took Bridie by the shoulders and eased her forward. He kissed her, not as long as they wanted, but enough for being in public. He took her arm and assisted her up the train stairs.

Kate and John looked at each other, without saying a word. They were not surprised by the kiss, but by the tenderness of it.

Tuesday, Margaret Holmgren received a letter from Brian, telling her the University was suspending classes the Friday of the following week for faculty meetings. He wrote he would return home for an extended weekend and wanted to surprise Catherine. She was elated and wanted Bridie to know as soon as possible. Margaret went to her desk in the corner of the dining room and cranked the telephone.

"Good morning, Margaret."

"Good morning, Cora. How could you be sure it was me?"

"Brian is away at school and Tom is at work."

"What if Tom was here, and not at work?"

"Then I'd be wrong. See how simple that is?"

"Cora, you're the most interesting telephone operator I've ever known. Please ring Bridie for me."

"Yes, my dear."

Margaret tapped a pencil on the desktop until she heard the usual clicking sound before Bridie answered.

"Hello?"

"Hello, yourself. How was your weekend in Galena?"

"I only need one word to describe it—Wonderful!"

"Is that how you would describe, Mr. Biff Arley?"

Bridie paused before answering. "I'd have to say, yes. I don't know where this relationship is going, but it appears to be moving forward."

"It sounds as if you're speaking from the heart. If he's what you want, then I'm happy for you and I hope it works. You certainly deserve a good man."

"Thanks. I guess time will tell."

"Does he know about Jack?"

"No. I think it's too early for that. I'll have no problem telling him, if necessary."

Margaret leaned back in her chair, ready for a lengthy conversation. "Biff is a good looking man, with a personality to match. I don't know how he stayed single all these years. There aren't many men like him around."

Bridie laughed. "I'm single. Aren't I good looking and pleasant?"

"Of course, my dear Bridie, that's understood. I was curious, that's all."

"Many people remain single due to circumstances beyond their control. You know why I'm single, and I'm just one of many stories."

"True." Margaret paused, "Has he kissed you?"

Bridie had trouble deciding whether to answer that question. "Yes."

"How often, and when was the first time?"

"Margaret! Do you need material for a novel you're writing?"

Margaret laughed. "No. I don't think I have it in me to write a novel. I'm only interested in your welfare."

Bridie took a deep breath. "Put your interest elsewhere. Is this why you called?"

"Actually, no. I just learned that Brian is coming home the weekend after next. There won't be classes that Friday, so he'd have three days at home … almost. Before I forget, he wants it to be a secret from Catherine."

"Good! She'll be delighted to see him, as will the rest of us."

"Plan on having dinner at my house that Sunday. Catherine can take Brian to the train station after we eat."

"Thanks, Margaret. I'll talk to you before then. Bye."

Friday, when Pina and Hillary arrived home from school, Pina removed letters from the mailbox. One was from Mr. Thompson, in Alton, Delaware. The other letter was from A. Roddy. Pina laughed, handing the letters to Hillary. "What do you know, nothing from Trish or Marnie. I wonder why?"

"He must have mailed this before we went to Galena last weekend, or I wouldn't have it already. Mail usually takes two weeks."

Pina smiled, slyly. "How does he sign his letters, A–Adam–A. Roddy, or with all my love, my sweet?"

Hillary slapped Pina's shoulder with the back of her hand. "He signs them, 'Hit Pina real hard for me.'"

Pina laughed and unlocked the front door. "Go to our bedroom and read your letters. I'll wait down here."

Pina sat on the living room sofa reading a school assignment until Hillary came downstairs. She closed her book and looked up at Hillary. "How are things in Alton and Galena?"

Hillary entered the room and sat in a stuffed chair, opposite Pina. "Iris and Vera were disappointed when they learned I won't get to Alton until next summer. In my last letter, I told them I'm attending the Bradbury School and wouldn't be able to see them soon." Hillary shifted in the chair, draping one leg over the armrest. "The truth is, I don't know if I'll ever be able to go back. I'm just pretending I'll go."

Pina laid her book on the sofa cushion next to her. "Have you asked Kate and John about returning to see your friends?"

Hillary appeared dejected, as she looked toward the ceiling. "Stupid me! I meant to ask them when we were there last weekend, but forgot."

"Did A. Roddy have anything interesting to say … something you can repeat?"

Hillary laughed. "I can repeat anything he writes. It's mostly about farm work, or a book he read." She remained silent for a moment, then added, "He asked when I would be coming home."

Pina laughed. "Well he found out, you were there last weekend."

Hillary slumped further into the chair. "I'll have to write him something, but I don't want to write about school."

"Tell him you enjoyed seeing him and his cousins, again."

Hillary leered at Pina. "I don't think he'll be thrilled if I wrote, 'I enjoyed seeing your cousins.' "

Pina rose from the sofa and started for her bedroom. "I'm sure you'll think of something that will make him happy."

Bridie was looking through the kitchen window, watching Jack at the boathouse. He was cleaning debris from the water before storing the boat for the oncoming winter. She watched his crippled body move about and remembered what a handsome, powerful man he had been, and how she'd looked forward to a life with him. Bridie never believed she would find another man she could care for in the same way. Now, she felt suspended between the man she wanted for a lifetime, and a man that could possibly give her the life she yearned for. She became confused and began to cry. *I have one heart for two men.*

CHAPTER SIXTEEN

A week later, Tom Holmgren met Brian at the train station and took him straight home. Bridie kept Catherine busy at their house, so they couldn't accidentally meet on the streets. Brian hugged and kissed Margaret, then asked when they were going to Bridie's house, so he could see Catherine.

A rapt expression covered Margaret's face. "It's nice to be young and in love. I'd like to see Catherine's face when she suddenly sees you." She gripped his arm, turning him toward the stairs. "Take your luggage upstairs and bathe, then run to her. Tom and I will come later."

As Brian ascended the stairs, Tom called after him, "Do you want me to get the buggy ready?"

Brian stopped and looked down at him, "Like Margaret said, I'll run to her. It's not that far and we won't be needing the buggy for anything."

Margaret raised her hand to Brian. "Wait! When do you think you'll be leaving here; in an hour or so?"

Brian laughed, continuing up the stairs. "In a half-hour at most."

"We'll take the buggy for them," Margaret said, on the way to her desk. "I'll call Bridie and tell her Brian is here, then call again when he leaves the house.

In a deliberate attempt to appear harried, Bridie rushed out to the back porch and stopped at the railing above where Catherine was removing weeds in a flowerbed. "That's enough for today," Bridie said, quickly. "I forgot, we're meeting Margaret at Kitty's in thirty minutes. Leave the garden tools there and I'll put them away. You go upstairs and bathe immediately, or we will be late."

Bridie carried the tools to the carriage house before returning to the kitchen and the telephone. After the second call from Margaret, Bridie waited by the living room window to watch for Brian, carefully listening for where Catherine was upstairs. Soon, she saw the six-foot youth trotting up the street. Bridie smiled, knowing how excited he must be, knowing Catherine would be in his arms within minutes.

Bridie stepped out to the front porch, signaling Brian to be quiet, then led him to the parlor where he could wait for Catherine. They greeted each other with a kiss and Bridie went to the kitchen to wait. When Catherine came downstairs, she stood in front of Bridie, asking if her green cotton dress was appropriate for their meeting with Margaret.

Bridie examined her, observing how beautifully she looked. "Believe me, Catherine, that dress is perfect for what you're about to do." Bridie walked to the back door and looked out of the window, glancing over her shoulder at Catherine. "Would you get my yellow scarf? It's lying on the parlor sofa." Bridie remained in place until she heard Catherine's squeal, followed by silence. She opened the door and stepped outside.

Tom and Margaret arrived at Bridie's house at five o'clock for a chicken dinner. During the meal, Brian and Catherine exchanged stories about their school subjects, while Bridie and the Holmgrens watched their excitement and interest in each other's experiences. When dinner ended, Bridie stood to clear the table. She noticed Catherine smiling at Brian. "You two go for a walk, or something. You don't have that much time together.

Tom removed a napkin from his lap and laid it on the table. "We rode over in the buggy, in case you and Catherine wanted to go for a ride?"

"It was my idea," Margaret added. "I thought you two might like to go for an ice cream at the parlor ... or whatever."

Brian looked at his parents. "Thanks." He took Catherine's willing hand and led her toward the front door. Without looking back, Brian said, "We won't be too long."

"Take your time," Margaret replied.

Brian helped Catherine into the buggy and looked up at her. "God! I miss you when I'm at school."

Catherine gave him a coquettish glance. "That's odd. I never miss you."

Brian laughed and took a step back. "If that's true, then get out of the buggy."

She smiled at him. "I'll decide whether that's true, while we're riding."

Brian untied Dandy and climbed into the buggy. Near the edge of town, they passed Temple Street, where Nerine Booker lived. Brian looked in the direction of her apartment, thinking, *I can never go to her bed again, and ruin what I have with Catherine.* He shook the reins to distance himself from Nerine's neighborhood.

They rode a short distance beyond town before turning down Wrenn Road, leading them to the east side of Newberry. They came upon a huge, gnarly old oak tree, with large branches spreading out over the dirt road. Brian stopped the buggy in the shade of the tree and took Catherine into his arms. "I love you and I want to marry you as soon as I graduate."

Catherine slid her arms around his neck and looked into his eyes. "That's what I want, too. I don't think Bridie and your parents will object, because they want us together."

They were kissing when a husky voice shouted at them. "Go home!" Brian looked about quickly, but didn't see anyone. He flipped the reins and hurried down the road for a quarter mile, then slowed

Dandy to a walk. He and Catherine looked at each other and began to laugh for being caught kissing.

Brian leaned back against the buggy seat. "Have you seen or heard from Monica recently? I was wondering if she's married now and when the baby is due."

Catherine hooked her arm with Brian's. "I haven't heard from her since Pina and I met her at Winnemac Park. Her parents were anxious to get them married because of the baby, so I assume they are married now." She smiled. "Can't say I know where they got married, or how."

Brian looked at her. "They got themselves into a difficult situation, but I wish them the best of luck. Monica deserves some luck. I don't know about Charles, but she does. We were so fortunate in our adoption, compared to her." Brian flipped the reins to hurry Dandy along. "When is the baby coming?"

It took Catherine a few seconds to calculate the months. "December, I believe. A nice Christmas present for them."

Brian guided Dandy around a bend in the road, leading them back to Newberry. "I think Margaret's suggestion of ice cream is a good one. Shall we go to Kitty's?"

"Yes, I'd like that. Besides, Kitty will be glad to see you again."

Passing a lily pond, two Pintail ducks flared upward and flew away. Brian watched them until they faded into the red and yellow sunset. "I'd say those ducks are working their way south for the winter."

Catherine looked up at the sky. "Hurry Dandy along. I want to be in town when it gets dark."

Brian had Dandy trotting through long shadows of trees spread across the country road. He squeezed Catherine's hand in his. "It's been an hour since I said I love you, so I thought I'd tell you, I still do."

Catherine laughed. "Imagine that." She laid her head on his shoulder.

They started up a rise, and when they got to the top, they could see Newberry a mile ahead. Brian kissed Catherine's forehead. "Tom and Margaret told me, they think Biff is a nice guy. Do you think Bridie likes him?"

Catherine lifted her head from Brian's shoulder and stared into his eyes. "I know she does. It appears he's interested in Bridie, too, but I'm not sure how deeply he feels for her."

Brian shook the reins again to keep Dandy moving. "Does Biff want children?"

"Kate says he does. She believes Biff pretends Hillary is his daughter. I wouldn't be surprised at that. He treats Hillary like a daughter."

"What about Bridie?"

"I'm sure she wants children, or at least one." Catherine laughed. "Hillary said Kate is trying to get pregnant now. Wouldn't it be funny if we, Bridie and Kate, were having babies at the same time?"

Brian smiled. "It may be funny, but it could very well happen."

Catherine laughed, again. "I can picture Kate a mother, but Bridie—feeding and cleaning a baby? That's quite an image."

They entered Newberry and went directly to Main Street and Kitty's Confectionary. He reached up, to help Catherine from the buggy. "I'd like to meet Biff. If I'm right, and he cares for Bridie, he'll be visiting her soon and more often."

When Catherine returned home from school the following Tuesday, Bridie was walking from the parlor, appearing somewhat flustered, as though guilty of something. Catherine sensed that Bridie had been at John McTavish's picture on the fireplace mantle. Slowly, she followed Bridie into the kitchen.

Bridie stopped at the table and turned to face Catherine, placing one hand on the back of a chair. "Would you like to go to Galena this coming weekend? It'll be three weeks since your last visit and winter is coming—meaning you won't be going as often."

Catherine laid her schoolbooks on the table and gave Bridie a curious glance. "My guess is, you want me to say, 'yes.'"

Bridie took a deep breath before answering. "I thought it would be nice."

Catherine sat at the table, looking up at Bridie. "Would you be going with us, as in, you haven't seen Biff in three weeks?"

Bridie smiled, sheepishly. "Was I that obvious?"

"Not really. I've been expecting we'd be going soon."

Bridie sat on a chair opposite Catherine. "Biff called earlier this afternoon and mentioned our going there. He'd already talked to Kate and John about it. He also suggested that he return with us and stay in Newberry two days."

Catherine laughed, politely. "Gee, I wonder why he'd want to be here for two days? Do you have any ideas?" Catherine leaned back in the chair and smiled at Bridie. "Last weekend, Brian said, that if Biff was truly interested in you he'd be coming here to see you. It appears he's interested in you, or he likes to ride trains."

Bridie looked at Catherine for a long moment and replied, "Enough talk about me and Biff. Ask the girls if they want to go and I'll make the arrangements."

Catherine folded her arms on the table. "Evidently, Margaret and Tom told Brian they liked Biff, because Brian said he was anxious to meet him."

Pleased by that statement, Bridie smiled and straightened her back. "I believe they do. Tom and Biff seemed to like each other straight-away." She reached across the table, patting Catherine's arm. "I imagine Brian and Biff will meet Thanksgiving Day. I intend on inviting the Galena people ... which reminds me, I'd better do it soon."

Catherine looked at Bridie, with raised eyebrows. "Well, if they come, we'll be continuing our visits of every three weeks. If we go there this weekend, they'll be coming three weeks later. It should be a very interesting Thanksgiving."

Bridie and the three girls went to Galena for another weekend in the country. It included more teasing of Hillary about A. Roddy and more bouts with Zelda. The girls rode Knickers in the corral, with

Catherine riding most of the time. Saturday evening, Biff took Bridie to a buffet dinner and dance at the Mason's Hall in Galena. As planned, Biff returned to Newberry to spend two days with Bridie. Both days, Catherine kept Pina and Hillary fully informed as to what she'd learned about them. Biff took a train home Wednesday morning, appearing pleased with his visit.

The following Friday, Jack was at the house doing chores that included chopping logs for firewood. His mother, Doreen, arrived an hour later to talk to Bridie. When Bridie opened the door, she was surprised by how pale Doreen looked. She helped Doreen take off her coat and hung it on the coat tree in the vestibule. "Would you like a cup of tea to warm yourself? I have hot water on the stove."

Doreen nodded. "Yes, I would. It must be about thirty-five degrees, an unusually cold day for early November." She followed Bridie into the kitchen and stopped at the table. "I came with a purpose, but I really don't know where to begin."

Bridie was at the stove adding wood to the fire, looking over her shoulder at Doreen. "Is it something serious?"

Doreen pulled a chair from the table and sat down. "I would put it in that category. To start with, my doctor said I have a bad heart and may not last another year. I'm sixty-eight years old, so I've had a long life. The end comes to everyone eventually."

Bridie understood why Doreen's face was so pale. She walked to Doreen, took her hand and kissed her forehead. "I'm so sorry. When were you told this?"

"Monday afternoon. The doctor has been telling me about my heart for a year and it's been worsening. I know my time is limited."

Bridie looked directly into her eyes. "You know if you need me in any way, all you have to do is call. We've been like family."

Doreen looked up at Bridie and smiled. "Thank you! You've been very kind and tolerant of Jack and me these past years. I imagine I'll be bed ridden, eventually. You won't be able to take care of us, your house, and your businesses."

Bridie returned to the stove and poured hot water into two cups. "Of course I helped you. Jack was to be my husband."

Doreen laughed weakly, watching Bridie at the stove. "You have a tender heart. Jack was incapable of being your husband many years ago, and you had no obligation to tie yourself to us and our problems."

Bridie dipped a tea ball into the two cups. "You like your tea weak, right?"

"Yes."

The hot water from the teakettle was beginning to steam the kitchen windows. Bridie picked up a dishtowel and wiped the window clear. "Jack's accident was unfortunate, but I still love him. He has been very good at doing chores around here, so I have no complaints."

Doreen nodded and mumbled, "No complaints and no children. You've dedicated your life to Jack. Very admirable, but you put a stop to your own life. I know you did it willingly, but it wasn't necessary—though we fully appreciate what you've done."

Bridie carried the cups of tea to the table, setting one in front of Doreen. "I loved Jack and I wanted him around."

Doreen warmed her hands against the hot cup. "Through the years, I've hoped you'd meet another man to make a home with and have the daughter you've always wanted. You have lovely Catherine, an adopted daughter anyone would be proud to have, yet I think you would like to have one of your own. That's natural. A daughter of your own and Catherine would be a very fortunate combination."

Bridie sensed that Doreen had a definite purpose to her visit. *Had Doreen seen or heard about Biff, being that she'd been around Newberry with him on different occasions?* "I never met another man I was interested in. If I had, who knows?"

Doreen laughed softly, again. "I noticed you used the word 'had.' What about now? You can't be accompanied around a small town without people noticing you on the arm of a stranger. You're too prominent a person in Newberry. I was in the grocery store one day and saw you walking with a handsome man. I must say you made a smart looking couple. I'd even say you two looked very happy together." Doreen stopped to sip her tea. "If you two were to love one another, I suggest you grab the opportunity so it doesn't get away. Before I'm gone, I'll find an institution for Jack, so you are free of him."

Bridie gasped at her decision. "Jack would hate being in an institution. It would probably kill him, or he'd run away and flounder somewhere. Who knows what would happen to him. If I were to marry Biff, I'd talk to him about Jack." Bridie paused. "Biff's the man you saw me with. We could build a proper bedroom for Jack in the basement. Biff has already seen Jack and understands his handicap."

Doreen's eyes narrowed, looking at Bridie. "You'd have your husband and babies to tend to. Jack would be a burden to your marriage. You can't ask this man, Biff, to accept Jack into his family."

They both paused, pondering a solution to Jack. Bridie sat back and said, firmly, "Jack can't be thrown to strangers, in an unfamiliar location. I don't see any other answer than he remain in Newberry."

Doreen decided not to discuss the situation any longer. She could see that Bridie would try to support Jack, no matter what. Even if she had arrangements for Jack's care, Doreen believed Bridie would intercede after her death and care for him in some way. She loved Bridie and knew she would have to take steps to prevent Bridie from adding Jack to her marriage. "You are a fine woman, Bridie. I guess you'll do what you think is right."

Bridie smiled, at what she believed was Doreen's resignation to the problem. "When you're gone, I'll be the only person Jack will be comfortable with. To put him with strangers would be very confusing for him."

Doreen leaned toward Bridie, her face glowing with interest. "Tell me about this man, Biff. Where is he from and how did you meet him?"

Bridie exhibited a smile she couldn't control. She looked down, staring at the table. "Biff lives near Galena, Illinois. He's the cousin of the man who adopted Hillary Cook, Catherine's girlfriend."

"I've met her," Doreen interrupted. "She's a lovely girl. As a matter of fact, all three of those girls are lovely. What a shame their parents aren't around to enjoy them."

"I agree," Bridie responded. "I met him during my first trip to Hillary's farm. From what I'm told, he loves children and pretends to be Hillary's uncle and spoils her. I was attracted to him immediately, but of course, I couldn't show it." She ceased staring at the table and raised her eyes to Doreen. "It wasn't long before I sensed he liked me. Our relationship seems to improve as time goes on. I guess we'll give it more time and see what happens."

Chapter Seventeen

Bridie opened the oven door to see if the Thanksgiving turkey was ready for serving. Margaret and Catherine were setting the dining room table. Hillary brought a glass of water upstairs to Kate, who wasn't feeling well and was resting.

John and Biff entered the kitchen, sniffing the air loudly, like two Bloodhounds.

Bridie lifted the turkey from the oven and placed it on top of the stove. She placed her hands on her hips and glared at them. "Aren't you overdoing your sniffing a bit? I understand you're hungry, but the bird needs carving. Any volunteers?"

Biff stepped forward, putting an arm around her waist, while removing the carving knife from her hand. He looked into her eyes. "I'd be glad to. That way, I get to nibble on the scraps before y'all get some."

Bridie slapped his hand and spun out of his grasp, before anyone else returned to the kitchen and witnessed his boldness. She removed a serving platter from the table and handed it to John. "Hold this for your cousin, the stove is too hot to put it there. I'm going upstairs to see how Kate is doing."

Tom and Brian came up the back porch carrying a block of ice and bottles of wine. Tom entered the kitchen first and opened the icebox door, so Brian could slide the ice inside.

Brian went to the sink and shook the rags that protected his hands from the frigid ice. "I'm glad that's done." He looked at Biff and John. "That bird sure looks good. Got a scrap, so I can test the quality?"

Biff turned to Brian and teased, "No need. John and I have tested it a few times, and we can tell you it's perfect."

Tom grinned, watching Brian's surprised, yet disappointed expression. "They're teasing you."

Brian relaxed and smiled, feeling somewhat silly for believing Biff. John handed him a slice of dark meat. "Thanks. It smells great."

Catherine and Margaret entered the kitchen for bowls of vegetables and candied apples. Margaret looked at the platter of meat John was holding. "A couple more slices, then we're ready to eat."

Catherine turned and walked away. "I'll go upstairs to get the other ladies."

John looked at the bird's carcass laying in the roasting pan "Ain't much left of that bird."

Tom chuckled. "There'll be a lot less in an hour."

Margaret tapped John's shoulder. "Follow me to the table and I'll show you where to place the bird."

The men followed Margaret into the dining room and sat around the table, saving a chair so their lady could sit next to them. Tom walked around the table filling the wine glasses. Soon, Hillary led the ladies down to the dining room. Kate sat next to John and patted his thigh. "I'm feeling better. The rest helped."

John kissed her head. "Good! Are you hungry?"

She glanced up at him. "Quite."

Bridie looked at her guests sitting around the table. "Take food that is in front of you and pass it clockwise."

While talking and passing food around the table, Hillary noticed the pile of food on Kate's plate. She nudged Kate's arm with her elbow. "You must be starved. You don't usually eat that much."

Kate glanced at John before responding. "I was hoping you wouldn't notice, but you are right. I'm eating more, because I'm eating for two."

All talking and passing of food ceased immediately. Everyone stared at Kate. The only sound that could be heard was a horse and buggy passing the house.

Hillary looked up at Kate and squealed loudly. "You're pregnant! My baby is coming!"

"That's wonderful," Bridie said, with an applauding smile. "That's wonderful."

Biff watched Bridie, perceiving longing in her voice.

Catherine looked at Hillary. "Your dream is finally coming true."

"Congratulations!" Brian called across the table.

Biff raised his wine glass to offer a toast to the occasion. "To the both of you, a dream come true, whether pink or blue, you start life anew." He laughed nervously at his modest verse.

Tom saluted Kate and John. "I wish you the best."

Margaret wiped an eye with her napkin. "That was sweet, Biff."

Hillary grabbed Kate's arm, before she put food into her mouth. "When?"

"Late May, or early June."

Hillary looked at Catherine. "Just as we get out of school." She patted Kate's back. "Good work."

John laughed. "I wonder if this news will make us hungrier or less hungry?"

Brian stuck his fork into a piece of meat. "I'm going to find out."

The following Monday evening, Wade Widner closed his desk drawer and grabbed his coat from the closet. He glanced around his office before turning out the lights. He walked out of Crossroads Shipping, deciding to stop at Doyle's Pub before going home. He turned up his coat collar and walked briskly to Union Avenue. When he entered Doyle's pub, he looked ahead through the tobacco smoke and saw Karl Polen standing at the bar. His thick, bull-like body was leaning against the bar, while one foot rested on the brass rail. Wade looked to his left, among the tables and chairs, and waved to a friend.

Wade stopped next to Karl and saw his beer mug was almost empty. "I'll get the next one, Pal." Wade held up two fingers to the bartender and unbuttoned his coat.

"Thanks," Karl uttered, in his deep, raspy voice. "Ain't seen ya in here for a while."

Wade looked into Karl's small beady eyes, staring at him from under the bill of his brown leather cap. "Any interesting news floating about?"

"Naw! Just that Bill Collier's wife died." Karl lifted his beer mug and drank the last of the beer. "Heard it was her liver. She liked to drink, ya know ... all day."

Wade chuckled. "There are a lot of people like that in Alton." He looked around the room and saw Meg sidestepping between tables, carrying a tray of drinks. She turned her body, slipping past a table of men, knowing if she didn't, she would get a pinch or pat on the bottom. Meg was a good friend of Kate's and he would lik to tell her Kate and John were doing well. Under the circumstances, though, he couldn't. He turned to face the bar, as the bartender placed two beers in front of them. He pushed a few coins forward.

Karl leaned close to Wade, whispering, "Talk is ya found John and Kate Hanley. Is that true?"

Wade looked surprised. "Where did you hear this? It's supposed to be a secret. I know you and John were close friends, but I can't reveal what I know." He raised his mug and took a quick drink. "Being that you two were friends, and you're curious as to their situation, I'll tell you they have a nice farm in a beautiful part of the country. They seem to be doing well. That's all I can say."

"I can't reveal where I got my information, either, but people talk when they shouldn't. I'm glad they have a nice place, but it ain't gunna do them any good if Tyler Sharpe gets after them."

"I know. That's what bothers me. I knew John and Kate fairly well, and I liked them. I've been trying to think of something to tell Tyler to change his mind, but he's a hot-tempered guy ... and stubborn. It was my job to find John, but I didn't like doing it. Now, my conscience bothers me."

Karl stood upright, pulling up his pants. "John told me what happened the night Jesse was killed. I'd like to tell you his tale, so you can tell it to Tyler. It may convince him that maybe John didn't kill his brother. I think it's worth a try."

Wade looked at Karl, with eager eyes. "He told you what happened that night?"

"Yes. And I'd be willing to tell Tyler, or you tell him the story and I'd back it up, hoping his hearing it from two people would be more convincing."

Wade wiped his mouth with the back of his hand. "It's all I've got to work with." He looked into Karl's eyes. "Tell me the story."

Karl shrugged his shoulders before starting. "John said he was standing at a bar in New Orleans, drinking and talking to a guy he didn't know well. This guy, I believe his name was Haggar, liked John's cap and offered him a steak dinner and more money than what it was worth. John liked the offer, so he sold it to Haggar, knowing he could buy another. Well, inside the cap was John's name—in case he lost it aboard ship." Karl took another drink of his beer and looked around the pub. "Next to them, was a high stakes poker game, with loads of money passed around. Tyler and Jesse Sharpe were in that game, and Jesse was flashing a big wad of money. When Jesse left for the outhouse, Haggar insisted he and John eat immediately because he was so hungry. It was dark, and Haggar had John wait for him across the street, while he went to the outhouse to take a whiz. A couple of minutes later, Haggar hurried toward John, slapped something in his hand, then brushed his hand against John's shoulder and ran on. John was confused at Haggar's actions. He didn't know what was in his hand, but it felt like sticky paper. John walked over to a streetlight and saw the money and the shoulder of his shirt were covered with blood. People at the side of the pub began calling for Tyler, yelling someone had murdered his brother. Then someone yelled John Hanley's full name, saying it was in the cap of the murderer. John panicked. He was standing there, with bloody clothes and money, while his hat was found at the murder scene." Karl chuckled. "He bolted just like you or I would have done."

Wade nodded in agreement. "You're right. I would have run, too. Now I must try and convince Tyler that it happened that way."

"Remember, I'm willing to tell Tyler and swear John ain't a guy that would murder someone." Karl raised his hand to the bartender, signaling for two more beers. "So, John and Kate are doing well, you say?"

"Yep, and they have that little girl living with them."

Karl nodded at Wade, "I know the girl. That's something else we can tell Tyler, to soften him—that they're raising an orphan girl."

Wade slid his mug back and forth across the bar. "You're right. That may help change his mind. Anything is worth a try, but he is, as I said ... stubborn."

In Newberry, that same day, Cora called Bridie to tell her that Doreen had collapsed at her back yard woodpile, while gathering wood for her stove. A neighbor saw her drop and her son got Doreen out of the cold and into her house. The doctor got there about an hour later and told her to get her affairs in order.

Bridie hung up the telephone and looked out her window at a freshly chopped pile of wood. She assumed Jack was at her house when Doreen had her attack. She gathered the ingredients to bake two loaves of bread and a large pot of vegetable soup for Doreen and Jack.

When Catherine got home from school, she was told what happened and that they would take food to Doreen's home.

Catherine went upstairs to change her dress and help Bridie prepare the food. When she returned to the kitchen, she donned an apron and began kneading the bread dough. "What will happen to Jack, if Doreen dies?"

Bridie looked at her with anguish in her eyes. "I'm the only one he has left, so I guess he'll live here."

Catherine was looking down, filling two bread pans with dough. She shifted her eyes to Bridie. "That's not exactly what you want, with Biff and all, right?"

Bridie was stirring the soup. She glanced at Catherine and took a deep breath before answering. "No, I would like things to be different, but they aren't, and life must go on."

Catherine opened the oven door and put the two bread pans inside. "Couldn't Jack go to a place where they take care of ..."

Bridie interrupted her quickly. "Doreen and I have already discussed this problem, and I don't want to talk about it again. I know what I have to do."

When they returned from Doreen's house, Catherine began doing schoolwork at the dining room table. Bride walked in and handed her a letter. "It's from someone named Carol Swane. I meant to give it to you earlier, but with Doreen's problems and all, I forgot. Is Carol a classmate?"

Realizing it was from Monica, Catherine had to keep from grinning. "Yes, a classmate."

After school the next day, Catherine met Pina and Hillary under the Willow tree to tell them about the letter from Monica.

"Three months ago, Charles and Monica were married in Galesburg, Illinois, not far from Knoxville, where they live. Charles's parents wanted as much respectability to this marriage as possible, so they're claiming Monica has relatives in Galesburg and her uncle gave her away at a church wedding, months earlier. That way, the ceremony would be away from Newberry and suspicious neighbors, especially with Monica being thick at the belly."

"Isn't the baby due soon?" Hillary asked.

Catherine smiled, and went on. "Monica wrote it should be born about mid-December. I can't wait until we see it. I know Monica will be glowing with pride when she shows it to us. She hasn't had many joys in her life."

Pina looked at her friends, "Remember, we have to keep quiet about what we know, for her sake."

"Not everything," Catherine responded. "Monica wrote, that since everything is respectable now, we don't need to keep her marriage and whereabouts a secret. Otherwise, it would look suspicious, like they were hiding something." Catherine laughed. "On the envelope, she had the name *Carol Swane* as the returnee, like she did before. She wrote it was a private joke for me."

Hillary looked at Catherine and frowned. "What about Mr. and Mrs. Peters? Isn't Monica afraid they'll make some claim to her, being they adopted her and now she's married into a good family?"

The girls cradled their books in their arms and began walking home. "Monica doesn't believe they'll try that," Catherine replied. "Especially since Clay Peters raped her."

Pina giggled. "I'm sure they'll keep their mouths shut." She hesitated and added, "Because there is a confusing question."

Hillary looked at her. "What are you talking about?"

Pina smiled, wisely. "Clay Peters raped Monica one day, then she was lying with Charles Belcher two or three days later. So, who is the father?"

CHAPTER EIGHTEEN

Friday night, Bridie and Catherine were upstairs trying on new winter clothes they had purchased earlier that day. When they finished complimenting each other on their choices, they put them away and went to the kitchen for a cup of tea and a slice of apple pie. When they finished eating, Bridie went by the sink and looked out of the kitchen window. "It's December second, and no snow yet. I'm sure it will come any day now."

Catherine looked up at her from the table. "I like snow, but I'm in no hurry for it–especially a big snow storm. Once it comes, we'll have its mess for months."

Bridie laughed. "You're right. It does get messy, and we have to wear cumbersome boots to go out. But a fresh snowfall is pretty." She stepped away from the window. "It's ten o'clock. I'm going up to bed."

Catherine watched Bridie walk away and called out, "Thank you for the new clothes."

Without looking back, Bridie said, "I enjoy you modeling clothes for me. It takes me back to when I was a girl. Good night."

Bridie had been asleep only an hour when the telephone next to her bed rang, waking her with a start. Being that it was at such a late hour, she assumed it was an emergency.

"Hello, Bridie?"

"Yes. Who is this?"

"It's Sheriff Mason. I have disturbing news, but stay calm and don't panic. I just got a call that the McTavish house is burning. The Fire Brigade is already there tending to it."

Bridie's shoulders sagged. There was anxiety in his voice. "How big a fire is it, Howard? I want the truth."

He didn't want to tell Bridie how bad it had been reported, so he lied, giving her time to adjust to the situation. "I don't know. I'm going over there now."

"So am I. I'll see you there."

Catherine came to Bridie's doorway, waiting to hear what happened. She could see Bridie was worried. "Who? What?"

Bridie hurried to her closet and grabbed some clothes. "Jack's house is burning. If you want to come with me, get dressed quickly."

"Oh, my God!" Catherine moaned, running back to her room.

Bridie and Catherine rushed out of the house and ran down the dark street, staring at the glowing sky five blocks away. When they arrived at the fire, men, women and children were standing around in their coats, asking questions. Some said one thing, some another—the way people do when they're guessing. It was a small frame house, with a big fire. She saw firemen standing on each side of a water wagon, pumping water, while two men manned the hose, spraying the house. Bridie's heart was pounding. While looking for Jack and Doreen, she called out, "Is anyone in the house?" She yelled again, "Did the people get out?"

People turned, looked at her and shrugged.

Bridie pushed her hair from her eyes, searching the crowd again, carefully examining every face. She saw women huddled together in groups, crying and murmuring, hoping no one was inside. Children wandered away from their mothers to join other children. They darted about, wide eyed and filled with excitement, their faces aglow from the flames reaching skyward. To them, it was just a lark, being up late and a chance to see friends and people they'd never seen before.

Other children stood and stared in wonder and awe at the spectacle that was too monstrous for them to comprehend. Scared by the horrific sight, some returned and stood by their mothers.

Sheriff Mason arrived, dismounted quickly and handed the reins of his horse to a fireman holding an axe. He spotted Bridie and Catherine and rushed to them. "Wait here, Bridie. I'll find out what I can."

Catherine put her arm around Bridie, searching for Jack and Doreen. "You've got to believe they got out. They were probably taken in by someone to get them out of the cold."

Bridie sighed, wanting to believe Catherine. "Yes. That's probably true. It would be easy to get out of that house." Bridie watched Sheriff Mason's face closely, as he talked to the firemen, hoping to see a smile or some sign that the McTavish's were safe. His face remained somber.

Catherine noticed a boy sneak up behind a girl and yank on her pigtail, then run away. "They don't understand this tragedy," she mumbled to herself.

Three men tried to get close to the house to see whether anyone was inside, but the heat was too intense. They backed away from the fierce flames, shaking their heads and chattering about how impossible it was to go in. Bright flames and thick black smoke engulfed the little frame house that was once white.

Sheriff Mason returned to Bridie and Catherine. "I don't know what to tell you, Bridie. Nobody knows if anyone is inside. Go home and I'll call you when I learn something."

Bridie's worried eyes stared at the house. "I need to stay until I know they're out. Thank God there are no houses close to it, or they'd be in trouble."

Sheriff Mason stood next to Bridie and looked at the black smoke. He knew thick, black smoke like that was from burning oil. He kept his thoughts to himself, knowing that Doreen heated the house with wood. He placed a hand on Bridie's upper arm and suggested, "I have friends that live down the street. I know they would take you in out of the cold. You could wait there."

Bridie smiled at him. "Believe me, this fire is keeping me warm."

Catherine nodded. "I'm warm, too."

Sheriff Mason placed a gentle hand against Bridie's chin and turned her face to his. He looked directly into her eyes and said, "Bridie, go home."

Bridie understood his meaning, and the futility of them standing there. She looked at Catherine. "He's right. We can't accomplish anything here." Starting through the gawking crowd, Bridie glanced back at Howard. "Call me as soon as you know something."

Sheriff Mason nodded. "I'll stop by when I learn all the details."

Catherine gripped Bridie's arm, and walked home, speaking words of hope, followed by moments of silence and tears. When they entered their house, Catherine helped Bridie take off her coat. "We aren't likely to fall asleep. Do you want more tea?"

"You need your sleep for school in the morning."

"It's Friday, Bridie. I don't have school tomorrow."

Bridie shook her head. "That's true. My mind is scattered a bit right now." She started up the stairs, "I'm going to wash my face and hands, while you're heating the water, but I don't want pie—just tea."

Catherine added wood to the stove, then went to the parlor and stood in front of John McTavish's picture. "I believe you've left us. I'll miss you." She hurried back to the kitchen before Bridie returned.

Bridie was wearing a robe over her nightgown. "I had to change clothes. What I was wearing smelled of smoke."

"I'll have to throw mine in the wash, too." Catherine carried the two cups of tea to the table and sat across from Bridie. "How are you feeling?"

"Numb. I believe Jack and Doreen are in the house."

Nothing was said for a moment. Catherine reached across the table and held Bridie's hand. "We won't know for sure, until the sheriff contacts us. I believe you're right, and he's giving us time to accept the situation."

Bridie smiled at Catherine. "If we're correct, you'll have to find someone else to give you away when you marry Brian." She stared at her cup of tea a moment. "It's odd that I should think of that, now."

"No. I've already thought of it, and of how happy you were when I told you I wanted Jack to give me away. It was important to you." Catherine retracted her hand from Bridie's and sat back in her chair. "We can still pretend I'm his daughter. Of course, that would be our secret."

Bridie grinned. "Pretend? I have been pretending since his accident in the river. A minute ago, I said I felt 'numb'—which is true. I don't feel pain, sorrow or grief—just emptiness. I'm ashamed to say it, but it feels more like relief, like I've been unchained." She sipped her tea and lowered her cup, slowly. "Yet, I loved him."

A tear ran down Catherine's cheek. "You loved him, but you didn't have him. That had to be painful all these years."

Bridie gave Catherine a melancholy glance. "It's like Jack has been at half-rest all these years. Here, but not here, alive, but not completely alive. Now, he's at peace."

Catherine chuckled. "We'll feel like idiots tomorrow, if Jack walks over here."

Bridie grinned. "I'm sure the sheriff will be here tomorrow to give us the bad news, in a gentle way." She carried her empty cup to the sink. "We can talk tomorrow, but right now I'm exhausted." Bridie went to bed, realizing it was December 2nd, Jack's birthday. Suddenly, her conversation with Doreen returned, recalling how Doreen wanted her to be free from Jack and have a daughter with Biff. Doreen's solution to the problem became clear. *She giveth life, and she taketh away.*

The next afternoon, Bridie opened the door for Sheriff Mason, looking into his eyes, knowing what he was about to tell her. He stepped inside and put his arms around her. "I'm sorry."

Bridie looked up at him. "Thank you, Howard. I've already accepted it as fact. Catherine and I both sensed they died in the fire. We discussed it last night before going to bed."

Howard stepped back, giving her a guarded glance. "There's more to it than what meets the eye. Can we talk?"

Bridie closed the door and started for the kitchen. "A few days ago, it was freezing weather, but today it is very pleasant. If you don't mind, we can talk on the porch and take advantage of this weather." When they got to the kitchen, Bridie asked, "Do you want something to drink?"

"Water will be fine."

Bridie slipped on a coat that was on the back of a chair, and filled two glasses with water. She led Howard to the porch, handing him one of the glasses. They sat in wicker chairs and sipped their water before Howard began speaking. "I suppose you knew Doreen had a bad heart?"

"Yes. We had a conversation about that a few weeks back. She was concerned about Jack, and what would happen to him, if she died. Doreen was planning to place him in an institution. I objected, saying Jack could live here and I would prepare a heated room for him in the basement, or upstairs of the coach house."

"What did she think about that?"

Bridie realized she would have to mention Biff, if they were going to talk about Jack. She took a deep breath before explaining. "I've been dating a man who lives near Galena, Illinois."

Howard interrupted her. "It's about time."

Bridie looked at him and smiled. "Doreen knew about Biff and was concerned Jack would be a hindrance to our relationship."

Howard interrupted her again. "Most of the people that know you are aware you're dating someone. It's a small town."

Bridie shook her head. "Yes, I guess that's true. But the point is, Doreen seemed determined to remove Jack from my life."

Howard leaned toward Bridie. "She did."

Bridie responded, sadly, "I thought of that, too."

"As long as you're thinking in that direction, I'll tell you what happened." Howard sat back in his chair, turning the glass of water in his hands. "From what an examination shows, Doreen poisoned Jack with cyanide, set the fire with oil, then poisoned herself. Both were dead before the fire got to them."

"How do you know it was cyanide?"

Howard sipped his water again. "When we suspected poison, we checked with the closest Apothecary. Doreen purchased cyanide from the Uslander Apothecary about three weeks ago. She told them she was buying it for rats." Howard rested his arm on the back of the wicker chair. "Being that the act was performed by one of the deceased, there will be no further investigation. There's no need."

"Good! Doreen had it her way, but she meant it as a positive act. Jack would have become more troubled without her."

Howard saw Catherine strolling along the pond, kicking stones into the water. "I just noticed Catherine by the pond. How is she taking this—being that you both sensed they died in the fire?"

"She's very upset. Catherine spent an hour in the coach house this morning, handling Jack's tools, while wearing his work jacket. As you can see, she's still wearing it."

Catherine glanced over at the porch and noticed someone with Bridie. When she realized who it was, she ran to them. "Howdy, Six Gun."

Howard laughed. "How's my number one girl?"

"Sad." She walked up the porch stairs and stood next to Howard, glancing at Bridie for a clue as to what happened to Jack and Doreen.

Bridie nodded. "We were right in our suspicions."

Catherine stepped back and leaned against the porch railing. "I've decided to keep this jacket. There will be other things of Jack's I'll want to keep."

Howard smiled at Catherine. "Even in that worn jacket, you look adorable." He turned to Bridie and softened his tone. "What should we do about a burial?"

"I'll get side-by-side graves and have Minister Blake give a grave-side prayer next Monday. There will be an announcement in the newspaper. It will be open to anyone who wants to attend. I'll mention this to Cora, the telephone operator. She'll know who to tell." Bridie laughed. "Cora will probably inform more people than the newspaper."

Howard stood and walked slowly toward the kitchen door. "Again, my condolences. I'll be at the funeral."

Catherine took his glass, as they passed through the kitchen. "Thank you for coming. I guess our lives will be a little different around here."

Howard looked at her and smiled. "Good news usually comes on the tail of bad news."

Bridie thought of Biff, as the coming good news. "Thank you for the information, Howard. We'll see you at the cemetery Monday."

Catherine waved. "Goodbye, Six Gun."

On Monday, December 5, 1900, twenty-eight people gathered at the graves of John and Doreen McTavish. Their thoughts were more occupied with Bride, and her tragic loss of John years before, than they were with the deceased before them. After the minister said prayers, Sheriff Mason gave a short eulogy.

Bridie stared at the headstone of *John McTavish* and said quietly, "Goodbye."

When Bridie and Catherine returned home, Catherine went upstairs to change her clothes. After hearing Catherine close the door to her bedroom, Bridie walked into the parlor and stood in front of the fireplace. She removed John McTavish's picture from the mantle, stared at it for a few seconds, then uttered softly, "Our dream was not meant to be." She carried the picture into the dining room and placed it in a buffet drawer under her best linens.

Biff rode to the Hanley farm and tied Creo to the corral fence, then walked over snow-covered ground to the house. When he knocked on the door, John answered with a hot mug of coffee in hand. "You can have this to warm yourself, after you take off your boots and put them on the rug."

"Standard procedure," Biff replied, removing his boots. "How is Kate feeling? Anymore baby sickness?"

"She's taking a nap, but not sick." He led Biff to the kitchen table where there was a dish of raisin bread. "Kate made this for you yesterday. It's on your list of favorite foods on the wall." He handed the mug of coffee to Biff. "Hillary called yesterday and suggested the raisin bread for her Uncle Biff."

Biff reached for a slice and hung his jacket on the back of a chair. "She's an angel. The last time I had raisin bread was at Laura's apartment." He sat down, looking at the clock Bridie brought as a gift. "It's almost noon and I haven't accomplished much today."

John chuckled at Biff. "It's our slow time of the year. Don't concern yourself. Take time to socialize with people like Alissa Newman, also known as widow Coakley."

There was a curious, hard smile in Biff's eyes. "Why did you mention her, especially with me getting tight with Bridie?"

John leaned back in his chair, unable to keep from grinning. "I was in Lengstrom's General Store this morning and met her there. We said a few words as we were parting, and she suggested I say "Hello" to you. Alissa also let me know she's working at Hibbard's Clothing Store. Her words appeared more like an invitation, rather than a casual comment." John was still smiling. "We were talking near a display of stove pipes. It made me think of a humorous story I heard, but then, you know that story."

Biff lowered his voice, so Kate couldn't hear. "And I know a father-to-be that had a great interest in a local flower named Meris Noolin. That would also be a funny story."

John's head went back as he drank the last of his coffee. "Funny for you, but not for me—so we're even." John stood and went to the stove for more coffee. "When Hillary called yesterday, she and Kate arranged a visit for the weekend after next." He turned and grinned.

"Bridie will be coming with the three girls. Does that make you happy?"

Biff nodded. "Yes, it does. I called Bridie last week and we discussed that visit. Of course, she had to talk to the girls before deciding. I'll call her tonight to acknowledge I know they're coming. I even have the sleigh ready for a ride in the snow."

John returned to the table and slowly lowered himself onto the chair. "A sleigh ride for *who* in the snow?"

"For anyone who wants to ride in the sleigh." Biff paused and looked into John's suspicious eyes. "You're right. I'm sure Bridie and I will have a ride alone."

"I imagine you will, but did you know we will be going to Newberry for Christmas?"

"No, I didn't, and I like that plan, too. It gives me an idea."

Chapter Nineteen

When Bridie and the girls arrived at the Galena Station, Biff was standing next to his black sleigh. He walked to the station platform to help them from the train. The girls alighted first then he assisted Bridie. As soon as her feet were on the ground, they kissed.

The three girls watched, somewhat embarrassed for doing so, but enjoyed the love scene.

Bridie noticed the girls staring at them, and smiled. "This isn't the first time we've kissed."

"It won't be the last time, either," Biff chuckled.

Bridie handed her bag to Biff and locked arms with him, as they walked. "You have more snow than us. It's lovely here."

"We got two inches yesterday, for a total of eleven this past week. I hope that's it for a while." At the sleigh, Biff announced, "You'll have to hold your luggage on your lap, or find space on the floor. Sorry, no luggage compartment, but you have blankets to cover yourselves."

Bridie enjoyed the sleigh ride and winter scenery, passing farms with white dormant fields, frozen creeks and profiles of black, leafless trees on rolling hills. It had a bleak, uninhabited look, typical of country during winter. To her, it was peaceful. She began thinking of how and where they would live, if she and Biff were to marry. *I love this country and I love Newberry. We could have both, but how? His business is here and mine are in Newberry. Then again, it is only a five-hour train ride between the towns and I don't have to be at my investments that often.* She smiled faintly, thinking of the prospect of a life with Biff and children.

"What are you smiling about," Catherine asked, interrupting Bridie's concentration.

Bridie's smile grew broader, glancing at the girls, realizing she was caught daydreaming. "Personal thoughts, not to be shared."

"I can imagine," Pina said, nodding up at Biff.

"Personal," Bridie repeated.

Hillary looked up at large white clouds. One, smaller than the others, was gray. She thought it odd that a single cloud should be a color different from the others. She wondered why that was. *It's like the proverbial, black sheep.*

"Brian would be with us, if we weren't coming this weekend," Catherine said, suddenly. "Kate invited him, but he won't be home for the Christmas Holidays until next week. I know he would like to see the farm."

"He'd like to be here with you, not us," Hillary corrected her. "He'll be here, eventually."

Bridie smiled at Catherine. "Do you and Brian still plan to marry as soon as he graduates?"

Catherine's face flushed a little, holding an image of Brian in her mind. "We plan to. As you know, right after graduation Brian will have a job with Mr. Holmgren, so there's no reason we should wait."

Intuitively, Bridie responded to Catherine's youthful desires. "You're right. You'll be eighteen, so there's no reason you shouldn't." Bridie appraised Catherine's sweet face and added, "Your first night together will be the most romantic moment of your life-savor it."

Hillary turned from the others, pretending to look at the barren fields. *I'll never have that moment with my husband.* She looked up at the clouds again, concentrating on the little gray one. *That's me, the cloud that's different. I must never tell anyone about what happened to me. That must remain my secret.* She bit back tears. *I hate you, Mr. Dragus.*

Biff shook the reins and looked back at the foursome. "Is everyone comfortable ... under *these* circumstances?"

"No," Hillary chuckled, "We're comfortable under *these* blankets."

"Boo! Poor joke," Pina moaned.

"We're fine," Bridie answered. "You're the one sitting up in the wind. How are you doing?"

"All's well up here. We're almost there and Kate will have hot beverages and sandwiches waiting for us."

Soon, they were following a path edging the vacant field between the Roddy house and the Hanley farm. Biff pulled back on the reins, stopping in front of the house.

Kate watched them through the window, before opening the door. She welcomed them and stepped back into the kitchen, giving them room to remove their coats and boots.

The first thing Hillary did, was go to Kate and place her hand on her abdomen. "I don't feel any movement."

Kate hugged Hillary and kissed her. "Too soon, my dear."

Hillary looked up at her, "Where's John?"

Kate pointed toward the window. "Here he comes now. He was feeding the animals."

Hillary turned and saw John walking through the snow a few yards from the house. She ran to the door and opened it, when she heard his boots banging on the porch. "Hurry in, Cowpoke. We don't want the cold in here."

They sat at the table eating pork and turkey sandwiches with hot tea and coffee, while talking about the baby and suggesting names for it. Kate and John decided to announce the names they'd already chosen. Kate looked at Hillary, pointing to Biff. "If it's a boy, he will be named Robert, for Uncle Biff. If it's a girl, she'll be named Laura, after your mother."

Hillary's eyes shifted momentarily to Bridie, wondering if she knew Biff had been in love with her mother. Bridie showed no emotion when the name "Laura" was mentioned, so Hillary believed she didn't know.

Pina noticed Biff looking across the table at Catherine, studying her. She intended to watch how often Biff gave her his attention. Pina wondered why nobody else noticed his interest in her, especially Catherine. Pina was concerned about what Catheine's situation would be, if Biff married Bridie, and was living in the same house with Catherine.

After breakfast the following morning, the three girls dressed to play in the snow. When Hillary opened the kitchen door to leave, Adam was standing there wrapped in heavy winter clothes. His arms were hanging at his sides, giving him the appearance of a statue. "I was about to knock. Do you want to play on our hill? We have three sleds."

Hillary looked at Kate standing by the stove. "Are we going for a sleigh ride this morning?"

"I don't believe so. The men are doing chores now, then Biff and Bridie will take the sleigh to town. Bridie wants to shop for things she can't buy in Newberry and have dinner at the De Soto Hotel. They'll probably return between five and six o'clock. Maybe you can go then." Kate waved her hand at Hillary. "Close the door. You're letting the cold in here."

Hillary and her friends raced outside, closing the door behind them. They crossed the field, watching Marnie and Trish sledding down the slope descending from their house. The children spent two hours sledding, until the cold got the best of them. Adam spent most of his time being attentive to Hillary, a fact that didn't go unnoticed by the other girls. It provided them with more fuel for, "A. Roddy" jokes.

Kate had a pot of hot vegetable beef soup on the stove when the girls returned for lunch. "That was fun," Pina said, walking into the kitchen. She noticed Kate's pale complexion. "How are you feeling?"

"I'm fine. Did you girls have fun?"

Pina walked over to Kate, removed her apron and tied it around herself. "You look tired. Go take a nap and we'll get our lunch."

"I think you should, too," Hillary agreed. "We want a well rested mother."

Kate did feel tired and decided to accept the girls offer. "Thank you. The soup and bread are ready to eat, so clean the dishes when you finish. The men will be eating lunch with me and Bridie."

Hillary watched Kate walk slowly down the hall to her bedroom. She hoped Kate wasn't having any problems with the baby. She dismissed those thoughts and turned to her friends. "You're my guests, so I'll serve."

Catherine drew a chair from the table and sat down, with her back to the early afternoon sun. When Hillary brought her a bowl of soup, she asked, "Did you get a letter from Iris and Vera recently?"

"About ten days ago. They're still wondering when I'll be going to Alton. Again, I wrote I'd try for next summer."

Pina sat at the end of the table, as Hillary brought her a steaming bowl of soup. "Have you asked Kate and John if you can go to Alton?"

Hillary ladled soup into her bowl and returned to the table. "Yes. Some time ago, but next summer would be the earliest. Kate suggested Biff go with me, because she doesn't want to go back there." She stirred her soup. "I was hoping she'd want to go to my parents graves with me, but I guess not."

Pina took a piece of bread and dipped it into her soup. She believed she understood Kate's reasoning, and said, "Remember, Kate will have the baby in May or June. She may have decided not to go because of the baby, being new and all."

Hillary looked at Pina and smiled. "You're right. I didn't think of that. That may be the reason."

That evening, when Biff and Bridie returned, John took the girls for a one-hour sleigh ride, while the sun was setting. They were thrilled at the big red ball sinking into the white horizon. When they returned,

Pina began clapping. "That was one of the prettiest sights I've ever seen."

John turned to Pina and clapped with her. "We don't get a red sun too often, so we were lucky it happened tonight."

Catherine was the first to climb out of the sleigh. "The contrast of the red sun and white snow was absolutely beautiful. I wish I had a picture of it."

Hillary faked a yawn, pretending she was bored by the sunset. "It was nothing special. I see it all the time."

Catherine scooped up snow and threw it at Hillary. "You're not kidding us. You loved it, as much as we did."

Hillary and Pina hurried out of the sleigh and began throwing snowballs at each other. John shook the reins and proceeded to the stable. He smiled to himself, thinking of his coming child, and what fun he was sure to have.

The next morning, the girls insisted on making a surprise breakfast. They told the adults to remain in their bedroom until breakfast was ready. The girls looked in the icebox to see what would make a delicious meal. Hillary reached for a basket of eggs. "I knew we had these, but I forgot about the hominy Biff brought Friday."

Catherine took the glass jar from Hillary and looked at the hominy. "We could stir this in with the eggs. It would be different, but it sounds like a good idea."

Hillary looked at Pina, as if appraising the idea. "That does sound good. What do you think, Pina?"

Pina nodded. "Let's do it."

Hillary carried a bowl of eggs and hominy to the stove. "One of you, grab the slices of ham for me."

Pina looked at her two friends. "We could cut the ham into small pieces and put that in the eggs, too."

Hillary looked back toward the girls. "Eggs, hominy and ham—why not? We want something different."

Catherine glanced into the icebox again, announcing, "There's a green pepper and an onion in here."

Hillary placed her hands on her hips, looking at the pepper and onion Catherine was holding. "That could be good, too. We want to be original, and it sounds like an appetizing combination."

Pina went to a cabinet next to the icebox and returned with the big mixing bowl.

Hillary got two large skillets. "This will have to be cooked carefully, in separate pans. It can't be soupy, or too firm—only just right. Our reputations as Bradbury cooks depend on success." She added more wood to the fire and began dicing the ham, while Pina and Catherine chopped the pepper and onion.

When the creation was ready to be cooked, the girls looked into the large bowl, as Hillary stirred the concoction. Hillary tapped the wooden spoon on the top of the bowl. "It's time."

Pina hurried to the stove, looking into the two frying pans. "The lard is melted, so pour it in."

Hillary stirred the eggs slowly, keeping an eye on its consistency as it cooked. "One of you, tell the adults to come for breakfast. It'll be ready when they get here."

Catherine went to the bedrooms and knocked on the doors. "Breakfast is ready."

Pina checked the tea water and coffee, before putting mugs on the table."

When Hillary decided the concoction was just right, she carried the frying pans to the table and set them on cloth pads. "I don't think we'd have enough, if Uncle Biff were here for breakfast."

John and Kate entered the kitchen, examining the food on the table. Kate looked into one of the frying pans. "It looks good. What is it-exactly?"

Hillary stuck her nose into the air. "Trey Pleasure, Madam."

John looked into the pan. "There are three things in that?"

As if insulted, Hillary answered indignantly, "How vulgar, three *things* ... in *that*. My dear man, it is a delicacy beyond your wildest dreams, and the trio represents the three chefs that prepared this pleasure—not the number of ingredients, which is five."

Pina walked over to John and elbowed him. "In other words, sit down and eat, then say how wonderful it is, whether you like it or not."

Bridie entered the kitchen, sniffing the aroma of the meal. "I like the smell of whatever it is. Where do you want me to sit?"

Catherine tapped the back of a chair. "Here, next to me."

Bridie looked inquisitively into a frying pan. "It looks inviting."

Hillary served the food, starting with the mother-to-be.

The adults commented on how good the meal was. The portions they ate, confirmed their words.

"Hillary was the one who actually cooked it," Catherine admitted.

Hillary waved her fork at Catherine. "We all decided on the ingredients. That's what makes it good."

Pina admonished, Hillary. "Waving that fork in the air isn't lady-like. Bradbury wouldn't approve."

Bridie looked at the three girls in turn. "You never made this before?"

"That's right," Hillary answered. "We took whatever we liked from the icebox and put it together. I must admit it is tasty."

Bridie moved a portion of her meal to the side of her plate. "Well, if this is the first time you made this, that means Biff had never eaten it. Therefore, I'll save some of mine for him." She smiled at Hillary. "Your uncle shouldn't be deprived of eating something this delicious. Write down the ingredients, so you don't forget them. Biff will probably want it added to his list of favorite meals hanging on the wall."

"I remember the ingredients," Catherine insisted.

Bridie sat back in her chair. "Good! Then we can make it at home."

The following Tuesday, Wade Widner was sitting at his desk when Tyler Sharpe brought him shipping orders for the next sailing. Wade poked through the papers quickly and looked up at him. "Send me there, too. I'd like to spend this winter where it's warm."

Tyler nodded. "I imagine you would, but what about Galena, Illinois? You said you loved that area, yet it has cold winters."

"I do like it there, and it's close to the Mississippi River which has good fishing. I can't get Kimby out of my mind, either." He could tell Tyler was confused by the name, so he explained. "Kimby is a beautiful horse I fell in love with."

Tyler chuckled, heading for the door. "Why would you want to be anywhere but beautiful, Alton, Delaware?"

Wade quickly raised his hand to keep Tyler from leaving. "Don't go yet!"

Tyler stopped in the doorway, facing Wade. "Is there something else?"

"Yes!" Wade leaned back in his chair, looking up at Tyler. "What do you plan to do about John Hanley?"

Tyler didn't appear pleased with the question, but answered. "I don't intend to get the authorities involved. I plan to pay him a personal visit in February. It's a very quiet time of the year. Many things die during winter."

CHAPTER TWENTY

Three days before Christmas, Catherine received a letter from C. Swane. She raced to her bedroom and quickly opened it, knowing it was from Monica. Catherine smiled, reading about seven pound, four ounce Andrew, and she would see him during the Christmas Holidays. She slid the letter into the envelope, anxious to tell Brian, Hillary and Pina. She sat in her rocking chair by the window, copied Monica's address and wrote a congratulatory letter, stressing how eager she was to see Andrew.

An hour later, Bridie returned from her office at the newspaper. She watched Catherine race down the stairs telling her about Andrew. Bridie was amused by Catherine's excitement. "That's wonderful news, and in a few months Kate will have her baby." She removed her coat and hung it on the coat tree. "In a couple of years, you'll be adding to the baby count, too."

Catherine grinned, "It'll be fun having babies around here. I'll love it."

Bridie removed her gloves and put them in her coat pocket. "Being that the painters haven't finished their work in the Holmgren house, as promised, we'll be celebrating Christmas here. Tomorrow, we shop for the Christmas dinner. I'll have Jack bring ..."

Catherine stepped forward and kissed Bridie's cheek, looking compassionately into her eyes.

"Old habits are hard to break," Bridie lamented. She removed her scarf and laid it over her coat. "I'm glad Brian is home from school. I'll call him to see if he can help with the groceries tomorrow."

"How many people will we be serving?"

"The Holmgrens and us, that's five, then four and a half from Galena, bringing the total to nine and a half people. The Campbells won't be here. They have another commitment for Christmas Day.

Christmas Day arrived with an occasional snowflake, drifting lazily to the ground. Everyone was in the dining room or kitchen, eager for the Christmas feast.

"Nothing like a fat Christmas goose," Biff said cheerfully, carrying a platter of meat into the dining room.

Hillary clapped her hands, applauding Biff. "And you shot it, Uncle Biff. It'll be delicious for that reason alone."

"It was a lucky shot," John quipped. "He accidentally pulled the trigger just as he sneezed with his eyes closed, and a bird fell to the ground."

Biff leered at John. "Put up some money and I'll show you what my sneezing can do for my bank account."

Brian pulled his chair closer to the table, leaning toward the meat platter. "I never ate goose, but always wanted to."

Biff watched Brian examine the goose. "If you like it, you can come up to Galena and we can shoot geese on the Mississippi and Galena Rivers."

Brian jerked his head toward Biff. "Honest?"

Many times, Tom heard Brian discuss hunting with fellow workers at the quarry. He rocked back on his chair and looked at Brian. "Now, there's a fabulous offer I know you like."

Biff nodded to Tom. "You can come, too, if you like hunting. John will be with us so I can teach him how to shoot."

John groaned. "Biff will teach you how to shoot with your eyes closed."

Margaret winked at Brian, knowing that hunting was something he wanted to do.

"Thanks, Biff … John, I would like that." His smile suddenly faded. "I'm away at school. When could I hunt?"

"When you come home to see Catherine," Kate responded, quickly. "You can bring Catherine with you." She looked at Bridie. "If that's agreeable with you?"

Bridie spread her napkin across her lap. "I think that would be acceptable, being that they would be with you people."

Kate covered her mouth with her hand and laughed. "I'm sure you'll be coming with them, making it totally acceptable."

"You're right," Bridie answered, with a grin. "I guess I would be with them."

The others laughed politely, knowing Bridie would always travel to Galena with Biff being there.

"I wasn't very convincing, was I," Bridie chuckled. "You know I love the farm." She turned to Biff sitting at her side. "I'm glad you called to tell us you were bringing this goose. Otherwise, Catherine and I would have purchased chicken or turkey."

Biff listened to Bridie while watching Catherine enter the dining room. He focused on the way she carried herself, her figure, her hair and complexion. More than ever, he wanted to accomplish his goal.

Catherine carried in a bowl of cranberry sauce and set it on the table. "All the food is on the table, and don't forget, the mother-to-be gets served first." She chuckled. "And I expect the same treatment when I'm pregnant."

Margaret handed the bowl of potatoes to Kate. "Is everything going well with the baby?"

"It appears, so. Other than needing naps, I'm doing fine. Ruth Roddy stops by regularly to see how I'm doing, and if I need anything. She's a very good neighbor."

"Does Tom Roddy takes care of your animals when you come here?" Tom Holmgren asked, John. "I know it's difficult for farmers to get away because of the constant attention farm animals need."

"Yes, he does. We rely on each other's help when necessary. It makes farming much easier that way."

Tom looked across the table at Biff. "Who takes care of your place when you're away?"

Bridie looked at Biff and smiled, knowing he had large farms to maintain.

Biff didn't want to brag about the size of his holdings, or the number of hired hands, so he simply replied, "I have friends that help when I'm gone."

Kate passed the cranberry sauce to Bridie. "How is your new handyman working out? Is he as reliable as Jack was?"

"Very much so. His name is Matthew Brown and lives with his sister, Courtney. Matthew married when he was twenty-three. His wife died of pneumonia within seven months of their marriage."

Kate gasped, "That poor man." She stopped from saying more, remembering Bridie's misfortune with Jack. "Life isn't fair for everybody," she said casually, wanting to avoid discussion about Jack, with Biff sitting there.

"He and his sister moved here from Columbus, Ohio, about a year ago," Catherine added. She looked at Bridie. "Didn't Matthew say he and his wife were school teachers?"

"Yes. He's a very nice, middle-aged gentleman who seems to be quite knowledgeable about any kind of repairs. He also bred horses when he lived in Ohio. My horse, Bree, took to him immediately."

"Was Courtney ever married?" Hillary asked.

"I don't know," Bridie answered. "He started working here just three weeks ago and we haven't discussed Courtney very much. I assume I'll eventually learn more about her."

With a quick motion, Brian sat back and sighed, "I *do* like this goose. Yes! I will have to buy a shotgun." He looked at Catherine, with a hopeful grin. "You'll have to learn how to roast a goose. I'll shoot it and you cook it."

Catherine gave him an unkindly stare. "That doesn't sound fair to me. You have fun shooting it, and I get to clean and cook it? Think that again, please."

"No, that's not what I meant," Brian responded, quickly. "I'll shoot the goose and clean it. All you'll have to do is cook it."

Catherine looked at the people sitting around the table. "See why I love him?"

Bridie tapped her water glass with a fork to get her guests attention. "Is there anyone here who doesn't like goose meat?" She glanced at everyone. "I want the truth."

After they all affirmed they liked it, Bridie made a suggestion. "I would like to propose that we have goose every Christmas. Does anyone oppose that idea?"

"Good plan," Tom replied, with the others following his lead. "Turkey on Thanksgiving and goose on Christmas."

"Enjoy our new tradition," Bridie said. "When we finish our meal, we'll go into the parlor and open our Christmas presents. Catherine and I will serve dessert after that."

Kate and Bridie were alone in the kitchen, putting the washed dishes into the cabinet.

Kate gently held Bridie's arm. "Sorry about Jack. I'm sure your years together have been difficult for you."

Bridie smiled. "Together, can have different meanings. For years, we were together physically, but not emotionally or mentally. I was young and in love and faithful to him. But since the accident, we were in two different worlds, and I shouldn't have devoted myself to him so thoroughly. I can see that now." She peered into Kate's eyes. "Looking back, I see them as years lost. Now, I want a life. I had a beautiful relationship with John, but once he became Jack my life became stagnant. I need to move on."

Kate understood Bridie was hoping for a full life with Biff and children. She hugged her. "You're still young, and I believe you can have a complete, more fruitful life ahead of you."

Two days later, Monica called Catherine to say that she would bring her baby to Bridie's house the next day, and would like to have Pina and Hillary there. Catherine guaranteed Monica it would be impossible to keep them away. Monica was to be there at two o'clock.

When the doorbell rang the following afternoon, the girls darted from the kitchen to the front door. They opened the door and all three heads clustered around Andrew, lying in his mother's arms. Monica drew back a portion of the blanket covering his head. The girls wailed with adoration, too occupied to notice Monica's face glowing with pride.

"Look at that little baby breath floating in the cold air," Hillary giggled.

Bridie came down from her bedroom. "Move out of the way girls, and let Monica come inside. It's cold out there."

The girls backed away from the door, still looking at Andrew. Bridie closed the door behind them, asking Monica if she could hold Andrew.

Pina watched Bridie lift Andrew from his mother's arms. *Why didn't I think of asking for the baby?*

Bridie walked to the parlor and the others followed. She sat on the sofa and parted the blanket around Andrew. Bridie reached up for Monica's hand. "Sit next to me." Bridie cradled Andrew, examining all his facial features, fingers and toes. She enjoyed how little he weighed. Bridie looked at Monica. "I guess we've ignored you long enough. Tell us how you feel, and about your new life."

Monica displayed a big smile, unable to contain her pride. "I don't mind being ignored. It happens every time I show the baby."

Catherine reached in and felt his fingers. "He's adorable, Monica."

"I'm going to have one of those around my house this summer," Hillary boasted.

"Then we'll have to visit you more often," Pina demanded, glaring at Hillary.

Catherine got down on one knee and lifted Andrew to her chest. She looked at Monica. "Do you mind if I hold him?"

Monica smiled. "No, but be careful."

Pina watched Catherine lift Andrew to her chest. *Why didn't I think of that, then I'd be holding him?*

Catherine walked in a circle, patting Andrew on the back. "You're a good-looking little guy."

Hillary was pleased Monica had something to be excited about. "Tell us about your new life, Monica."

There was a rapt expression on Monica's face, as she began explaining. "Everything has moved so fast, changing my life completely. I'm not sure how to explain. I have what I believe is a beautiful life, especially compared to what I had before. Charles is a proud daddy and seems to love me. And now we have a beautiful son. He has a good job and we have a nice apartment. My life is the best it's ever been."

Bridie smiled at Monica. "You couldn't have explained it better. Your life has changed dramatically for the better, and we all wish you happiness." She looked up at Andrew, thinking, *It's my turn to have my needs met.*

Hillary took Andrew from Catherine and did the same, walking and patting him on the back.

Pina planned to take Andrew from Catherine, but waited too long. "I'm next and last to hold the baby," she insisted, loudly.

Bridie rose from the sofa and started for the kitchen. "Who wants tea?"

"I do," Monica answered.

"Me, too," Pina responded. "Thank you."

Bridie continued toward the kitchen. "I'll make enough for all of us."

Pina and Catherine sat on the sofa with Monica, while Hillary continued walking with Andrew. Monica began to whisper, "I have something to tell you three. It has been bothering me, because I want you to know the truth." She looked at each girl to be sure they were listening. "You know what Mr. Peters did to me. Then, soon after that, I was with Charles when I ran away. I don't know if you were wondering who Andrew's father is, or even if you thought that it could be Mr. Peters, but I want you to know I hadn't ovulated until I was living with Charles. So, I know who the father is."

Pina stood and reached for the baby. "My turn." She cradled him in her arms and began circling the room. "I love holding him."

Monica smiled, and continued. "It's amazing how my life has changed because Mr. Peters raped me. Many times I've thought, if that hadn't happened, I wouldn't have run away and joined Charles. I'd still be working long hours and living in a small, dilapidated house, with no possible chance for a happy future. Now, I have Andrew, a nice apartment and a husband with a good occupation, and it all happened in less than a year. And to think, I almost refused being adopted by the Peters. I wonder where I'd be now, if I hadn't gone with them."

Pina stopped abruptly in the middle of the room and stared at Monica. "You'd be where my brother Marcello and Jason are—somewhere unknown."

Catherine placed her index finger across her lips. "Shhh! Andrew is asleep. Talk softly."

Pina looked at Andrew once more, then bent forward and handed him to Monica. "Here's your most precious possession."

Hillary stood, so Monica could lay Andrew beside her. "What's your most precious possession right now, Pina?"

"That's easy to answer, Eileen and Richard Campbell, not that they are possessions, but they are the most precious people in my life. They have been very good to me and improved my life completely. They're even sending me to Bradbury School, which is not an easy expense for them. Everything I have, came from them." Pina looked at Hillary. "Leaving Alton, Delaware was the best thing that could have happened to us. Don't you agree?"

Hillary nodded. "Yes, but I had to leave my parents to do it. I'd like to be near their graves, but I guess I can talk to them from here." She thought of the times Mr. Dragus was with her, then responded vigorously, "You're right, I am much happier in Galena, and for many reasons."

Pina went on to finish what she had to say. "My life has changed so completely, living a life I never dreamed I'd have. I went from all work and no play, to a nice home, loving parents, Bradbury School and beautiful friends. I couldn't be happier."

"We love you, too," Catherine added, quickly.

Hillary looked into Pina's eyes, "We all love you and realize you are a very happy person ... you live it."

Monica lay Andrew across her lap and looked up at Pina. "I don't know you as well as the others, but you are fun to be around. That's a good friend."

Bridie could hear most of their conversation from the kitchen, so she decided to serve the tea and go upstairs, giving them privacy while making memories. She carried in a tray of tea and lemon and apple squares. The girls moaned with delight and thanked her for the wonderful treat. Andrew's eyes opened slightly and Bridie carefully stroked his cheek with her finger. "He's adorable."

Monica smiled. "Thank you. I like him."

Bridie laughed. "I'm sure you do." She stepped back, watching the girls take a napkin and lay it carefully across their laps. Bridie was pleased the Bradbury girls displayed proper etiquette, while serving each other and eating with appropriate poise. *The school is doing a fine job preparing them for society. Sending them to Bradbury was a good idea.* Bridie turned from the girls. "I'm going upstairs to read, while you girls continue doing whatever you were doing."

Knowing Hillary lived on a farm, Monica asked her what her most precious possession was.

Hillary laid her fork on the saucer and glanced at all of the girls. "I would have to say the memories of my parents. Except for a cathedral clock my father bought my mother one Christmas, that's all I have of them. Nothing else I have could be more important, because I loved them dearly. I feel cheated because they died at a young age."

"Oh, good answer," Catherine, sighed. "The memory of my parents has to be mine, also." She sat back into the sofa. "I'm sorry for interrupting. Do continue."

"You're forgiven," Hillary smiled. "Of course, I love Kate, John and Biff ... and you girls. But as we know, people aren't possessions, so Knickers and Bradbury follow after my memories and the clock." She looked at Andrew and grinned. "Next important will be Kate and John's baby, who I love already."

The other girls laughed, fully understanding her yearning for the baby.

Hillary looked at Pina. "Like you, I am so happy to be away from Alton, for many reasons. I wasn't unhappy there, because I was young and didn't know any better. All the children worked long hours, six days a week, but that's how it was in Alton. I had fun on Sundays with Iris and Vera, even forming our private club, Wildflowers, pledging ourselves friends for life, because we believed we'd always live in Alton. As with Pina, I never imagined this kind of life." She looked at her friends. "I'm so happy we're here."

"We are the lucky ones," Monica sighed. "Often, I recall the faces of other children who rode the Orphan Train with us, and wonder what kind of life they are having?" She smiled at Catherine. "Remember little Becky with the brown curls, always clutching her raggedy doll? The lady who took her home was crying with joy, so we know Becky got a good home."

Catherine couldn't contain her smile. "I remember her very well. It was an emotional moment I'll never forget."

Pina removed the folded napkin from her lap and placed it on the coffee table. "Catherine, what is your greatest possession—besides Brian, that is?"

"Nothing," Hillary laughed.

A willing smile appeared on Catherine's lips, as she addressed Pina. "Hillary would be correct, if we included people as possessions."

Catherine poured tea into her cup, as she began explaining. "I agree with Hillary, the memories of my parents would have to be first. Being this house and the horse and buggy are Bridie's, I can't include them, so I'd have to say my Flying Geese blanket is my favorite possession." She looked at Monica to explain, being she was the only one present who hadn't seen it. "It's a patch quilt made by a negro slave, many years ago. It has a lot of history attached to it, but I won't tell you about that now. It would take too long." Catherine paused to sip her tea. "My education from Bradbury School would have to be next. Other than that, all else I would rate equally."

"Andrew is asleep again," Hillary announced. She looked at Monica, inquisitively. "Is he always this good?"

"To be sure, he is *not*. We've been lucky." Monica noticed the clock on the fireplace mantle. "It's later than I thought. We'd better go to the Belcher house. Dinner is in fifty minutes."

The three girls helped Monica with her coat and wrapped Andrew in the blanket. "We'll walk you home," Catherine, suggested.

The girls went to the foyer and put on their coats. Catherine called upstairs to Bridie. "We're walking Monica to the Belcher house. I'll be back in about an hour."

CHAPTER
TWENTY-ONE

The following day, Biff, Hillary and her parents boarded the train for Galena. Hillary and Biff would return to Newberry ten days later, so Hillary could go back to school, and Biff would spend two days with Bridie. Hillary sat next to Kate, with the men behind them. They rolled past farms and small towns, sitting quiet for a time, almost oblivious of each other. Hillary examined the interior of the coach closely. It was much like the one they rode the day they left Alton, Delaware. She interrupted Kate, watching the passing scenery. "Could this be the coach we rode when we left Alton? It looks like it."

"It couldn't be. It's a different railroad company." Kate glanced around the coach. "I see what you mean. It is similar."

Hillary looked down at her folded hands, gathering the nerve to ask what she knew could be a delicate question. "The day we left Alton, did you see Mr. Dragus, while Uncle Biff and I waited for you at the train station?"

Kate hesitated before answering, wondering why Hillary asked that question. She didn't believe Hillary knew about Frank Dragus's death. To protect herself, however, she decided to lie. "No, I didn't see Mr. Dragus. I went there for some things I left in my desk drawer. You saw me walking from the mill, remember?"

"Yes, I saw you, but wondered why you went there."

Kate responded quickly, to avoid appearing she was creating a story. "Like I said, I went for things in my desk drawer."

Unsure whether she believed Kate, Hillary decided to withdraw from that subject. "That makes sense." Quickly, she changed the discussion. "Can you go back to Newberry with us next week?"

Kate smiled at Hillary. "I don't think so. Remember, Biff is going back to have time with Bridie?"

"You're right. That was a dumb question. It's a shame Biff and Bridie won't be celebrating New Year's Eve together." Hillary sat back in her seat, thinking about the first letter she'd received from Vera, months ago, telling her Mr. Dragus was murdered the Sunday they'd left Alton. *Who else would have been there?* She thought. *The Mill is closed on Sunday. Does Kate have a secret? If she does, we both have an evil secret regarding Mr. Dragus. He was a pig and I'm glad he's dead.*

The beginning of the year, 1901, was being celebrated wildly at Doyle's Pub in Alton, Delaware. Wade Widner leaned against the bar, looking at the poor people around him, dressed in shabby clothes and spending their hard earned money on drink, as they always did. He began thinking about Galena, Illinois, a tidy town surrounded by beautiful country, with hard working people who built themselves a nice life. He envied them.

Karl Polen ambled his thick, muscular body across the room and stood next to Wade. "Happy New Year, Mate."

Wade raised his mug to Karl. "Same to you, friend."

Karl removed his brown leather cap, scratched his scalp, and replaced it on his head. "You don't look very chipper for someone celebrating New Year's Eve."

Wade turned and leaned against the bar, so he could face Karl. "I'm not. I feel guilty for finding John and Kate for Tyler. He intends to go after John in February, but I'm not to tell anyone—got it?"

Karl's eyes widened. "I got it. That ain't far off, thirty-one days, plus whatever. I think we'd better tell John's story to Tyler, so he'd give up on that idea. Time is running out, I'd say."

"That's what I was about to suggest to you. The sooner, the better, so he has time to think about what we tell him."

Karl drank the last of his beer and flashed two fingers at the bartender. "Tyler may be hung-over from celebrating New Year's Eve, so let's talk to him in two days, when he should be in a better mood—whatever that is. I'll meet you and we'll walk to his office together."

Wade nodded. "I agree. Come to my office about five o'clock. We must change his thinking." He finished his beer and pushed his mug forward. "I've seen what John and Kate have and I would hate to spoil it for them, especially with them caring for that orphan girl. We have to convince Tyler of John's innocence."

Two days later, Wade walked into Tyler's office, with Karl following. Karl closed the door and they sat in two of three chairs spread before Tyler's desk. "Got a minute?" Wade asked. "We've got an important story for you. A true story."

Tyler was somewhat confused about their quick entry and abrupt manner. "It depends on what it is."

Wade sat back in the chair and crossed one leg over the other. "It's about John Hanley."

Tyler's eyes rolled back and forth between the two men, then he stared at Wade. He was obviously upset with Wade for mentioning this in front of Karl. "What's Karl got to do with John? This is between you and me, only."

"Because Karl knows more about the John and Jesse story than we do," Wade said firmly, hoping to convince Tyler what he was about to hear, was true. He looked directly into Tyler's eyes, "Karl doesn't know about anything we've discussed." Wade continued to gaze at Tyler. "Some time back, John told Karl what happened the night your brother was murdered." Wade was about to lie to give strength to his story. "That was long before you came to Crossroads Shipping. Karl will tell you the story, which makes sense, and you should realize that you could be wrong about your convictions."

Tyler removed a handkerchief from his pocket and wiped his mouth. "I'll decide that."

Wade looked at Karl. "Go ahead."

Karl proceeded to tell Tyler about a man named Haggar, buying John's hat with his name in it, and going to the outhouse where Jesse was, leaving the hat on the ground. Haggar slapped bloody money into John's hand and kept on running.

Wade looked at Tyler and lied again. "John had told me that same story, and it was just by chance that Karl and I mentioned it to each other. As you can see, it's a feasible story. A bad guy frames a good guy. It's that simple. Karl and I know John could never kill a man under those circumstances." Wade placed his hands on the armrests of the chair and began to stand. "We'll leave now, and you think about what we told you. I'll discuss it with you in a couple of days."

Minutes after the men left, Tyler reached across his desk, picked up a glass paperweight, then threw it against the door.

The girls finished their first day of school after the Christmas break. Catherine was standing under the willow tree, rocking back and forth on her cold feet. Hillary and Pina could see Catherine waiting for them, her steamy breath swirling about her head. They wanted to get out of the cold, so they ran to her and walked at a fast pace toward their homes.

Pina elbowed Catherine and grinned. "Hillary got a Christmas card from A. Roddy last Friday."

Hillary rolled her eyes. "Yes, big mouth. I got a card from A. Roddy. Tell Bridie about it, maybe she'll put that important information in the newspaper."

Catherine laughed. "Better to get the card late, than never ... I guess. Did you send him a Christmas card?"

Hillary leered at Catherine. "Very funny."

Pina looked at Catherine from the corner of her eye. "I have yet to see a letter from Trish or Marnie. I wonder if Adam ever shared Hillary's address with them, or if they even know he's writing Hillary?"

Hillary wanted to divert the conversation from herself, so she entered Monica into the conversation. "What do you think about Monica's explanation about the father of her child?"

"I believe her," Catherine replied. "I think if it was Clay Peters baby, she'd have admitted it, though I wouldn't have."

"Hurry across the street before that coal wagon comes," Pina suggested on the run.

On the other side of the street, Hillary pulled up her coat collar. "Andrew has a slim face like Charles, while Clay has a round face. I agree with Catherine, Monica would have admitted it, if it had been Clay's baby."

Catherine looked at Pina, sympathetically. "Sorry to change the subject, but have you ever received a letter from your brother?"

"No," Pina answered, somberly. "But it would have been a wonderful Christmas present. I wonder what kind of Christmas Marcello had?"

"Think he had a happy one," Catherine suggested. "It's a greater chance Marcello had a good one, than a bad one."

"I suppose, but I wish I knew in detail what kind of life he is living. It's been two years since he was taken from me, and no letter, yet. I don't think I'll ever know where he is."

Catherine looked at Pina, with an evil smile. "Since you mentioned Christmas, I never told you about the bracelet Biff gave Bridie. It's made of gold and silver, with a rose engraved at its center. It had to cost, dearly."

"And he was with her this weekend," Hillary added, quickly. "He went back to Galena yesterday afternoon. Those two are getting pretty cozy, I'd say."

Pina glanced back-and-forth at her friends. "Isn't that what we wanted? Do you think he'll buy her a small, round piece of jewelry in the near future?"

Catherine looked off into the distance, analyzing their relationship before answering. "I wouldn't be surprised. And my guess is, she would accept it."

Ruth Roddy had her three children walk a path through the snow-covered field to the Hanley farm, in case Kate needed her in an emergency. She didn't have a telephone, so she used a telescope to watch Kate's kitchen window that would display a large piece of red paper, if she were needed. After crossing the field and Kate's barnyard, she stepped onto the porch, stomping snow from her boots, before knocking on her door. Ruth brought two loaves of oatmeal bread she'd baked that morning. When Kate opened the door, Ruth grinned. "I'm sure you knew who was at your door in this weather."

"I was ninety-nine percent sure," Kate chuckled.

Ruth handed her the loaves of bread and removed her boots. "They're oatmeal."

"Thank you. We love oatmeal bread." She laid the bread on the table and started for the stove. "I have coffee and tea. Which would you prefer?"

"I'll have coffee this time." She placed her coat over the back of a chair and gave Kate a side-glance. "You're growing right on schedule."

"Yes, and I dread getting bigger. I feel awkward already."

Ruth laughed. "It's not a barrel of fun, but the results are worth it. When you hold your newborn, you'll all but forget the ... inconvenience."

Kate carried the beverages to the table and sat across from Ruth. "Hillary is as anxious for this baby, as John and I are. She's looking forward to playing mommy this summer. It'll be fun watching her."

Ruth spooned sugar into her coffee and stirred it. "Today is Hillary's first day back to school, right, the same as my children?"

"Yes. She loves being with her friends, and school, and being here. Yet, her world isn't perfect. Her parents are almost always on her mind. They were two beautiful people." Kate looked down into her cup, slowly turning it on the table, thinking about when she'd first met Laura and Jeremiah, and the fun they'd had through the years. "Life can be so unfair."

Ruth watched a change come over Kate's face, generated by loving memories of dear friends. She decided to change the subject and move on with the present. "How are Biff and Bridie getting along? From what little I see of them, they appear to be quite happy with each other."

Kate smiled at Ruth. "Yes, they seem to be getting along nicely, but both have a personal problem that needs to be resolved before they can get serious." She tilted her head, slightly, looking at Ruth. "It's not my business to explain that last statement."

"No need. If they want to be together, they'll work it out."

Kate looked out of the window to see if John and Tom were returning from town. "Daylight is fading and I don't like John on the road after dark, especially during winter."

"Tom brought his rifle in case they encounter a bear or wolves. Actually, he hopes they run across a deer, so he can bring meat for our larder." She reached across the table and patted Kate's hand. "Of course, you'd get half the meat. John told us you make excellent deer sausage."

Kate laughed, "He only said that, because it's true." She reached to the end of the table, pulling the kerosene lamp and stick matches toward her. She lit the lantern, watching the flame dance for a moment. "Is Adam a complete Roddy now, or is he still stuck in the past?"

Ruth couldn't contain her smile. "Yes! Ever since he learned Hillary and her friends had been orphans, he's adjusted quite well. We are one family now. He needed to see the love shared between your three girls and their families, to believe what I'd been telling him all along—simply, that we love him as our own." Ruth paused, before asking what might be a sensitive question for Kate. "Are you aware that Adam is sweet on Hillary?"

Kate laughed. "I was about to ask you the same question. He doesn't hide his feelings very well." Kate raised the wick in the lantern, increasing the glow. "We also know his feelings can change at any time, being children are whimsical."

Ruth nodded and slowly smiled. "I'm sure we won't miss anything that may develop between them."

Three weeks later, Catherine received a Valentine and letter from Brian. She was in the foyer sitting on the steps, when Bridie came home and saw her reading. Catherine waved the letter at Bridie. "Brian sent me a Valentine *and* a letter. I like the letter more because he wrote it—not some printing company. They came three days early, making sure they'd be here by Valentine's Day."

Bridie removed her coat and hung it on the coat tree. "That would be my guess, as well. He does love you." She removed her scarf and stuffed it into her coat pocket. "I assume you sent him a card?"

"And a letter." Catherine responded.

Bridie chuckled. "Who's trying to keep up with who?"

"I can't wait until he's home for Easter."

Bridie started for the kitchen. "You'll have to."

Catherine followed Bridie and sat at the table. "Do you miss having Jack around the house?"

Bridie placed the teakettle on the stove. "Do you want tea?"

"No, Thank you." Catherine waited for Bridie to answer.

Bridie looked over her shoulder at Catherine. "Surprisingly, very little. Matthew does the work needed around here, and I have accepted Jack's death completely. It wasn't difficult, being he hadn't been John for many years. I loved him through the years, but it wasn't a complete love, like you share with a healthy man. We can't change our past, so I'm looking forward to a better life." Bridie slowly dipped the tea ball into the cup of hot water. "Biff is that opportunity, and I truly love him. I know he cares for me, but how deeply, only he knows."

Bridie carried a cup of tea to the table and sat across from Catherine. "If we were to marry, I'm not sure who he would be to you—step-father, step-adopting father, adopting step-father, step-guy … him?"

Catherine laughed. "How about, Biff?"

Bridie nodded. "I could accept that."

CHAPTER
TWENTY-TWO

Bridie heard Catherine close her bedroom door, as she opened the front door for Brian. "Welcome home."

Brian kissed Bridie's cheek. "Thanks. Mom and Dad will be here shortly." He looked up the stairs, waiting for Catherine to come into view. When she did, Brian brandished an eager smile. "Here comes my Easter Bunny."

Catherine held the handrail, rushing down the stairs, "Yes, forever and ever, I'll be your Easter Bunny."

Knowing her presence wasn't needed, Bridie turned for the kitchen. "You can kiss her, if you like." Bridie smiled. "I haven't said that for a long time."

Bridie walked into the kitchen, where Pina and Hillary were preparing the salad, relishes and desserts. "Catherine will be back to help when she finishes saying 'hello' to Brian."

"That could be quite a while," Pina snickered.

Hillary smiled. "That's good. They need time together."

Bridie inspected the food on the table, then the baked ham on the stove. "You girls are doing a great job. Everything looks delicious." Bridie picked out a sliver of ham lying on the bottom of the roasting pan and tasted it. "It appears Bradbury School will have you girls ready to entertain your guests when you're married."

Hillary pointed her thumb toward the parlor where Catherine and Brian were still greeting each other. "Catherine will be the first one married—being that she graduates in a few weeks and has a man to marry."

"You'll have your turn," Bridie assured them.

Pina held a hand over her heart and pretended to swoon. "Living with the man you love must be wonderful."

Bridie walked over and placed her hand on Pina's back. "Marriage can be wonderful, but imagining a life with a man, is different from living with one. There are disappointments and you have to be forgiving and understanding. Then, when children come, they are a joy, but also a lot of work. Marriage isn't all roses." Bridie paused, thinking about the empty life she'd had. "But, it's better than living alone."

Pina sliced pickles and placed them in a relish dish. "That first night with your man must be magical, getting lost in each other's arms for hours?"

There won't be a first time with my husband, Hillary thought, slicing a loaf of wheat bread. She clamped her teeth together, so she wouldn't cry. *Bastard!*

Bridie went out to the back porch and onto the lawn where her guests were having a drink, enjoying the warm weather. The men were wearing dress jackets and the women had shawls around their shoulders. The temperature was forty-eight degrees, but it seemed warm compared to the winter that had just passed. "We'll begin eating when the Holmgrens arrive. Brian and Catherine are in the parlor saying 'hello' to each other."

Her guests laughed, and Eileen Campbell raised her glass of wine. "Good for them. A toast to young love."

The others smiled, raising their glasses.

"Nothing wrong with mature love, either," Biff whispered to Bridie.

"Any stage of life," Bridie whispered back.

Brian stepped out onto the porch. "Tom brought a surprise with him," Brian announced, eagerly.

"Good. I like surprises," Eileen said.

Brian looked at her, sheepishly. "Sorry. It's a surprise for the men."

Richard Campbell raised his glass of beer. "I'll drink to that, too."

Eileen looked at Richard. "You'll drink to anything." She looked at the others. "The truth is he rarely drinks. I shouldn't have said that."

Richard placed his arm around Eileen and addressed the others. "We rarely drink, so when I do, she thinks it's too much."

"Surprise," Tom Holmgren shouted, bursting through the kitchen door. He had two shotguns in his raised arms. "As suggested, we're going to shoot goose and turkey for all the holidays."

Biff laughed and clapped his hands. "Good, another way of having fun together."

John and Biff huddled around Tom, examining the shotguns.

"Don't point them at anyone," Margaret shouted from the porch.

Tom looked at Margaret, crossing the lawn. "There aren't any shells in these guns."

"Good." She replied. "Guns are new to you."

"You bought good, quality guns," Biff remarked, turning a gun in his hands.

"Only one thing wrong with these," John snickered. "They have gun sights. You don't need sights, if you're going to shoot, Biff style … you know, with your eyes closed."

Brian and Tom laughed, watching Biff leer at John.

Biff waved his finger at John. "We'll go target shooting one day, for a dollar a hit. When we're finished, I'll own your farm."

"We don't have to wait for someday," Tom responded, quickly. "We can go to my quarry this afternoon and practice. There are many things we can use as targets. Besides, doves love flying around quarries."

"This afternoon?" Margaret moaned. "But it's Easter."

Tom glanced at the other ladies to appeal his case. "Most of you go back to Galena tomorrow. If we don't practice today, it may never happen. Besides, it's a half-hour to get there, an hour of shooting, and a half-hour back for a total of only two hours."

Biff glanced at Bridie for her response. She smiled and nodded toward Brian. "How could I refuse that eager face?"

"Good!" Tom said. "We should go right after dinner."

"That would be best," Kate agreed. "The girls prepared the dinner, so us bigger girls will clean up after dinner, which will take about an hour."

"Are you really going to bet money?" Eileen asked.

Biff glared at John. "Definitely."

"Do you have shells?" Richard asked.

Tom winked at Richard. "I have boxes of them in my buggy. You can shoot, too, if you'd like?"

"I believe I'll stand back and watch," Richard answered. "I doubt that I'll be hunting in the future."

"I'm afraid," Margaret whined to Tom. "You don't know anything about guns."

Catherine opened the kitchen door and called, "Dinner is ready."

At the end of April, Wade Widner boarded a train that would take him back to Galena, Illinois. He put his luggage in the overhead rack and sat next to a window, just as the train began rolling from the station. He looked about the coach and saw that it was half occupied, mostly by men. He pulled up on the money belt under his shirt to keep it from pressing against the bottom of his ribs. When he was comfortable, he removed a telegram from his jacket pocket, reviewing the directions he was to follow in Galena. In another pocket was a Derringer pistol he'd purchased years before, when he was an Artillery Officer.

After reading the instructions, Wade sat back and watched the small country towns and farms and open prairies disappear behind him, and thought about his future. He decided to wait a few days before riding Kimby to the Hanley farm. He was pleased that Tyler Sharpe convinced him to take this assignment. It was going to be a financial boost for him.

The first weekend in May, Biff met Bridie and the three girls at the train station. It was early afternoon and a spring shower had just ended.

As they rode out of town and onto the dirt road, Hillary sat with her hands clasped around her knees. "In three weeks, when school ends, I may have a baby to play with it."

Pina laughed. "You won't have time for the baby. You'll be too busy answering the door for A. Roddy."

Bridie smiled and nudged Hillary. "She knows better. I think she's jealous."

Hillary raised her nose into the air, "Bridie's right. You'll be jealous, and I may not let you play with him or her."

"Okay. I envy you because you'll have a baby at your house. I'm sorry. Please forgive me. Now, can I play with it?"

"If you behave." Hillary answered.

Suddenly, Biff yelled, "There's a band of wild horses in the field on our left."

All heads turned in that direction. "Pick one," Bridie said, to Catherine. "It'll save me money."

"I'd love to, if we had a chance of catching them." She looked at Bridie, "Are you still planning on buying me a horse?"

Bridie's eyes rested on Catherine. "You still want one, don't you?"

Catherine smiled. "Yes, but we haven't discussed it for such a long time, I wasn't sure if it was definite."

Bridie grinned. "It's definite. I've been waiting for warm weather. We can talk about it when we get home."

Catherine wanted to scream for joy, but controlled herself, for it wouldn't be lady-like.

Minutes later, they pulled up in front of the house. Kate was sitting in a rocking chair on the porch, waving to them. As soon as the buggy stopped, Hillary jumped to the ground, yelling, "Stand up," then ran to Kate.

Kate knew what Hillary wanted to do, so she obliged her, rising to her feet. Hillary kissed Kate, then leaned over and placed he ear and hand against Kate's abdomen. Suddenly, she stood with a canyon-sized smile. "He-or-she moved."

"I'll drink to that," John said, stepping out of the house. He waited for Hillary to come and embrace him. "Welcome home, Sugar."

Hillary looked up at him. "Are you getting more excited with each day?"

He peered at her happy face. "Yes, I am, and we're going to have fun with him … her."

Pina and Catherine stepped from the buggy, "Thank you for having us again."

Kate looked at Catherine. "Congratulations on your coming graduation, and you only need to wait one year for Brian to graduate."

Catherine's face glowed at the thought. "Soon after that, I'll be Mrs. Hampton."

Kate laughed at her ardor. "The next time you come here, Brian should be able to come with you."

Bridie stepped out of the buggy and walked over to Kate. "If my math is correct, there's only a month left, right?"

"Yes! I feel like a watermelon." Kate faced Catherine and Pina. "Knickers has been waiting for you girls, so change your clothes and have fun."

Catherine beamed at the suggestion. "Good."

Hillary was pleased Catherine shared her love of horses, then they could ride together in the future. She picked up her bag from the ground and said, "Follow me girls, we've got riding to do." They carried their baggage inside and the men took the buggy to the stable. Bridie sat in a chair next to Bridie. They looked at each other for a moment, without speaking. Both thinking the same; where they were in life. Kate having a baby, Bridie's prospect of marrying Biff, and possibly being a mother in the near future, and how in so many ways, adopting the girls had changed their lives for the better.

Kate folded her fingers together and laid them on her lap. "I'm very content with my life."

Bridie smiled at her. "You look it. I hope to be the same as you some day."

Kate knew, by how deep Bridie was looking into her eyes, that she wanted a clue as to Biff's intentions toward her. She didn't want to make up something, just to make her feel good, so she decided to tell only what she knew. Yet, there remained the Laura and Catherine look-alike problem and Kate didn't know if Biff could resolve that. In a reassuring voice, Kate said, "Biff appears to be very interested in you. He's a private man and doesn't easily talk about his feelings. What he has in mind for the future, I really don't know. I also know, he'd like to have a family, but he isn't the type to marry a woman without loving her. So, if he does ask you to marry him, you can be sure he truly loves you and you can give him your soul."

Bridie turned her head, looking at the girls walking Knickers into the corral. "Thank you for your honesty."

The following day, Wade Widner rode Kimby to the Hanley farm. When he arrived there, he slowed his horse to a rhythmic gallop. Wade could see three girls and two women at the corral standing around a horse. He recognized Kate. She appeared to be pregnant, but he wasn't sure, because of the distance between them. He saw Kate turn from the horse and face him. She didn't wave, as she did the last time he rode by. She stood like a pillar, looking his way. He continued on, realizing he couldn't go there while they had guests. Wade saw one of the girls mount the horse and ride along the corral fence. He decided to return after the weekend to see if they would be alone.

Kate watched the rider pass on, behind a cluster of trees. She had no doubt he was the rider she and John had seen months before. He was big and sat tall in the saddle. The image was identical, as before. As she wondered about the man, Kate placed a loving hand over her unborn child. She recalled Helen Harte's description of the tall man claiming to be a friend and wanting to visit them. Yet, he never came. *Is he after John, or me?*

The house was dark after everyone went to bed. Kate reached for John's shoulder and whispered, "Remember Mrs. Harte describing the man who asked about us months ago?"

John turned onto his back. "Yeah, of course I remember. That's why I take the gun into the field with me. Why do you ask?"

"Do you remember the tall stranger who rode past our farm about that time, and we waved to him?"

"Yeah, he waved back and moved on. I remember."

Kate propped her pillow against the headboard and laid her head on it. "Well, I saw him again this afternoon, when the girls were riding in the corral. He didn't wave this time, nor did I. He continued on, without looking back." Kate hesitated a moment, trying to see John's face in the dark. "I know it was the same man. My eyes and gut tell me that. If he lived nearby, we would see him more often, but we haven't. There's something very mysterious about him that scares me."

Late the next morning, Biff took Bridie and the girls to Barbara's Café, for what most people believed to be, the best breakfast served in Galena. He explained Barbara Cane was born in Galena, and had become a famous singer and dancer performing in many of the major theatres in Illinois, including a few in Chicago. Pictures of Barbara in various costumes were displayed on the walls of the café. After placing their breakfast order with the waitress, the girls circled the café looking at pictures of Barbara in wide brimmed hats with plumes, and flirtatious gowns.

"She was beautiful," Pina commented. "I imagine she had many men sending her flowers after her performances."

"My guess is, she's had many proposals of marriage," Hillary added.

Catherine grabbed her friend's arms, "The waitress is serving our table. We'd better get back."

During their meal, Pina noticed Biff looking at Catherine again. The corners of his mouth turned up ever so slightly, revealing he had found some sort of pleasure in whatever he was thinking. She continued watching Biff until they finished eating, but he didn't do it again.

At the train station, the girls pretended not to watch Biff and Bridie kiss.

Catherine lowered her head and rolled her eyes toward her friends, whispering, "I would say that was more meaningful than just "goodbye.""

Biff helped Bridie up to the first stair, then stepped back. "I'll see you in three weeks for Catherine's graduation."

Bridie smiled back. "I hope Kate doesn't have the baby before then."

CHAPTER
TWENTY-THREE

Tuesday evening, Wade Widner rode up to the Hanley house and tied Kimby to the corral fence. No one came to the door, so he assumed they hadn't heard him ride up. He stood at the fence a few moments, inspecting the farm. He smiled, pleased he had come to Galena. The sun was low, causing long shadows across the snow covered ground. As he started for the house, light from a lantern began to glow through the kitchen window. He could see Kate standing next to a table, with a lit match in her hand. He needn't wonder any longer. She was pregnant.

Wade continued on, hoping to surprise her and John. Kate stood erect when she noticed a man walking toward the house. Wade was near the porch when Kate opened the door and stepped outside. She was smiling, as though ready to greet a friend. When he was a few feet from Kate, her smile was displaced by a look of fear. He wondered what was going through her mind, knowing she and John had been discovered.

"Don't scare the baby," Wade chuckled. "This is a friendly visit."

Kate stared at Wade, confused, not knowing if she should be concerned.

He wanted to erase her fears, so he stepped up to Kate and gave her a hug. "Don't be scared. All is well. I've been looking forward to seeing you and John."

Kate looked up at him, frowning, "How did you find us?"

Wade assumed Hillary should not have been writing friends in Alton, Delaware, so he avoided answering. "Let's pretend I'm a good detective, because I'm not answering that question."

"Is Tyler looking for John?"

"Let's go inside and I'll answer all your questions." Kate turned and Wade followed her into the house. "Is John home?"

John finished bathing and was in the bedroom dressing. He yelled through the door, "Is that Tom?"

Kate looked at Wade. "I guess that answers your question. Tom is our neighbor." She stepped toward the hallway. "No. It's a surprise visitor."

"A surprise visitor?" John repeated. "Is it the Pope? He'd be a surprise."

Wade could see Kate was still upset as to why he was there, but he didn't want to explain until John joined them. Wade figured she would relax, talking about the infant. "When is the baby due?"

"About a month. I'll be glad when it's over." Kate began shaking her head. "I still don't understand how you found us."

John walked quickly down the hallway toward the kitchen. He stopped abruptly, seeing Wade by the table. His shoulders dropped, as he stared at Wade. "The Pope would have been less of a surprise."

Kate pulled a chair from the table. "Let's sit. My legs feel weak." She faced John. "Wade says this is a friendly visit."

Wade reached into his jacket pocket. "I have something for you." He removed an envelope from the pocket and handed it to John. "It's a letter from Karl Polen. He wanted to say 'hello.'"

John smiled. "He's a good guy, thanks." He sat in a chair and laid the envelope on the table next to him. "Does Karl know where we are?"

"No. Only Tyler and I know. Don't worry about Tyler. Karl and I convinced him you didn't kill his brother. He's given up on revenge."

John slumped in the chair and, for a moment, laid his head back, as though reveling in the good news. They were "free." He slowly lowered his head to look at Wade. "How'd you do that?"

Wade unbuttoned his jacket and sat at the table. "Being as ornery as Tyler is, it was a challenge, but we told him what you told Karl about being framed in New Orleans. We both said you told us that story before Tyler came to Alton, you know, like there was no reason for you to lie before he came to town, so it must be true. We lied, but we needed to do what was necessary to convince him you didn't kill his brother. After explaining your story, we simply said, 'a bad guy frames a good guy.' It was an easy explanation, but a rational one. He knew he couldn't prove you did it."

"How did you find us?" Kate asked again.

"I won't tell you, for personal reasons." Wade glanced out of the window. *Our secret, Hillary. You owe me a hug.*

Kate looked at the men. "Do you want coffee?"

John stood, placing his hand on Kate's shoulder to hold her down. "I'll get it. Do you want coffee, Honey?"

"No, thanks."

Wade began to laugh. "By the way, Kate, you make a beautiful squaw."

"You," she bellowed. "You're the guy who went to the photography shop and asked where we lived?"

Wade nodded. "When I saw that picture, I knew I'd found you. I just needed to know exactly where. The lady was quite helpful."

Kate pointed her finger at Wade. "Did you ride by here last Saturday?"

"Yes. You and others were standing by the corral. I saw you turn and face me, but from that distance, I couldn't be sure if you were pregnant."

John placed a cup of coffee in front of Wade. "So, what you're telling us, is, we don't need to hide anymore."

Wade tapped his mug against John's, as a salute. "You can relax. You're free as a bird. Consider it a wedding present from me and Karl."

Kate and John held hands and gave each other a look of relief.

John smiled, "We can't thank you enough. Tell Karl we thank him, also." John felt excited. A jumble of thoughts, and plans, and memories streamed through his mind. "You're a good friend."

Now that John was safe, Kate wondered if anyone was looking for her. Without thinking, she quickly asked, "Are they looking for Frank Dragus's murderer?" As soon as those words passed her lips, she sat back, clamping her mouth shut, knowing that she'd given herself away by knowing of Frank's death. She felt her face getting warm, afraid of what would happen next. She stared into Wade's eyes, nervously waiting his response.

John's eyes shifted from Kate to Wade. "Frank Dragus was murdered?" He looked at Kate again. "How did you know that? Frank wasn't dead when you left Alton."

Wade peered into Kate's anxious eyes, knowing she was petrified for revealing her knowledge of the murder. Now, he knew Kate killed Frank, as he'd suspected. He glanced at John. "I told Kate about his murder when we were on the porch."

Wade knew by the way Kate was looking at him she was saying, "Thank you."

Wade sipped his coffee and smiled at Kate. "You will have a baby to take care of soon." He said that, so Kate would understand he wouldn't reveal her crime and she could continue with her life as it was.

"So, Dragus was murdered?" John mumbled aloud. "Do they know who did it?"

Wade looked at John and answered slowly, "No, and nobody seems to care. After his death, it was learned he molested many young girls working in his mill, so no tears were shed for him." He paused and gave Kate a quick glance. "Public opinion is, some parent killed him when they learned of their daughter's rape. And since Frank had no living relatives around, no one seems to care who did it. Considering what he did to children, some people are glad it happened."

Kate tilted her head to the side, breathing a silent sigh of relief. "I'm so happy we're away from Alton. Life is good here."

As if confused, John looked at Wade. "Did you come all this way just to tell us that we're free from Tyler Sharpe?"

Wade sat back in his chair and chuckled. "No! I would have sent you a telegram for that. The truth is, I live here."

Kate and John looked at each other, then at Wade again.

"You live here ... in Galena?" John questioned.

Wade leaned forward, resting his arms on the table. "Not exactly Galena, but I live nearby, in Paxton. I'm now working as a dispatcher for the Mississippi Barge Company."

John picked up Wade's empty coffee cup and his own, and started for the sink. "Tyler is no longer looking for me, and you have a new job. We must celebrate with something stronger than coffee." John looked over his shoulder at Wade. "Continue about your new job."

"It's not a complex story," Wade said. "When I was here months ago, I fell in love with this area and the horse I rented to find you." Wade nodded toward the window. "That's her out there—Kimby. One afternoon, I looked in the newspaper and saw the barge company's ad. I had shipping experience, so I went for an interview. They needed someone to fill a position immediately, but another man was moving out of state months later. That was the position I requested, but wasn't completely convinced about moving so far west." He paused, as John poured him a shot of whiskey. He then went on. "It was Tyler Sharpe who convinced me to take this assignment, being how I continually expressed my fond feelings about this area. Actually, I believe he wanted me away from Alton, since I knew about his evil plan of revenge toward you. You know—better I be gone than able to talk about him in Alton."

John raised his shot of whiskey to Wade. "Thank you, for what you've done for us, and telling us about it."

Wade raised his glass in return. "We were friends before, so we can continue to be." Wade smiled at Kate. "Do you know any available women I may like?"

John snickered, "That's an important issue you don't want to waste time on."

Kate gave Wade a tender look. "A man like you won't have trouble finding a woman."

John pointed outside toward Wade's horse. "You already have a lady you love. How many females do you want?"

Wade grinned. "Yes, I do love her. She's my prize possession." He stood and pushed his chair to the table. "I have to ride to Paxton, so I'd better be going. Come outside and I'll show her to you."

John rose from his chair. "Yes, I'd like that." John went through the door first and headed for Kimby.

Wade stopped at the door, as Kate came up behind him. He smiled into her eyes. "Better days are coming for you."

"Thank you, for covering for me."

"Our secret," Wade responded. "Think of it as another wedding present."

They stepped onto the porch and Kate looked directly into his eyes. "Do you want to know why I did it?" The anguish she'd suffered over Hillary's rapes reappeared in her face.

Wade answered, softly, "I believe I know. Love is a strong emotion. Consider it another secret between us."

Kate rubbed her hands together, wanting to explain. "The only reason I went to his office, was to confront him before we left Alton, and tell him what I thought of him. We got into an argument and he made an ugly comment about young girls being physically old enough for him, as though they were merely toys and not human beings. I was so mad, I reacted without thinking."

Wade raised the palm of his hand to her. "Conversation over and forgotten."

Kate sat in the porch rocker, gripping the armrests. "If I were a weeping woman, I'd cry with happiness."

Wade walked away. "I'm glad you're not. I hate crying."

Kate watched the men fuss over Kimby and laugh a few times, before Wade climbed on his horse and rode past her, waving. She stood and waited for John to return to her, before entering the house.

John poured himself another shot of whiskey and sat next to her. "What a wonderful day. No more hiding."

Kate sealed the whiskey bottle. "That's enough for tonight."

He leaned forward and kissed her. "I agree, Mother."

After hearing the good news, there was a new peace and happiness that settled into their home. John reached for Kate's hand. "Happy?"

Kate looked up at him and smiled. "Very."

Two weeks later, John, Kate and Biff went to Newberry to attend Catherine's graduation, and bring Hillary home for the summer. It was late Friday afternoon when Brian met them at the train station and drove them to Bridie's house. When they arrived, Bridie had just finished spending the day rushing about the house and the markets, making sure the preparations for the next day's graduation party were in place. When they walked into the kitchen, Bridie was sitting at the table checking her list of tasks.

Bridie was startled when they entered the room. She stood and walked directly to Kate to give her a hug. "My God! I was so deep in thought, I didn't hear you people come into the house." She looked at Kate's swollen abdomen and shook her head. "You look as though you're about to burst." She smiled and sighed deeply. "Excuse me, I've got something important to do. I'll be right back." She walked up to Biff and kissed his smiling face. "I don't want you to feel ignored."

Biff laughed. "If Kate is about to burst, I'd rather you concentrate on her."

Bridie looked at Brian standing silently behind the others. "Catherine's upstairs bathing. Take Biff to your house now, when you return she'll be ready." Bridie glanced at the others. "Brian hasn't seen Catherine for two hours, so *he's* about to burst."

Biff took two peanut butter cookies from a plate on the stove and handed one to Brian. "We're not wanted. Let's go."

John carried their luggage upstairs to the guest bedroom, while Kate remained in the kitchen with Bridie.

Bridie stood behind Kate, placing a gentle hand on her shoulder. "Do you want a cup of tea?"

"No, thank you, but a glass of water would be nice."

Bridie walked to the sink, asking, "Are you nervous about the baby coming ... abruptly? You know, like when you're on the train."

Kate laughed. "I've certainly thought of it. But no, even though I'm a balloon, I have no inkling it will be soon." She looked down at her abdomen and rubbed her hand over it. "But then, you never know."

Bridie set a glass of water in front of Kate and sat across from her. "You don't have to worry while you're here. If the baby does surprise us, I know a good doctor to contact immediately." Bridie lowered her head to relieve an ache in her neck. "I've been running all day to be ready for tomorrow. It feels good to sit for a while."

Kate looked at Bridie a long moment. "How do you feel about losing Catherine after having her only three or four years? It's a question that popped into my mind recently, while thinking of my baby and how fast they age."

Bridie raised her head slowly and smiled. "I've thought about it many times, but even though Catherine will be married next year, she'll be nearby, giving me grandchildren." She leaned forward, looking at Kate with raised eyebrows. "But, if she ever moved far away, that would devastate me."

"What's uncanny," Kate chuckled, "is that you and the Holmgrens got your children on the same day and will lose them on the same day."

Bridie laughed with her. "That's true. I didn't think of that. But it will make our long friendship more like family." She looked up toward the ceiling, "I hear Catherine stirring. She must be getting dressed. I'll go upstairs, take a bath and change clothes." Bridie rose from her chair and glanced at Kate. "Do you need anything before I leave?"

"No, I'm feeling fine."

Moments later, John returned to the kitchen and stood next to Kate. She was so quiet that he became concerned. "Is something bothering you?"

"No. Nothing is bothering me, but I was thinking about Hillary going to Alton to visit her parent's graves and the other two Wild-flowers. I know she wants to go, because she mentioned it a couple of times."

John looked at her. "We knew that time would come. It was only a matter of when."

Kate put her hand on his arm. "The way I see it, the time is now. Hillary is free from school and the baby isn't born yet. Some time back, I asked Biff if he would go with her and he said he would. Then today, on the train, I realized this is the best time for her to go."

Even though Wade Widner said no one was looking for Frank Dragus' killer, Kate didn't want to take the chance of someone questioning her about his murder. Being she was well into the pregnancy, it was a good excuse for not going. Kate removed her hand from John's arm and breathed deeply. "It would be exciting for her to see Iris and Vera again. I'm not due to deliver for two weeks and the first baby usually comes late. If Hillary went next week, she could be back before the birth."

John thought for a moment. "I believe you're right. She should go as soon as possible. Once the baby is born, it will be difficult for her to leave. Let's talk to Hillary this weekend."

The following afternoon, the small Bradbury auditorium was filled with people from different parts of the Mid-West. Brian looked up at Catherine, sitting on the stage, waiting for her diploma. He couldn't imagine loving anyone, as much as he did her. What a wonderful future they had before them. Brian recalled the days in New York City when he slept with women to earn money, and the times he went to Nerine Booker's apartment. Fortunately, these affairs had remained a secret. He pledged to himself, that he'd never again do anything to hurt Catherine.

Bridie felt pride, watching Catherine approach the podium and receive her diploma, as she had done, years before. The ceremony brought back memories of friends she'd graduated with, and the fun they had those two years at Bradbury. It was a short time later she'd met John McTavish and fell in love. They had ambitious dreams of having a family and living in a fine home. Life was exciting then, as it is for Catherine now. Then, her dreams were crushed in one terrible moment, on one terrible day, leaving her without the man she loved. Bridie glanced at Biff sitting next to her, the man she loved now. She was elated with Biff, but regretted the years of her life that were lost being a caregiver rather than a wife. She wanted a full life, and if Biff asked her to marry him, she would do everything she could to make him happy.

After the ceremony, people gathered outside of the auditorium congratulating one another, saying "goodbye" and wishing each other "good luck" in the future. Eventually, the crowed thinned, as people dispersed in different directions.

Immediately after returning home, Brian took Catherine by the hand and whispered, "Quick, come with me." As the others filed into the house, talking and laughing, Brian sneaked Catherine to the rear porch stairs and sat her down.

Catherine was perplexed. "What are you doing? Why are we back here?"

Brian sat next to her and held her hand. "Congratulations on finishing school, and with honors grades, too. I'm very proud of you."

"Why are you telling me this, here?"

"Because I wanted to get away from the others to talk to you." Brian looked up to see if anyone had entered the kitchen. He looked at Catherine again and said, "In a year, I'll finish school, ready to earn a living. We will have gone from poor orphans to college graduates, with a promising future. We've wanted to be together since the moment we met. You can't deny that. The two years we've lived here ..."

A tear slid down Catherine's cheek, as she interrupted him. "Are you attempting, what I think you're attempting? Because, if you are, you aren't good at it, so just ask me and forget all the fancy dressing."

Brian gave her a sheepish grin. "You're right. I am stumbling." He removed a ring from his suit pocket, looked into her eyes and said, as genuinely as he could, "I love you with all my heart. Will you marry me?" He squinted at her. "Don't tell me you want to think about it like you did last time."

Catherine smiled, looking at the diamond ring he was holding, "It's absolutely beautiful, and you remembered that I like the emerald cut." She presented her hand to Brian. "Yes, I'll marry you. And yes, I've loved you since the moment we met."

He slipped the ring on her finger. "I wanted us to be alone when I gave you this ring as a graduation present. We'll be engaged for a year, then get married right after I graduate next year, just like we planned." He held Catherine and they kissed deeply. "I brought you back here, because here is where we promised ourselves to each other, and told our parents we'd be together forever. Now, we can tell them we're definitely getting married."

Catherine thought it a beautiful sentiment. "You're right. We should tell them. I'll go first." Catherine moved up against Brian and looked up at the sky. "Mom and Dad, Brian will be your son-in-law as I promised, and I love him completely. Life has been good to me and it's getting better. I love you both and will never forget you." Catherine looked at Brian, waiting for him to begin his prayer.

"Mother! Dad! Catherine and I will be married next year, like we said. We hope you will be with us. She makes me very happy and I will love her forever. I think of you always."

They noticed the kitchen light go on and heard voices. Catherine stood and took Brian's hand, pulling him from the stairs. "Let's not tell anyone. We'll see how long it takes for someone to notice the ring."

Brian looked at her and smiled. "Good idea. Let's go back to the front door. Maybe no one will have noticed we were gone."

As they ran to the front stairs, Pina and her parents were entering the house, so they walked in close behind them. Catherine tapped Pina's shoulder. "One year from now, you will be graduating."

Pina smiled. "Yeah! And I'll be 16, ready to …" She became mute when she noticed the ring on Catherine's finger.

Catherine placed a finger in front of her lips. "Shhh! No one knows yet. We want to see how long it takes others to notice."

Pina rolled her eyes and swooned. "It's not like this wasn't expected, it's just that … there it is, on your finger, and it's beautiful. I can't wait until Hillary sees it."

Brian closed the door and whispered to the girls, "I don't think it will be a secret very long, being Pina noticed immediately."

"I'm more clever than most," Pina teased. She went into the kitchen to join Hillary. "How can I help? I'm not being nice, it's just that I'm hungry and want to hurry things along."

Bridie looked at her. "Thank you, Pina. Help Hillary carry the food to the dining room table. I'll get Catherine to help."

Bridie entered the dining room and raised her hand, signaling Catherine to come to her. "Help the girls set the table, please."

Pina watched Catherine enter the kitchen, anxious to see if someone would notice the ring. Within a couple of minutes, all the food was on the dining room table and the guests began seating themselves. Pina was amazed the ring hadn't been discovered. She sat next to her parents and asked Catherine, who was across the table from her, if she would pass the bread to her.

Catherine kept her left hand on her lap and passed the plate of bread to Pina.

Next, Pina asked Catherine to pass her the potatoes that were at her left. To her disappointment, Brian lifted the bowl of potatoes and set them in front of her.

Bridie stood at the head of the table, holding a glass of wine to propose a toast to Catherine's graduation. The others raised their glasses. "This toast will be simple, but to the point." She looked at Catherine, with a loving smile in her eyes. "To my daughter, who I love dearly. I'm proud of your accomplishment of graduating from Bradbury School with honors. You have been a pleasure to me since you came into my home, and now you are about to embark on a new life." Bridie glanced at the people sitting around the table and smiled. "If you don't understand what I mean by 'new life,' look at that ring on her finger."

Hillary's eyes widened. She stared at the ring from across the table. She pushed her chair back and ran over to Catherine for a better look. "Oh, Catherine, it's magnificent!" Hillary kissed her cheek and gave her a hug, as others congratulated them. She turned to Brian and kissed him. "I'm so happy for you."

Catherine held her hand over the table to show her ring. "Oh, this old thing? I've had it twenty-three minutes already."

Tom and Margaret looked at Brian. "Congratulations, Son." Then smiled at Catherine. "We wish you both, a life of happiness."

John raised his glass. "Good luck to you two."

Eileen Campbell and Kate went to Catherine to admire the ring and wish them happiness.

Biff smiled at them. "May you have health, happiness and children."

Bridie looked at Biff when he mentioned "children." She interpreted it as, Biff's belief children were important in a marriage.

Eileen Campbell backed away from examining Catherine's ring and turned to Kate. "What names have you picked for your baby?"

Before Kate could answer, Pina answered her mother's question. "You and father must be the only people who don't know. Sorry, I thought I had told you. Laura and Robert."

Eileen looked at Kate and John, as she started back to her chair. "Nice! I like both those names."

Bridie was enjoying the excitement that existed between Catherine and Brian, and the anticipation of Kate and John's baby. She watched her guests, smiling and talking. Catherine was saying something to

Brian, while looking down at her ring. Kate had a hand resting on her abdomen. A deep peace and happiness could be felt in the room.

CHAPTER
TWENTY-FOUR

Later that evening, after the Holmgrens and Campbells went home, the three girls were washing the dinner dishes, an agreement they made if Hillary and Pina could sleep there the next two nights. Bridie was in the dining room arranging it to its original condition. Kate wanted to help, but they wouldn't let her. She was told to go sit in the parlor and relax. Since she wasn't allowed to help, Kate decided it was a good time to talk to Biff about taking Hillary to Alton. Walking to the parlor, Kate saw Biff standing on the sidewalk in front of the house. It was almost dark when she stepped onto the porch. Biff came to assist her down the five wooden stairs. She raised her arm to him, so he could steady her. "Where is John?"

"He left me to use the bathroom. John was gone a long while, so I went upstairs and found him sleeping on your bed."

Kate chuckled. "That sounds like him. When the sun goes down, so does John."

Biff smiled. "Such is the life of a farmer."

She took Biff's arm and started to walk. "I'd rather walk than stand in place. Shall we go to the corner and back?"

"If you'd like." He eyed her keenly, sensing she had something on her mind. "Is there a problem you'd like to discuss?"

Kate nodded. "Yes. I wanted to discuss Hillary's trip to Alton. Are you prepared for this?"

"I would imagine so. My time is flexible."

She began speaking lightly, as they walked. "John and I decided that since Hillary is out of school and the baby isn't born yet, this would be a good time for her to go." Kate looked up at his face, gauging his reaction to what she was about to say. "Like in a couple of days."

He grinned. "Do you mean Tuesday?"

"No, not that soon. I don't want to be ridiculous." She smiled back at him. "How about Thursday?"

He cast a brief look at the houses around him and laughed. "Oh, that's much better." He put his arm around her shoulders. "Like I said, I'm flexible. You know I have a crew of men to take care of things when I'm gone. Besides, I agree, it is a good time under the circumstances. Once the baby comes, she won't want to leave."

"If you left Thursday, you'd be there so Hillary could have a full Sunday with Iris and Vera, the only day the girls aren't working. Hillary could go to her parents graves Saturday evening, then again Monday morning before returning on the train."

"You're right," Biff uttered, contemplating the work for his coming week. "Iris and Vera do work six day weeks. I'd forgotten about that." He kissed Kate's forehead. "Then we leave Thursday."

Kate looked at him, with grateful eyes. "Thank you. I haven't discussed it with Hillary, yet, but I'm sure she'll agree with our reasoning."

The next morning, Brian phoned at 10:00 a.m. to learn if his bride-to-be was up and dressed. "She's awake," Bridie said, "But up and dressed? No. Remember, her friends slept here last night and they're doing girl things until they decide when to dress."

"It's a sunny, beautiful Sunday morning. Tell her it's a Bonnie Day and I want to share it with her."

Bridie chuckled. "Bonnie? We haven't used that word around here for a long time. Besides, if it were dreary and raining, you'd still want to share the day with her. Be patient, Catherine will want to spend time with Hillary today because she goes home tomorrow."

"By the way, Bridie, Biff is on his way to your house. He left here about ten minutes ago. I hope *you* are dressed."

Bridie's back stiffened at his improper remark, but decided it was just youthful thoughtlessness. "Of course, I'm dressed. Yesterday, Biff said he would be here around ten o'clock. He's joining me and the Hanleys for breakfast in town."

Brian couldn't think of anything more to say, except for a request. "Would you ask Catherine if they would like to go for a buggy ride this afternoon? Please! I'll call in an hour."

"I will." Soon after Bridie hung up the receiver, there was a knock on the front door. She could see Biff through the glass panel of the door. Gently, she opened the door and Biff entered with a smile. When Bridie closed the door, he put his arms around her and they kissed. It reminded her of when Catherine would open the door for Brian, and she would say, "You can kiss her if you like."

Biff looked at her, his eyes eager and happy. "Do you want to go for a buggy ride and dinner this afternoon—just the two of us?"

Bridie was pleased he asked her to spend time alone with him, even though she had guests. "Well, since you are leaving tomorrow, I guess we could do that."

He looked into her eyes. "And if I wasn't leaving tomorrow?"

She smiled at him. "I guess we could do that."

It was noon when the adults returned from breakfast. Brian was standing in the foyer waiting for the girls to get ready for the buggy ride. John and Biff walked through the foyer and on to the kitchen for a cup of coffee. Kate wanted to take a nap. As she was going up the stairs, the three girls started down. Hillary went down last, so she could stop to kiss Kate and rub her abdomen. She smiled at the others. "The baby has been very active lately." She looked at Kate. "Soon, maybe?"

Kate groaned, "I hope so."

Bridie stopped them from going beyond her. "Be back by 3:30. Biff is taking me for a ride and dinner at the Highlander Restaurant."

"We will," Brian assured her. "We're only going to Kitty's and a short ride."

Bridie closed the door behind them and went upstairs to see if Kate needed anything, before going to sleep. She knocked lightly on the door and whispered, "It's Bridie."

"Come in."

Bridie approached Kate, leaning against two pillows propped up against the headboard. "Do you want anything, water, tea or coffee, or just sleep?"

"Actually, resting for a while is all I need." She patted the bed. "Sit for a while."

Bridie sat on the edge of the bed and held Kate's hand. "I imagine you're excited—being you will have a baby in a matter of days."

Kate laughed softly, pointing to her abdomen. "I'm tired of carrying the baby here. I want to carry it in my arms."

Bridie laughed with her. "I don't doubt that." She paused and carefully asked, "What will you do if the baby comes while Hillary is in Delaware, and John is in the fields working? You should have someone with you, at least for the first few days."

Kate squeezed Bridie's hand, gently. "Ruth Roddy will be around to help." She noticed Bridie's smile fade, as though disappointed.

"Ruth has her family to care for, so she can't be with you all of the time. And you never know when there may be an emergency."

Kate realized what Bridie wanted. She hadn't been around newborns and would like the experience, just in case there was going to be children in her future. Besides, Bridie was right, she could help with the baby and be available to Biff at the same time. The idea of having someone around all day appealed to her. Kate looked at Bridie and nodded. "That's true, Ruth can't be there all the time."

Bridie was satisfied with Kate's response and casually suggested, "If it would be helpful, I could come when you have the baby and assist you for a while. I wouldn't mind. As a matter of fact, I'd love it!"

Kate pretended with her, hesitating as if giving it consideration. "You're right, that would be a good idea, if you don't mind? Being that it's my first baby, I really don't know what to expect. And as you say, in an emergency I'd need someone with me."

Bridie straightened her back, while patting Kate's hand. "Good! Then I'll come as soon as the baby arrives."

The children returned at three o'clock, gabbing excitedly and laughing. The adults were sitting in the parlor discussing Hillary's trip to Alton. Pina entered the parlor first. "Kitty is so sweet. When she saw Catherine's engagement ring, she had tears in her eyes."

"Yes, she is a sweetheart," Bridie agreed. "You'll have to invite her to the wedding. She would be hurt if you didn't. She loves all four of you."

Catherine took Brian's hand and looked at him. "Of course, we'll invite her. Won't we?"

Brian nodded. "Yes! Sure we will."

Biff looked across the room at Brian. "Would you give Bree water? I'm sure she's thirsty after pulling you four around. I'll feed her when Bridie and I return from dinner."

"Sure, I'll do it now." He spun around and headed for the door.

The girls turned to follow Brian. "Hillary," Kate called. "Stay here, I want to talk to you upstairs." Kate wanted to be alone with Hillary when they discuss her going back to Alton. She didn't know if the discussion would open old wounds where Hillary would become emotional, especially if the conversation included Frank Dragus.

Hillary looked puzzled, glancing back at Kate. "Is it about the baby?"

Kate stood and walked toward her. "Partially." She turned to Bridie and the men. "Excuse us for a while."

Biff rose from his chair, as they left the room. "Bridie and I may be gone before you return. We should be back between seven and eight o'clock."

Kate led Hillary up to the guest bedroom and sat on the bed. She watched Hillary flop onto her stomach next to her. "I brought you here to discuss your trip to Alton."

Hillary turned over quickly and sat next to Kate, her legs dangling over the edge of the bed. "I'm going to Alton? When?"

Kate looked at Hillary's soft, wavy blond hair and long, curled eyelashes. "This Thursday."

Hillary stared deep into Kate's eyes. "But you may have the baby, while I'm gone."

Kate took a long breath. "I've discussed this with Biff. We both know that once the baby is born, you will find it difficult to leave. Therefore, since the first baby usually comes late, we figured you could have your trip and be back before it is born."

Hillary looked down at the floor. "I'm not sure what I want to do." She jerked her head toward Kate. "Wait a minute! What about the man who thinks John killed his brother? I thought we were hiding from him."

Kate put her arm around Hillary. "We don't have to worry about him anymore. That man learned John didn't kill his brother, so now you can go to Alton. For a long time you've been wanting to go to your parent's graves and visit the other two Wildflowers. Now is your chance. You'll have all summer to play with the baby until you go back to school."

Hillary looked down at the floor again, "You're right. It does make sense to go now. I do want to visit my parent's graves and my friends, but I don't like going back to Alton. It's an ugly place."

Kate agreed. "It isn't a pretty town."

Hillary looked out of the window and began rubbing her hands together. "How Alton looks isn't what I meant. It was the ugly life I had there, working twelve hours a day, children hurt by the machines, the poverty, drunks and children wearing tattered clothes." She sat silent for a moment, before looking up at Kate. "If it weren't for you and John, I don't know where I'd be today. I love my life here."

Kate saw anguish in Hillary's face, because of her memories of Alton. She wondered what was going through Hillary's mind at that moment. *Will she ever talk freely about Frank Dragus?* She laid a hand on Hillary's shoulder. "I had wondered if your life in Alton had faded from your memory, but I see it hasn't."

"I'll never forget," Hillary mumbled. "I remember everything. All I have to do is think about the boys that had their hands and toes ground up in the machines, little Ellie Tuzik killing herself, and why she did it … and other things that happened. Then everything comes back to me. Those memories will be with me all my life."

Kate knew what Hillary meant by, "other things," and wanted to free Hillary of any guilt she may be carrying because of Frank Dragus. She removed her hand from Hillary's shoulder and said, "You can't dwell on the past, Hillary. Things happen in our lives that we have no control over. You're a beautiful girl getting a fine education. One day, you'll meet a nice young man who'll love you forever. The past is over and you must look to the future."

Slowly, Hillary turned her head to look at Kate. "I know my past, but I don't know my future."

Kate placed her forehead against Hillary's forehead and looked into her eyes. "You're happy now, aren't you? What you are living now, was your future when you lived in Alton. So your future is better already." Kate sat back and sighed. "There is a beautiful world out there and a beautiful life waiting for you. Go after it."

Hillary smiled, weakly. "That's true. My life is better already, thanks to you, John and Uncle Biff."

Kate smiled when Hillary called Biff, "Uncle." "Then is it settled, you'll leave Thursday?"

Hillary began swinging her legs. "Yes."

It was 8:30 when Biff and Bridie returned home. Bridie stayed with Biff, while he unhitched Bree from the buggy and put hay into her trough. When he finished, Bridie took him by the arm and they walked to the house. Biff hung their coats on the coat tree in the foyer before they entered the kitchen where Kate and John were drinking coffee.

"Where are the children?" Bridie asked.

Kate pointed upstairs. "Brian went home and the girls are in Catherine's bedroom."

Biff sniffed the air. "The coffee smells good." He looked at Bridie. "Do you want a cup?"

Bridie stepped up to the table under the ceiling light. "No, thank you."

A sparkle of light caught Kate's eye. Its brilliance glistened against Bridie's black dress. Kate smiled and rose from her chair to hug Bridie. "My God! It's wonderful. I'm so happy for you."

Bridie couldn't contain her smile, as Kate held her. "Thank you." She glanced over Kate's shoulder to look at Biff. "I'm sure you're not as happy as I am."

Biff smiled back at her.

John looked up at Biff standing next to him. "What's Kate so happy about?" He paused a moment, "And why are you grinning, so goofy-like?"

Kate walked over to Biff and kissed him. "Congratulations! I hoped this would happen."

John looked bewildered. "Congratulations for what? Did Biff shoot another bird with his eyes closed?"

Kate gave John a disgusted look. "'Congratulations' and 'I'm so happy for you.' What else could it mean?"

John's eyes widened, realizing what had transpired. He glanced at Bridie's left hand to affirm what he was thinking. "My God," he said. He stood and turned to Biff. "Congratulations, for sure!" He shook Biff's hand. "You never said a thing to me."

Kate laughed. "He wasn't supposed to say anything to you. He had to say it to Bridie."

John grinned and waved his hand at Kate. "You know what I meant." John walked over to Bridie and kissed her. "Welcome to the family. Your union with Biff will make many people happy." He turned to Kate. "Shall we call the girls down from the bedroom? They will go crazy when they find out."

"I'll get them down," Kate said, eagerly. She walked through the hallway and stopped at the foyer stairs. "Do you girls want hot chocolate?"

She could hear mumbling voices from behind the bedroom door, before Catherine yelled, "No, thank you."

Kate looked back at the others in the kitchen, smiling at her failure to bring the girls down. She decided to offer them something else she didn't have. "Would you like a slice of lemon pie?" Again, she could hear the murmur of the girl's voices.

Catherine repeated her answer. "No, thank you."

Bridie walked to where Kate was standing and the men followed her. "I'll get them down." She looked up the stairs and called, "This is Bridie. Do you want to see my engagement ring?"

There was a moment of silence before they heard a thump from someone jumping off of the bed, followed by six feet stomping across the bedroom floor. The door whipped open and three screaming girls raced through the hall and down the stairs.

Bridie looked at Kate. "I knew that would get them down."

The girls crowded around Bridie to look at her ring and marvel at it. They hugged and kissed Bridie and Biff, congratulating them and expressing their happiness. When Hillary hugged Biff, she whispered in his ear, "I love you so much. I want you and Bridie to be the happiest people on earth."

Biff whispered back, "You've been my happiness. Now we'll share it with Bridie."

Hillary looked at him, with tears in her eyes. "I don't mind sharing it with her. Bridie is perfect for you."

Kate heard their whispers and smiled at the irony of Hillary showering, love and best wishes, on a man who shared a love with her mother. Biff and Hillary had shared a special love where he'd treated her like a daughter and, if Laura hadn't died, he would have been her father. She closed her eyes for a moment. *That's another story.*

Pina sat on the stairs rocking back-and-forth. "This has to be the greatest weekend ever—two engagements and a graduation. I can't wait to tell my parents!"

Catherine looked at Bridie. "We should let the Holmgrens know, right away. Why don't you call them?"

Bridie glanced at her watch. "It's just after nine o'clock. We've been up late before, so I guess we can do it again." Bridie went into the kitchen and cranked the telephone. Five minutes later, she returned. "All three are coming, and they're bringing Champagne."

Pina rose from the stairs and leaned against the railing. "Where will you be living?"

Biff crossed the foyer and stood next to Bridie. "We've decided to build a new house for us, and keep where I live now, as a guest house."

Uncertain of her immediate future, Catherine beseechingly looked at Bridie. "Then, we'll be living in Galena?"

Bridie smiled at her. "No, my dear. We will keep this house. It's only a five-hour train ride between here and Galena. What we'll do in the distant future, we don't know yet. You'll be long married before I get rid of this place."

"Brian and Catherine could live here, if you were to move permanently to Galena," John suggested. "Then, you'd still have both houses."

Bridie spun around to face him, "That's a good idea. We'll have to discuss that."

Kate placed her hand on her abdomen. "It appears the baby is excited, too. It's kicking up a storm."

Hillary rushed to her. "Is it coming?"

"No," Kate assured her. "It's just being active."

John looked at Biff. "Ready for a cup of coffee?"

Biff nodded. "One more before the Champagne arrives." He glanced at Bridie. "Do you want coffee?"

She smiled. "No, go ahead."

Catherine started for the front door. "I'm going to the front porch and wait for the Holmgrens."

"Good idea," Pina agreed, following Catherine.

When the girls were on the porch, Kate stepped next to Bridie. "I thought of something recently. Do you remember what I said to you, the day we first met at the Highland Games? As I was leaving the refreshment tent to find John, my last words to you were, 'You'll love Uncle Biff.'"

Bridie had to laugh with her. "Yes, I do—very clearly. When you said that, I actually felt it was true, you know, like a premonition. Because of that, I wanted to meet him. And when I did, I knew he was special."

CHAPTER
TWENTY-FIVE

The following evening, Kate was sitting in her rocking chair on the front porch, thinking about the baby. Biff came out of the house and stood next to her. "I'm going home. I'd appreciate it, if you would thank Tom Roddy for taking care of Creo for me while we were in Newberry."

Kate watched Biff slip on his denim jacket. "I will." She leaned back and studied him. "You appear to be a content, happy man since you've become engaged. It shows what the right girl can do for a man."

Biff grinned. "Yep! Bridie affects me that way. The truth is, I never expected it to happen again."

The word "again" immediately revived Kate's memory of Laura, the first woman Biff loved. She wondered whether his being around Catherine would be a problem in the future. She watched Biff step down to the ground, "Before you go, I'd like to ask you something." She waited until he turned to face her. "Have you resolved your secret dilemma—the Laura and Catherine look-alike situation?"

He went back up the three steps and stopped by Kate, kissing the top of her head. "Yes. It took a while, but I finally succeeded. Every time I've been near Catherine, whether we were outside or at a dinner table, I would constantly watch her, trying to identify her as Catherine, only. The transition was almost complete last Christmas, but by Easter, it was done. It seemed the more involved I became with Bridie, the more I accepted Catherine as her daughter, an individual separate from Laura. Now, Laura is in my memory only."

Kate reached for his hand. "She always will be, especially with Hillary's presence to remind you." Kate smiled, "It's uncanny. Hillary almost became your daughter, but now she's mine, and John's; people from the same family. I've loved Hillary since she was an infant."

Kate noticed a hurt look in Biff's eyes. "I'm sorry. I have to alter that statement. In reality, Hillary has been a daughter to all three of us."

Biff stepped back and started down the steps again. "I like to think that."

Kate called after him. "If my baby is a girl, would it bother you if we named her Laura?"

Biff continued walking, without turning around. "It would bother Hillary if you didn't. Good night."

Kate smiled. "Good night!"

At noon the next day, Bridie returned home from a business meeting at the Newberry Times newspaper. The sky was gray and rain was imminent. While she was gone, Catherine made a small pot of vegetable soup for their lunch, occasionally looking out of the window to watch Matthew prepare the flowerbeds for the new plantings.

While they were eating, Bridie suggested, that at the end of the week, they go to Paul Johnson's Horse Ranch to see if they could find a horse for her.

Catherine beamed. "I can't believe it, my own horse." She finished her remaining spoonful of soup, then asked, "Are you sure you want to do this?"

Bridie put her spoon into the empty bowl and sat back in her chair. "Definitely. I knew by the way you handled Knickers the first time you rode, that you're a natural rider and should compete. Once we find the right horse, we'll get an instructor. How well you succeed at riding, is up to you."

Catherine carried their bowls and spoons to the sink and began washing them. "It's a shame Pina didn't like riding Knickers. If she had, it would be something we could enjoy together."

Bridie laughed. "Pina didn't like it at all. Actually, she looked scared, as she rode."

Catherine removed her apron and hung it over the back of a chair. "I'm going upstairs to wash my hair and sew a button onto a dress ... and think about horses."

Bridie smiled at her. "That sounds appropriate." She rose from her chair and started for the back door. "I'm going out to have a chat with Mister Matthew Brown, before the rain comes. I want to arrange the flowers differently this year."

As Catherine entered her bedroom, the telephone rang. Bridie answered it, but Catherine couldn't hear the conversation.

Minutes later, Bridie climbed the stairs, walking slowly into Catherine's bedroom. "I'm afraid we can't shop for a horse this week."

Catherine stood motionless, staring at Bridie's somber face. "Why not? What happened?"

"We have to change our plans." Bridie couldn't hold back her smile any longer. "Laura, was born."

Hillary was sitting on the green parlor sofa holding Laura, when Bridie and Catherine arrived at the house, carrying gifts. John knew they were anxious to see the baby, so he immediately led them to her. Hillary's broad smile showed she was as proud of the baby, as her parents were. Laura was wrapped in a soft, pink and white blanket, her roving black eyes trying to capture the movement before her.

Hillary peeled back the blanket exposing the baby's red, spindly legs and black hair. "Isn't she beautiful?"

Bridie placed the wrapped presents on the floor, next to the sofa, as she and Catherine leaned forward to look at Laura. "She certainly is beautiful."

They watched Laura's small fists beat the air, while Catherine grabbed her kicking, bare feet and held them. "I never expected her to have black hair."

John laughed. "I want Kate to explain that."

Hillary leered at John, for what she thought was an unfunny joke. "Kate told me her hair color would probably change."

Bridie glanced at Hillary and John. "The Holmgrens and Campbells are dying to see Laura. They said, I should have you people come to Newberry, as soon as possible."

Catherine laughed. "Pina was so excited, I bet she doesn't sleep until she sees her." She began stroking Laura's soft legs and glanced at Hillary. "I can understand why you didn't leave for Alton. She's too exciting."

Hillary slipped her hand under Laura's head to support it. "Biff and I are leaving Thursday, giving me another four days with her. I couldn't make myself go right after she was born."

Bridie stood and smiled at Hillary. "I can certainly understand that. I couldn't leave Laura, either." She looked at John. "Is Kate sleeping?"

"I don't think so. Peek into the bedroom and see."

Catherine glanced at Bridie, as she knelt before Laura. "I'll be with you in a few minutes."

Bridie walked quietly to the bedroom and rapped lightly on Kate's door, waiting for a response.

"Come in, Bridie."

Bridie opened the door and stepped into the room. "How did you know it was me?"

"Half by your walk, half by intuition."

Bridie sat on the bed and patted Kate's leg. "She's adorable."

Kate sat up against the headboard. "We like her. Hillary is constantly with Laura when she's awake. I'm not sure if Laura knows who her mother is, because she smiles every time Hillary talks to her. Yet, she doesn't for anyone else." She looked into Bridie's eyes. "How do you feel, knowing you could be a mother in the near future?"

Bridie couldn't contain her smile, looking down at the blue blanket covering the bed. "I think of it all the time. For years, I attended to Jack, believing I would never be a mother. And yet, I love Catherine so much, I feel she is my daughter. Then, when I met Biff, new horizons opened for me. The years are moving on, and we both know we'd better start a family right away." She gave Kate a fleeting glance. "Seeing Laura, makes me more anxious to be pregnant."

Kate understood the sincerity of her words, knowing Bridie was longing to be a mother. She laughed and responded quickly. "I think you'd better get married first." She smiled at Bridie. "Biff said you plan to marry this summer—meaning you'd marry within a few months."

Bridie was unaware of the sudden glow of happiness in her face. "A garden wedding at my house in August."

Kate laughed again. "That means you could be a mother a year from now?"

Bridie laughed with her. "Yes! And I could be pregnant at my daughter's wedding. Wouldn't that be a sight?"

The bedroom door slowly opened and Catherine peeked into the room, smiling at Kate. "I love her."

Kate smiled back and held her hand out to Catherine, wanting her to come closer. "Thank you. It appears this is the beginning of many babies we'll be having the next few years."

Catherine walked to Kate and kissed her. "I agree. Between you, Bridie and me, we'll help the Illinois population grow." Catherine turned to Bridie. "Biff just arrived. He's in the parlor with Laura."

"I'm getting up," Kate said, whipping back the blanket. "I've rested enough. Let's join the others in the parlor."

Catherine helped Kate put on her robe, then winked at Bridie. "Biff seems to enjoy carrying the baby."

Bridie stood, and started for the door. "I'll do what I can to keep him supplied with them."

As they entered the parlor, Biff was walking away from them, carrying Laura against his chest, bouncing her ever so slightly. Laura's dark eyes were peeking at them over his shoulder.

Bridie and Kate looked at each other, amused by Biff's total involvement with Laura.

When Biff reached the end of the room, he turned to retrace his steps and saw the ladies watching him. He was at a loss for words, so he merely said, "Look what I've got."

Bridie smiled at him, then looked to Kate. "Do you mind if I hold your daughter?"

Kate hesitated a moment before responding. "You need to get permission from Hillary, not me."

Hillary's face beamed at Kate's remark and looked at Biff. "It's Bridie's turn to hold *my* baby."

Biff bowed his head. "Yes, Mama." He gave Bridie a kiss, then handed Laura to her.

Bridie held Laura against her chest and began circling the parlor. She looked at Kate. "I assume Ruth has been here a few times."

Kate sat on the sofa next to Hillary. "Yes. She was here when Laura was born and every day since, usually with her daughters. The whole Roddy family came to see Laura the day after she was born. I could tell by the look on Adam's face, he thought that wrinkled little thing was grotesque. But then, his interest is only in Hillary."

Hillary put her hands over her ears. "Please, no more A. Roddy jokes." She shook her head at them, then leaned forward to tap Catherine's arm. "You can carry Laura when Bridie is finished."

Catherine laughed. "Thank you, Mama."

They watched Bridie walk around the room with the baby. Laura's eyelids began to flicker. Soon after, her arms fell limply to her sides.

Hillary gave Catherine a sad look, "You can carry her another time."

The following four days, Kate and Bridie took short walks to the creek, talking about family life, their men, and living in Galena. Hillary and Catherine rode Knickers when they weren't amusing themselves with Laura. John and Biff were free to work their farms, knowing Kate and Laura were well cared for.

Wednesday evening, Kate, Bridie and Ruth were relaxing on the front porch chatting, waiting for the sun to set.

Catherine was inside, helping Hillary pack clothes for her trip to Delaware. Hillary was pensive, thinking about the life she lived in Alton. She was anxious to get to her parent's graves and talk to them, and be reunited with Iris, Vera and the Thompsons. Hillary tried to put aside the ugly memories of Ellie Tuzik's death, the children mauled by machinery at the mill, and most of all, the times she was alone with Frank Dragus. There were moments she wanted to laugh, and times she wanted to cry. Hillary appreciated Catherine's help packing her clothes, but wished she were alone, so she could give in to her emotions. Hillary pulled out a dresser drawer to decide which sweaters she would take on the trip. Looking at an old sweater, she recalled the night her mother died, and how she filled her apron and coat pockets with stones, ready to walk into the Clarion River. If the boy named, "The Pocket Merchant," hadn't been there to stop her, she would never have known the wonderful life she was experiencing now ... and little Laura.

Ruth sighed, pointing toward a pink, red and blue horizon spreading before them. "The prettiest part of the sunset is about to begin. Watching sunsets is one of the things I like most about living in the country."

Kate agreed and looked to Bridie. "See what you have to look forward to. Sunsets are difficult to see when you live in a town."

Bridie smiled. "There will be many sunsets for me to enjoy. Their colorful displays seem to celebrate the performance of another day, like fireworks, the last hours of the Fourth-of-July." She laid a hand on Kate's arm. "Or, it could mean the celebration of a newborn."

Kate laughed. "Well, if that were true, I was too busy to see Laura's sunset."

Ruth leaned forward in her chair, looking at her friends. "It could also include, as in our case, children starting of a new life with a different family—like Adam and your girls coming to us. Their lives turned dark with the loss of their parents, then they began a bright, colorful life with people who love them and give them hope."

Bridie folded her hands together and laid them on her lap. "I've thought of that many times, but not only how their lives changed, but also, ours. Love has blossomed from pain and sorrow, giving all of us a better life. Catherine and Brian found each other on an Orphan Train bound for Newberry. Pina and Hillary were reunited, bringing me and Biff together. The Campbells have Pina and Adam is with you, Ruth. Monica is married now, and has a child."

Kate looked at Bridie. "I don't mean to be critical, but you forgot the Holmgrens and Brian."

Bridie laughed. "Please, don't tell Catherine."

Ruth slumped back into her chair again. "I guess we can interpret sunsets any way we want? All I know is, they're as beautiful as our children."

Bridie looked down at her hands. "I wonder what goes through a child's mind when they lose their parents? It must be a very empty feeling, having such a loss, and then not know what will happen to you." She raised her head and looked at her friends. "And for us, the apprehension of adopting a child we know nothing about. You wonder how far you should go with discipline and love, not knowing how they will react to decisions you make for them. You ponder what their lives were like before they came to us, and what memories they carry with them."

Kate gazed at the bright colors spread across the horizon. "It's a gamble when you adopt a child, but what intrigues me most is—what *secrets* do some children have painfully buried inside their hearts?"

OoOoO

978-0-595-43628-6
0-595-43628-5

Printed in the United States
94904LV00002B/64-90/A